Walter Goodman

The Keeleys on the stage and at home

With two photo-engravings from pictures by the author and other illustrations

Walter Goodman

The Keeleys on the stage and at home
With two photo-engravings from pictures by the author and other illustrations

ISBN/EAN: 9783337280260

Printed in Europe, USA, Canada, Australia, Japan

Cover: Foto ©Raphael Reischuk / pixelio.de

More available books at **www.hansebooks.com**

PORTRAIT OF MRS. KEELEY AT THE AGE OF 93

Mary Anne Keeley

THE KEELEYS

ON THE STAGE AND AT HOME

BY

WALTER GOODMAN

AUTHOR OF

'THE PEARL OF THE ANTILLES,' 'PEOPLE I HAVE PAINTED,' ETC.

WITH TWO PHOTO-ENGRAVINGS FROM PICTURES BY THE AUTHOR, AND OTHER ILLUSTRATIONS

LONDON

RICHARD BENTLEY AND SON

Publishers in Ordinary to Her Majesty the Queen

1895

Dedication.

TO THE MANY ADMIRERS AND PERSONAL FRIENDS

OF

THE KEELEYS

AND TO THE

DRAMATIC AND MUSICAL PROFESSIONS

THIS VOLUME IS RESPECTFULLY INSCRIBED

BY

THE AUTHOR.

INTRODUCTORY

From the Author to the Actress.

' MY DEAR MRS. KEELEY,

'You have been often asked to write your reminiscences, but have always declined to do so from a natural dislike to sing your own praises in print, and because such things must necessarily be more or less egotistical. Besides, I remember your once saying, "What can it matter to anyone when I was born, who were my parents, and what I did as a child?"

'It might not matter, perhaps, were you an obscure person whom nobody ever heard of. But you are an actress who has achieved many a histrionic triumph in your time, who has lived not merely the allotted span of three score and ten, but the best part of an entire century. And our gracious Sovereign has thought fit to invite you

to visit her presence, because I understand that
she remembered you when you were in your
prime, and entertained for you a feeling of sincere
admiration and personal regard.

'So I have ventured to jot down some of the
pleasant gossip at the easel which you and I have
had when recalling memories of the stage of your
time, with such stories or anecdotes as you were
good enough to relate, and a few biographical
notes which I have collected from various sources.
If my book is defective, or has failed to do you
justice, let the blame rest upon my own head.

'I believe you never took formal leave of the
stage, but retired into private life without even
the usual benefit performance. In the same
manner the humble writer of your biography
takes no formal leave of his principal subject, but
merely says, "Good-bye and God speed till we
meet again," as I hope we shall for many years
to come.

'And so for the present, dear Mrs. Keeley, I
remain,

'Yours most sincerely,

'WALTER GOODMAN.

'236, THE GROVE,
   'HAMMERSMITH.'

From the Actress to the Author.

'Many thanks, dear Mr. Goodman, for your very kind and complimentary letter. I cannot remember to have done anything particular to deserve such encomium, except having lived at the beginning and the end of the century : I was born in 1805, and I write this in 1895. Very grateful I am, for I have lived to see, amongst other things, well-deserved honour conferred upon one of the truest friends and one of the most perfect gentlemen of the age—Sir Henry Irving. Do not be astonished at this outburst ; you know my sentiments in that quarter.

'I value your friendship, and shall always remain,

'Yours most sincerely,

'MARY ANNE KEELEY.

'10, PELHAM CRESCENT, S.W.'

Postscript by the Author.

All that now remains is to thank friends who have kindly assisted me with notes and interesting recollections of their playgoing days, not forgetting those who have been good enough to lend pictorial souvenirs of the Keeleys for reproduction in these pages. For the latter favours, I am particularly indebted to Mr. George A. Delacher and the members of the **Green** Room Club; to the proprietors of the *Illustrated London News*, the *Gentlewoman*, the *Illustrated Sporting and Dramatic News*, *Woman*, and *St. Paul's;* and to M. Adolphe Beau.

CONTENTS

LIST OF ILLUSTRATIONS

THE KEELEYS

ON THE STAGE AND AT HOME

CHAPTER I.

MY FIRST DRAMATIC LOVE.

THERE is, as everyone knows, much virtue in the first of anything, whether in respect of earliest impressions or initiative achievements, always excepting, of course, those which relate to one's birth and marriage. For inasmuch as the first of these highly important events does not occur more than once in a lifetime, while the last may never happen again, they can scarcely be included in the same category as our first kiss of love, our first school-fight, our first cigar—pantomime—cheque or professional success.

Personally I may, perhaps, be allowed to lay claim to a 'double first' on my own list, from the fact that the very first drama that profoundly interested me was 'Jack Sheppard,' while the

I

actress who created the principal character was eventually my first theatrical portrait subject. So, although other people beside myself may cherish the same fixed impressions of Buckstone's popular hero, I do not think that it has fallen to the lot of many to have made his acquaintance, on and off the stage, under the same peculiar circumstances.

I have ventured to begin with these preliminary remarks because it is obviously desirable that a writer of theatrical biography should at least have seen and heard, if he did not actually know, the people whom he proposes to describe ; so, should the reader of these lines be of the same way of thinking, it may be a satisfaction to him to be informed at the outset that the present scribe saw and heard, time out of number, no less than four of the principal characters figuring prominently in this history, and that he is intimately acquainted with one of them.

But my personal experiences of the leading lady in this book do not go as far back as her birth, or anything like that remote date.   Nor was I in at the birth of any of her best impersonations.   I must, therefore, plead this as my excuse for not beginning at the very beginning, in conformity with biographical custom, by stating when and where the lady was born, who were her parents, and so forth.

For these reasons I must ask my audience to wait till my subject herself appears upon the biographical scene to tell the story of her child-hood and earliest conquests upon the stage in her own inimitable manner. Meanwhile, I will do my best to give the audience my view of her from the front of the house.

It was on Monday, April 30, 1855, that George Webster—a nephew of the celebrated Benjamin—opened Sadler's Wells for the summer season, and for the first week he had no less an attraction than his ' uncle,' who, in conjunction with the equally famous Madame Celeste, ap-peared for the first three nights in the ' Green Bushes,' followed by the comic piece, by Planché, ' Who's Your Friend ? or, The Queensberry Fête,' and the last three nights in ' Tartuffe,' and in the ' French Spy ; or, The Fall of Con-stantine.'

The next managerial announcement was, ' Mrs. Keeley, as Jack Sheppard. For a limited number of nights.'

I had heard much of Mrs. Keeley's realistic rendering of Jack Sheppard, and had been told how completely she identified herself with the part, till I began at last to regard the actress and the character as one and the same persons, just as everybody afterwards did in the case of Sothern

and Lord Dundreary, or Jefferson and Rip Van
Winkle.

At the time the drama was first produced, the
public had gone temporarily insane over W.
Harrison Ainsworth's romance of 'Jack Sheppard,' which had been running as a serial story in
Bentley's Miscellany, and was reprinted in three-
volume form about the same time that Buckstone's
dramatic adaptation appeared upon the stage.
But if one may judge by the adverse criticisms
of the press of the period, the dramatic version
was regarded with far more favour than the book.
However, the dramatic critics of that day might
have been more grateful to the original author for
having furnished the materials for an Adelphi
drama of interest, and affording thereby another
opportunity for a versatile actress to display her
gifts in a totally different direction.

That Mrs. Keeley did this to the complete
satisfaction of the first-nighters may be gathered
from the fact that after describing the opening
act in terms of high praise as regards its scenic
effects, one of them raises his critical curtain upon
Act ii. by saying: 'There stood Mrs. Keeley,
dressed in the best style of Hogarth's apprentice,
with apron rolled up, large flapped drab waistcoat,
high-heeled, high-quartered shoes, and a red neck-
handkerchief loosely tied ; and there hung on the

walls those orthodox ornaments of a carpenter's shop—the ballad, the almanac, the seven golden candlesticks and the history of the chaste Susannah.'

In reference to her performance, the same enthusiastic writer says : 'Nothing could be more exquisite than Mrs. Keeley's acting ; the naïveté, the assurance, the humour and the boldness of Sheppard were excellently delineated ; the slang was given without the least admixture of vulgarity, while in many passages, especially at the tomb of his mother and the scene with Thames Darrell, the pathos was almost touching. Well did she merit the general call for her appearance at the fall of the curtain '—a sentiment that was echoed by another first-nighter, who writes : 'At the fall of the curtain there was a universal uproar of applause. Mrs. Keeley was called for and led on by Mr. Yates, made her bow to her admirers, and retired amidst their acclamations of gratitude at her performance.'

What a line, or series of lines, the above ' opinions of the press ' would have been for the managerial advertisements of to-day! But in those more modest times managers appeared satisfied with a simple announcement in the daily papers, so that it was difficult to judge by it whether the new piece was or was not an ' enormous success ' and drew 'crowded houses.' In fact, it was apparently found not more necessary to pay for lengthy puffs than it was to raise the salaries of star performers. Mrs. Keeley was probably receiving at that remote period something like £15 a week for her services. Is it too much to say that such an actress would be considered worth to-day that amount *per night* ?

It need hardly be mentioned that with the mania for Harrison Ainsworth's novel which existed in 1839 there was more than one dramatized version going at the minor theatres. Surrey audiences were naturally dying to see the story on their stage ; so the management, as represented by G. B. Davidge, shortly announced, 'Ainsworth's original Jack Sheppard,' as a distinguishing title, and opposed to Buckstone's version, while as a further inducement to see this edition, the public were informed that 'the whole of the scenery was superintended by George Cruikshank, the original illustrator of the original book.' This interesting announcement, supported by a printed copy of a letter from 'Captain' Ainsworth to Mr. Davidge, saying that he had read the version as requested, and that it met with his complete approval, was no doubt sufficient to fill the Surrey for some considerable time.

Then the gods of the Victoria were made happy, and perhaps virtuous, by the contemplation of 'Jack Sheppard; or, The Progress of Crime.' In this case the hero was a real man named Harding, while Jonathan Wild was impersonated by Mr. Hicks, a melodramatic comedian of the good old school. At the Queen's Theatre in Tottenham Street, 'Jack Sheppard,' pure and simple, was in the bills, with Miss Rogers as the notorious one, while at Sadler's Wells there was coupled with the leading title, 'The Housebreaker of the Last Century.' Mrs. Honner was the Jack, which naturally gave rise to a Cockney joke having reference to the proverbial 'Honour among Thieves,' and Mr. Hall was the thief-taker. A namesake, if not a daughter, of Mrs. Honner, called Miss F. Honner, took the subordinate part of Rachel in the Adelphi version, so that the same personal joke might have been applied to her.

The Adelphi edition enjoyed a pretty long and prosperous run for those fastidious days when programmes were changed at least once a week, and sometimes every night. It was in the bills till quite the end of the year, or the beginning of the next, and at Christmas it was put on as a first piece to a seasonable extravaganza.

When announced for revival some twelve years

later, a distressing incident happened which rendered it necessary to postpone the piece indefinitely. It seems that while rehearsing the Flash Ken scene, Mrs. Keeley's foot slipped in descending a ladder placed against the set, and, according to the reporter of the accident, the actress 'suffered a severe sprain of the ankle, but was expected to appear next evening.'

This was on July 12, 1852, and the mishap took place on the previous day at the final 'call.' But on the 13th the promised revival was again postponed till the 15th, and on that day till the 19th. So it went on till the 26th, when the postponing announcements took a leap, and declared that the injured lady would not be in a condition to appear till August 2, in evidence of which the management issued a medical certificate, rather oddly worded, and signed by Dr. Cahill and Mr. Pollard, stating that 'the injury to Mrs. Keeley's ankle is not sufficiently recovered to admit of her resuming her professional engagements on Monday, July 26, without the risk of danger.'

After that 'Jack Sheppard' was taken bodily out of the Adelphi bills, and the public heard no more, either of the piece or of the postponement, till September 6, when it was announced at the Haymarket, in conjunction with 'Paul Pry,' with nearly the same cast as at the Adelphi, except that O. Smith was down for Jonathan Wild in place of Mr. Lyon, Sam Emery for Mendez, and Miss Laura Honey and Miss E. Chaplin for two of the principal female characters.

Of course, the accident to the Jack Sheppard of Mrs. Keeley had been the talk of the town ever since its occurrence, and even the daily papers— which did not, as a rule, give more than one comparatively meagre notice of any dramatic event— condescended to devote a line or so of their valuable space to the 'severe ankle sprain,' and about half a dozen lines to the Haymarket revival. The longest critique began by grumbling at the Haymarket prices, saying that they were 'not considered suitable to Adelphi audiences, so that halfprice had to begin at eight instead of nine, and then the house was crammed.' Next the writer found fault with the immoral tendency of the piece, declaring that it was likely to influence banefully the evil-disposed of the gallery, and to contaminate the pious pit, not to mention the upper boxes.

But the same virtuous scribe was pleased to find that many of the objectionable passages peculiar to the original version had been suppressed, while in reference to Mrs. Keeley's Jack he remarked : 'It is a piece of personation that no other actress could approach. She is indeed a finished artist, and every characteristic of the

audacious, spirited, spoiled, daring young criminal
was admirably rendered.   Much that in other
hands would have been stagey and theatrical was
rendered with the truest feeling and the nicest
nature.   We are not surprised at the pertinacity
with which the lady has pursued her resolution to
assist at this revival, for it shows her extraordinary
abilities in a very prominent manner.'

It showed something besides this—namely, that
the vigorous lady had now completely recovered
from the effects of the 'severe sprain to her ankle,'
as it was called.   But in those days interviewing
was an unknown luxury in this country ; otherwise, some enterprising journalist might have
discovered by personal inquiry—as I myself did
many years after—what was the real nature of
the accident.   It is, however, not impossible that
the wily management purposely suppressed the
particulars, in order that the public might not
think that the actress had lost any of that lightness and elasticity of step for which she was
always so famous.

She had assuredly not lost it when I saw her
three years later at Sadler's Wells, and when
George Webster informed me that Mrs. Keeley
was coming our way, it was like hearing that Jack
Sheppard, the highwayman and housebreaker, was
about to visit the neighbourhood of Pentonville.

The impression of the two people rolled into one remained more fixedly still in my mind when I came to see the actress in the prohibited play of my childhood, and as I never met Jack behind the scenes, except once for a moment by accident in passing the stage, the pleasant illusion was kept up to the very last.

Yet I had seen Mrs. Keeley previously in many pieces, and even at Sadler's Wells under young Webster's management she appeared in the old Adelphi drama, 'Sea and Land,' and again in one of her favourite farces, 'Pas de Fascination,' together with 'Uncle Tom's Cabin,' in which the versatile actress played Topsy. But in my own estimation it was quite another Mrs. Keeley whom I then saw, and in no way resembled the Jack Sheppard one. As for my more juvenile views of the lady, it was usually 'the Keeleys' we were accustomed to see at the Adelphi, the Haymarket, or wherever the inseparable couple of that united name happened to be engaged. I had, moreover, never before seen the better half of the Keeleys in a boy's part, so that I did so at Sadler's Wells for the first time.

Though at first announced for 'positively six nights only,' the great Adelphi drama remained in the bills for another six nights after that; and it was played also for an 'extra night' upon the

occasion of the manager's benefit at the fag-end
of his season, on June 4.

After witnessing ' Jack Sheppard ' for those
twelve consecutive nights and the extra performance, I became so familiar with the fascinating
drama that at last I could repeat, almost line for
line, everyone's part in it.

CHAPTER II.

THOSE who can remember Mrs. Keeley, the actress, and 'Jack Sheppard,' the play, will not need to be told what each was like individually, and both collectively. But as the majority of my readers may not have seen either the one or the other, I propose to run through such portions of the drama as relate to the popular hero and to the equally popular creator.

In the original version, as performed at the Adelphi in 1839, an entire act is devoted to certain stirring events which take place at a time that Jack Sheppard and his friend, Thames Darrell, are babies in arms, and in the opening scene Mrs. Sheppard is discovered nursing the infant highwayman. But when the play was produced at Sadler's Wells, it began with the second act, which is supposed to have taken place some twelve years after the first, and this was, I believe, the way the piece commenced when revived in 1852.

The scene at the opening is a carpenter's shop in Wych Street, Drury Lane, kept by Owen Wood, who has adopted young Sheppard and taken him as an apprentice. Upon the rise of the curtain, little Jack is seen standing on a box placed over the work-bench, in the act of putting the finishing touches to his name, which he has been carving upon a wooden beam. He is at present in his shirt-sleeves, with a carpenter's apron rolled up to his waist, a long drab waistcoat, knee-breeches, high-heeled shoes, and a red hand-kerchief tied loosely round his neck. When more fully attired, he sports a brown coat of the period of George II., and a three-cornered hat, cocked carelessly over his short-cropped hair.

While engaged in carving his name, to the neglect of his proper duties, the young scamp gives evidence of his criminal tendencies by sing-ing an old cracksman's song of the last century, beginning :

> When Claude Duval was in Newgate thrown,
> He carved his name on the dungeon stone.
> Quoth a dubsman who gazed on the shattered wall,
> ' You have carved your epitaph, Claude Duval,
>   With your chisel so fine, tra, la !'

Having finished the song and his name, Jack springs nimbly from the box, and seating himself on the bench, says :

MRS. KEELEY AS JACK SHEPPARD, 1839.

To face p. 13.

'There, that'll do. Claude Duval himself couldn't have carved it better. I've half a mind to give old Wood the slip and turn highwayman.

WOOD (*who has overheard him and comes forward*): The devil you have! What, you'll rob the mail, like Jack Hall, I suppose, eh, you young dog? (*Cuffing him.*)

JACK: Yes, I will, if you beat me in that way.

After further conversation to the same effect, Jack promises to be a good boy for the future, and in evidence of his intention to be industrious, he takes up a carpenter's plane and goes to work with energy.

The planing business in this scene was always received with a round of applause, as the audience liked to see real planing done on the stage, especially by a woman. And it was no pretended work, either, for the actress was quite expert at the business, and the curly chips seen by the audience were the result of *bona-fide* hard work at the bench.

The same close attention to details was shown in the next important scene, or 'illustration,' in which Jack quarrels with his friend Darrell over the latter's sweetheart, and offers to fight him. Mrs. Keeley here placed herself in the orthodox boxing attitude, and her sparring movements clearly suggested that she had some knowledge of pugilism, and must certainly have been coached in the art, which, indeed, was actually the case.

The next interesting event occurs when Jack and Darrell are imprisoned in the Roundhouse, the latter having been falsely accused of theft, and the other of complicity in the supposed act. It is here that the actress's wonderful animal spirits and keen sense of humour are seen at their best, while her close imitation of the gaoler, Mendez, who speaks a sort of Dutch-English with a 'dash' of Welsh in it, was most amusing and created roars of laughter. In scenes of this kind, Mrs. Keeley always impressed one with the idea that she was enjoying the joke quite as much as the audience, and yet was unconscious of being the cause of their merriment. This gave a spontaneity to everything she did or said, making her acts and words appear perfectly natural, or unstudied.

Of course Jack effects his escape and that of his friend from the Roundhouse. But the filing of his friend's handcuffs and his own, the picking of the lock of their prison-door, and all the other business necessary for their freedom, are done gradually, impressing the spectator with the belief that the bolts, bars, and manacles are no theatrical shams, but genuine articles of the kind.

Jack sings and talks to Mendez while freeing himself from his fetters, and the audience are almost as much deceived by this singular case of art concealing art, as the gaoler himself is supposed to be.

'I knew I could file off your ruffles,' at last says Jack to his comrade, and they are heard to fall with a heavy thud behind the iron grating of the room where the lads are confined.

'Vat's dat?' says Mendez, with some alarm.

JACK: My fellow-bird trying to get off his ruffles.

MENDEZ: Ho! ho! Dat is no easy matter.

JACK: No, dat it ain't.' [Holding up the handcuffs aside to the audience, who, of course, shout with laughter.]

The escape from the Roundhouse brings the curtain down upon Act i., and when it rises again, after a supposed interval of nine years, we are introduced to a 'Flash Ken' in the Mint, where Blueskin and his pals are assembled, anxiously awaiting the arrival of Captain Sheppard, as he is now called. Jack has just made his escape from Newgate, and after a hearty welcome from his friends and his two wives, Poll and Bess, silence is proclaimed by Blueskin, and the company are told to 'clear their pipes for a chorus' to a song which the Captain has been invited to sing.

2

It is here that Mrs. Keeley essays the famous
ditty by Herbert Rodwell, of ' Nix my Dolly,' the
first verse of which is :

> In a box of the stone jug I was born,
> Of a hempen widow the kid forlorn.

BLUESKIN.   Fake away !

JACK.   And my noble father, as I've heard say,
> Was a famous merchant of capers gay.

BLUESKIN.   Nix my dolly, pals, fake away.
> *Chorus*—Nix my dolly, pals, fake away.

Towards the end of the fourth verse of this
favourite song, which was always enthusiastically
applauded and uproariously redemanded, all the
characters dance to the tune, including Jack, and
while doing so Mrs. Keeley afforded, by the
grace, lightness, and refinement of her movements, another striking example of her versatility.
She showed, however, to even greater advantage
in the last act, where Jack Sheppard makes his
final escape from Newgate ; so much so that,
when the little hero, who has been sitting peace-
fully for his portrait in the prison-cell, leaps up
after the sitting, and exclaims, ' Now for an
achievement compared with which all I have yet
done shall be as nothing,' the prophetic words
were quite as applicable to the actress as to the
scene about to be represented.

Before describing this, it may be as well to

refer to one or two incidents bearing upon it.
Jack Sheppard goes to the house of the thief-
taker in the Old Bailey, disguised as Arnold
Quilt, and he arrives there at the moment in
which Wild and Sir Rowland Trenchard are plot-
ting the murder of Thames Darrell. As soon as
the sham Quilt enters, Wild says to him, in
reference to the capture of Jack :

'Well, Quilt, have you succeeded ?

JACK (*in Quilt's voice*) [which the actress so
well imitated.] : All's right—he's safe in the hold
again.

JONATHAN : My excellent Quilt, the reward is
yours ; remain with him in the hold till I come to
you ; it is not safe to turn your eyes from him.
(*Shuts the door upon Jack.*) That's all right ; he
can't elude me, daring and active little devil as
he is.

But the daring and active little devil enters
again softly, and, concealing himself behind a
cloak suspended by a nail on the wall, overhears
the story of his high birth and that of his friend
Darrell, and learns by it that their respective
mothers were the sisters of Sir Rowland, and
rightful heiresses to the estate. He also sees
Jonathan take from his pocket a packet of papers,
one of which contains an account of Jack's birth.
These important documents the Captain deter-

mines to possess himself of, and taking advantage of a moment in which Sir Rowland and Wild are whispering together, he comes forward, and diving his hand nimbly into the pocket where the papers are deposited, withdraws them, and then quickly returns to his place of concealment.

The workmanlike manner in which this business was effected afforded one more striking example of the actress's close attention to details. The abstraction of the documents from Jonathan Wild's pocket was so rapid and dexterous as to appear the accomplishment of a practised hand at pocket-picking. Indeed, it looked so like the real thing that the audience were afraid lest the unwary thief-taker should turn round and catch the young culprit in the act, and there was quite a sigh of relief when Jack had safely landed the rightful proofs of his birth.

The pickpocket incident was the result of careful study on the part of the actress, assisted by some instruction from an expert in the ways of thieves. The actor of Jonathan Wild seldom, if ever, felt the small, flexible hand of Mrs. Keeley as it dived neatly into his pocket, and was hardly aware that the trick was done.

In spite of Jack Sheppard's many delinquencies and his fame as a notorious highwayman, the sympathies of the audience are with him in the

drama from first to last. This is due in some
measure to the knowledge that he is of high
birth, and to the fact that he has been driven to
misdeeds by the force of circumstances over which
Jonathan Wild has had no inconsiderable control.
The audience therefore regard the lad—for he is
only one-and-twenty in the last act—as simply a
young reprobate or gentleman scapegrace, and the
painstaking actress assisted them in this impression by representing their hero with a certain
picturesqueness of manner and refinement of
speech, which caused his lowest slang and most
depraved ditties, if perfectly true to nature, to be
wholly without vulgarity. So the moral of the
stage story appeared to be, 'Train up a child in
the way he should go,' and don't drive him to do
wicked things.

But the hero of Buckstone's piece has also a
good heart, and proves himself besides a stanch
friend to those in need of his assistance; while
the occasional loving references to his unfortunate
mother show him to be possessed of some filial
devotion, though it must be confessed that his
regret for all that she has suffered on his account
comes somewhat late in the day. At the opening
of Act iii. Jack is discovered lying on his recently-
departed mother's grave, attired in a black coat
and white waistcoat, and his little soliloquy, ear-

nestly delivered by the actress, was not without its appeal to the hearts of the audience.

'Oh, Jack, Jack!' he cries, 'you have broken your poor mother's heart, and here she lies buried by her last request in Willesden churchyard. Poor mother! when I heard Wild tell Sir Rowland you were in Bedlam, and driven there by my misconduct, neither he nor I knew you had been three days dead! They tell me she forgave me before she died—bless her! Oh, villain, outcast, condemned felon that I am!'

There was not a dry eye in the house when the actress gave out these semi-pathetic lines; and certainly not at the back of the pit, where the present writer was doing his best to set the example.

Jack Sheppard has now made up his mind to turn over a new leaf, and he proposes to retire from the business of housebreaking by setting sail for a foreign clime, there to begin life afresh as an honest lad. It is not too late, he thinks, and if the law will only give him another chance, he will never again act as a charmingly picturesque and delightfully fascinating young villain—at any rate, upon the stage, greatly to the regret, be it said, of the audience.

But unfortunately the law, in the shape of Jonathan Wild, won't let him, the more so be-

cause the thief-taker has sworn a terrible oath
that he will bring Jack to the gallows, as he did
with his father before him. So Wild makes one
last attempt in this direction, and he is so far successful that, after an affecting scene between the
hero and his new-found cousin, Thames Darrell,
whom Jack has been instrumental in restoring to
his rightful estates and his sweetheart, the young
highwayman is seized and eventually overpowered
by no less than half a dozen well-armed constables,
who, with the greatest possible difficulty, accompanied by rounds of applause from the sixpenny
gallery and shilling pit—to say nothing of the two
and three shilling boxes—hurry him off to Newgate.

Safely landed in his old quarters, Jack is
strongly handcuffed and chained to the stone
floor. But he has presently to endure that which
to some persons would be considered as a form of
slow torture, for he has been prevailed upon to sit
for his portrait to no less an artist than Sir James
Thornhill, the picture being destined to figure in
the collection of no less a person than King
George II. The great Hogarth also takes a
sketch of him at the same time, while Gay, the
poet, and Figg, a prize-fighter, look on and pass
critical remarks.

Of course, sitting for a portrait on the stage is

a very different thing to the same performance in
a studio, and as the audience were well aware of
this, their sympathies for Jack Sheppard's suffer-
ings were not reawakened on this account.   But
to pose for your likeness with manacles upon your
wrists and heavy rings of iron on your legs is
quite another matter, and it was doubtless for this
reason that when the scene shifted and the 'notorious highwayman' was discovered in the act of
having his head taken off on canvas as a preliminary exercise to be followed by hanging by
the neck, there was more than one suggestive
shudder among the spectators.

How little did one spectator, who contemplated
the performances from the back of the pit, imagine
that the time would come when the impersonator
of the notorious one would be sitting to that spectator for her portrait in a far more realistic fashion
than she ever did upon the stage, and that it—the
picture, not the highwayman—would be hung on
the line at the Royal Academy! But, in the
words of the novelist, let us not anticipate.

It is immediately after his artist-friends and
teacher of boxing leave the stage that Jack pulls
himself together, and prepares for the 'achievement compared with which all that he has yet
done will be as nothing.'

By way of beginning, he sets free his hands

from the handcuffs that have hitherto clasped his
wrists—and really clasped them, for the scrupu-
lously particular actress used from first to last a
pair of genuine manacles, the exact facsimile of
those worn by the real Jack Sheppard, and they
were not only placed in orthodox fashion upon
her slender wrists, but properly locked into the
bargain. All the same, Mrs. Keeley contrived every
night to squeeze her flexible fingers and palm clear
of them, though how she did it I did not precisely
know till many years after I had witnessed the
somewhat painful operation.

While so engaged, to the breathless excitement
of the audience, Jack sings :

> Though with neither a chisel, a knife, nor a file,
> Yet the dubsman shall see that I do it in style !

He continues to sing while taking off his shoes
and dancing in his fetters, till he suddenly stops
as his foot comes in contact with a painful but
serviceable nail. Then he laughs, and again
sings :

> Oh ! fortune ne'er played me so pleasant a trick
> As to drop me a nail my lock to pick !

Which the prisoner is soon busy in doing. First
he picks the padlock of the floor, which releases
the chains attached to it ; then he twists the chains
round till the centre link snaps, and after this he

draws the fetterlock up his legs, binds the broken chain round one leg with a scarf from his neck, and fastens another to the companion leg with his pocket-handkerchief.

All this time Jack is singing cheerily, and the business looks so real that the audience are kept on tenter-hooks to know what next he will do. But their suspense is of brief duration, as the gaol-bird presently takes up a blanket from a recess at the back of his cell, and, going with it to the chimney, is soon seen ascending that convenient aperture for prisoners in want of a practical loophole for escape.

The scene is then shut in by a 'front cloth,' representing a room in Wood's house, where Thames Darrell and his sweetheart, Winnifred, meet and are made happy, and when poor Jack is next visible the scene has changed again to the highest leads of Newgate. Here Mrs. Keeley is seen in the act of descending a wall by means of a blanket, which has been securely fastened to a nail. Jack is now pale and exhausted, and when he alights safely upon the leads he leans somewhat feebly upon an iron bar which he has brought with him.

At length the runaway, who is still burthened with his fetters, grows weaker and weaker as he flees from one street to the other, till in the last

scene but one he staggers in without his faithful
bar, and says :

'It's all up! They unkennelled me from Wych
Street. I've darted from them, but now where
can I run? I'm surrounded on every side. Yes,
it's no use—it's all up with Jack. Very hard,
though, after the bold tug I've had for it. I've
lost my best friend, and now my heart seems
breaking. I can do no more—they must come
and take me. To-day will end my life—my short
and wretched life! For let guilt be as bold and
as brave on the outside as it may, all is surely
misery—bitter misery—within! The poor Lon
don lads will, I hope, be warned by me and my
fate, for here is the end of sin !'

But this highly-respectable moral speech is not
quite the end of the drama, as in the next and last
scene of all we are shown the exterior of Newgate
in the Old Bailey, with Jonathan Wild's house occu-
pying most of the stage. The thief-taker has
been imprisoned in his own house for some days,
along with his accomplice, Mendez, and Blueskin
has sworn to make them pay dearly for their
various acts of villainy, should Jack Sheppard be
captured and taken to the gallows. So, finding
that their beloved Captain has been run to earth
and is already on his way to Tyburn, Blueskin
and his pals carry out their threat by setting fire

to Wild's domicile. This being done, the wretched
inmates of the burning house meet with a fate
which completely satisfies the audience, who have
been all along thirsting for their blood ; for Wild
and Mendez are buried alive in the smouldering
ruins when the interior of the house falls, and this
last episode, of course, brings down the other
house and the curtain.

CHAPTER III.

THE PALMY DAYS OF LEGITIMATE FARCE.

SMIKE was generally pronounced to be the
actress's next best boy impersonation after Jack
Sheppard, which immediately followed it, and it
was on November 19, 1838, that 'Nicholas
Nickleby' drew its first breath upon the stage of
the Adelphi, just three days before the commemoration of Mrs. Keeley's own birthday.

It is, however, not easy to picture Mrs. Keeley
as a half-starved school-drudge, after having witnessed her dashing young highwayman; the
more so because, when the present writer saw
Jack at Sadler's Wells, his figure, if small, neat
and graceful, was decidedly well developed, and
his limbs were quite statuesque in their symmetry,
while his face was perfectly round, not to say
plump. Yet it is said that the artist's make-up
as the attenuated lad in Dickens's story was positively startling in its accuracy, and that in general

appearance she was the exact counterpart of the well-known drawings by Cruikshank.

The same trustworthy authority states that when Smike was seen for the first time, huddled up over the wretched fire in the dimly-lighted kitchen of Do-the-boys Hall, the audience scarcely recognised the actress, and were for some time in doubt whether to laugh or to weep at Smike's woe-begone appearance. At last they took a humorous view of the situation, perhaps because the piece was called simply a ' farce ' by its adapter, Edward Stirling, and presently there was a roar of laughter in the house. But when the actress rose and walked totteringly to the footlights, where she remained still speechless and staring blankly at vacancy, the laughter gradually subsided, and long before Smike's opening lines were over, there was hardly a dry eye in the house. Then, when the lines came to an end, the walls of the Adelphi rang again and again with thunders of applause at the artistic conception of the character.

There was no more laughter after that as con- cerned Smike, but only the keenest sympathy for the wretched outcast, varied by occasional thrills of horror at his shameless treatment. This appears to have been particularly noticeable towards the end of the first act, where Smike, who has run away from his persecutors, is

SCENE FROM 'NICHOLAS NICKLEBY.'

O. SMITH (NEWMAN NOGGS).   MRS. KEELEY (SMIKE).   J. WEBSTER (NICHOLAS).

NOGGS. 'Is this the boy of desperate character? Poor fellow! Poor fellow!'

To face p. 29.

captured and brought back to the loathsome school, where, in presence of the other boys and the schoolmaster's family, Whackford Squeers prepares to thrash him with a cane.

' Let every boy keep his place,' says Squeers, striking his desk with his flexible weapon. ' Nickleby, attend here. Now, sir (*to Smike*), have you anything to say for yourself? (*flourishing cane*). Stand a little out of the way, Mrs. Squeers, my dear; I've hardly got room enough.'

SMIKE: Spare me, sir; I was driven to do it.

SQUEERS: Driven to do it, were you? Oh, it wasn't your fault; it was mine, I suppose, eh?

MRS. SQUEERS: What does he mean by that?

SQUEERS: We'll try and find out. (*Seizes Smike, and is in the act of striking him, when Nicholas comes forward.*)

NICHOLAS: Stop!

SQUEERS: Who cried stop?

NICHOLAS: I. This must not go on.

SQUEERS: Must not go on?

NICHOLAS: No; I say must not—I will prevent it.

Which he does most effectually, and to the intense relief and delight of the audience; for, after wresting the cane from the schoolmaster,

Nicholas thrashes him severely with his own weapon, and so the curtain falls on Act i.

In the second and last act Smike and Nicholas, who have decamped from the hateful school, prepare to walk to London. On the way they meet honest John Browdie, who befriends them, and with the money he lends the wanderers, they are enabled to journey to town by coach. The farce then introduces the audience to some really laughable scenes at the Mantalinis', followed by other amusing incidents at Newman Noggs's humble lodgings, and so on till the characters assemble at Ralph Nickleby's luxurious home, where he is denounced by Newman, who restores the persecuted orphan to his legal rights, and the play ends.

Dickens's immortal story is too well known by every novel-reader to need more than this brief outline of Edward Stirling's adaptation, which followed that portion of the original pretty closely, though it was neither submitted to the author nor produced with his sanction. But the reader of the present record will have a good notion of what a dramatized version of the book was like by reference to its more recent adaptation by Andrew Halliday, who wrote and produced it some twenty years ago ; and taken in conjunction with the revival of his piece five years later, which

SCENE FROM 'NICHOLAS NICKLEBY.'

Miss Shaw (Madame Mantalini).   Fred. Yates (Mantalini).   Miss Cotterill (Kate).

almost any young playgoer may remember, he will have an excellent idea of how the version was acted.

Commenting upon the inconsistent behaviour of the 1838 audience, a modern journalist remarks :

'Something besides the power of Mrs. Keeley will probably have struck the reader, and that is the singular ignorance of the audience. Dickens was at the height of his popularity ; everyone, it might have been supposed, had read " Nicholas Nickleby," or, at any rate, knew all about it, and therefore all about Smike, one of the most pathetic of Dickens's creations. The playbills show that Mrs. Keeley is playing Smike, and when the wretched boy appears they roar with laughter !'

The farce was brought out on a Monday, which seems to have been the favoured day of the week for first representations at that time. On the previous Saturday Mrs. Keeley was playing in 'A Model Man,' and in the 'Blue Jackets,' so that our managerial predecessors were apparently not given to close their houses for final rehearsals. The pieces just named followed, upon the same evening, Miss Pardoe's stirring drama of 'Louise Rignarolles ; or, A Lesson for Husbands,' and for once the management thought fit to supplement their usually simple announcement by stating that the excellence of the drama

3

was 'nightly attested by the tears and sympathy of the audience.' As this piece afterwards preceded ' Nicholas Nickleby,' it may have been another reason for the unseemly conduct of the spectators. They had already shed copious tears over Miss Pardoe's production, and they had none left for the after-piece!

When first produced in 1874 at the new Adelphi, and revived at the same theatre in 1879, it would, with one notable exception, be difficult to beat the cast, and in my own humble opinion I do not think that in the 'palmy days of the drama,' when Webster produced the piece, the cast, taken as a whole, was half as good as that of fifteen and twenty years ago, in spite of the fact that in Stirling's edition the public of 1838 had for the Newman Noggs O. Smith, who is reported to have looked the part to perfection, and 'played it to the life'; for the Mantalini, no less a person than Yates, who, according to the best authority of the day, ' made the part a caricature of a caricature,' and for the other characters, Mr. Wilkinson (Squeers), Mrs. Fosbroke (Mrs. Squeers), Miss O'Niel (Mrs. Nickleby), Miss Cottrell (Kate), Mr. Cullenford (Ralph), Mr. Beverly (John Browdie), and Mr. J. Webster (who is described as 'tame') in the title *rôle*.

For Halliday's version, which is considered far more interesting as a play than the first attempted, and introduced other characters and scenes, to the exclusion of Mantalini and his business, we had Mr. Terriss in the title *rôle;* Mr. Fernandez as Ralph; Mr. George Belmore as Newman Noggs (afterwards played by Mr. Hermann Vezin); Sam Emery (and in 1879 Henry Neville) as John Browdie; Mrs. Alfred Mellon (Miss Woolgar) as Mrs. Squeers; Miss Lydia Foote as Smike; and last, not least, Mr. J. G. Taylor, who both looked and acted Squeers to the life when he appeared in 1879, the part having been previously filled (1874) by 'Johnny' Clarke. It is worth a passing note that the very day after the revival of Halliday's version, on October 30, 1879, the author of 'Jack Sheppard,' J. B. Buckstone, breathed his last.

In noticing Mrs. Keeley's Smike when she enacted it for the first time in 1838, a dramatic critic of the day remarked:

'It was on Mrs. Keeley's shoulders that the weight of the piece for dramatic effect was principally thrown. Her small and pretty figure did not suit well for the representation of the overgrown boy of nineteen, but her dress was perfect, her look inexpressibly wretched, and her voice and manners truly heart-rending. Nothing could be more natural or moving than the boy's shudder when Squeers announced, in answer to his timid inquiry whether he had any news for him, that nobody asked about him. Then, again, the joyous expression with which he dwelt upon his childish notions of liberty, contrasted with the desponding tones in which he pictured the approach of gloomy death, without even the satisfaction of beholding the friendly faces of home, which the diseased imagination of another boy—his companion—had conjured up around his bed before his decease, hushed the house into complete stillness, which was only broken by the most rapturous plaudits.'

Another first-nighter refers to the actress's 'silent by-play, quiet and simple,' as being a 'very study,' and concludes by saying : 'The house called long enough for Mrs. Keeley (at the fall of the curtain), but she did not come forward.' The piece was, however, 'announced for repetition amidst loud cheers,' a proceeding on the part of the management which nowadays might be considered superfluous. Fancy appearing before the curtain upon the first night of the latest Adelphi success, in which at least two star performers had made big hits, to say that the new piece would be presented again !

The piece which I propose now to describe was

SCENE FROM 'NICHOLAS NICKLEBY.'

Mr. Wilkinson (Squeers).   Miss O'Niel (Mrs. Nickleby).   Mr. Cullenford (Ralph).

To face p. 34

far better entitled to the name of farce than the
one just referred to.

This was called 'Pas de Fascination; or, Catching a Governor,' by J. Stirling Coyne. It was a
favourite with the actress as well as with the
public, for in it all Mrs. Keeley's best qualities
as a low comedian, and her useful accomplishments of dancing and singing, were seen to
advantage. The piece was originally produced
at the Haymarket in 1848, where it was entitled
' Lola Montez ; or, A Countess for an Hour,' but
the title was afterwards changed for political
reasons in connection with the King of Bavaria,
and because such a person as Lola Montez
actually existed, and was the talk of the
town.

The cast was a strong one, with Mrs. Keeley
as Katherine Kloper (played in 1857, at Boston,
by Mrs. John Wood) ; 'Bob' Keeley as Michael
Browsky ; Mr. Tilbury as Count Muffenuff, the
Governor ; Miss E. Harding as Lola Montez,
under the assumed name of Zepherine Joliejambe
(afterwards played by Mrs. Buckingham White) ;
and Messrs. Rogers, Clark, Braid, and other
Haymarket favourites in minor parts. I could
well imagine how Mr. Keeley would play Michael,
the State barber, from having seen him in so
many characters of the kind, and also because

I was sufficiently familiar with the play when I saw it at Sadler's Wells, with James Rogers as Michael Browsky, and Mrs. Keeley in her original *rôle* of the 'clear-starcher, gofferer, washer of laces, and confidential agent.'

I saw quite enough of ' Pas de Fascination ' to be able to describe it now. So, for the benefit of readers who may not be familiar with the ' plot,' I venture to give a brief outline of it, together with a specimen of the dialogue, leaving those who may happen to have seen Mrs. Keeley when some thirteen years ago she emerged from her well-earned retirement to appear in ' Betsy Baker' for Mr. Toole's benefit, to picture her in the part about to be described.

The farce is in two distinct scenes, and at the rise of the curtain Katherine Kloper, who appears to be a cross between a Russian peasant and a British-born maid-of-all-work, is discovered ironing at a table in her Slavonic home, and singing some ' quite English ' verses to the American tune, ' My skiff is on de shore.' After the song, the cheery, industrious little woman has a long speech, in which she refers to her sweetheart Michael, the Court barber, who has lately ' begged her acceptance of an affectionate heart and a pot of genuine bear's grease,' and whom she has consented to take—along with the ' four bears

that he has fattening in his cellar.' Then she
remembers to put in the window the business-
card bearing the N.B. : 'Confidential communi-
cations treated with the utmost secrecy ;' and she
has scarcely done so when a customer enters in
great alarm to say that she is in danger of losing
her liberty, and perhaps her life, owing to a
misunderstanding with the manager of the St.
Petersburg Theatre, where she was engaged to
dance a favourite *pas* in the ballet, but owing to
an appointment that night to sup with Prince
Dunbrownski, she declined to appear. The
manager, suspecting the truth, applied to the
Minister of Police, and the latter in turn sent
an old colonel of dragoons and a file of soldiers
to request the dancer's immediate presence at the
theatre.

The clear-starcher is, of course, very sympathetic, and at once offers to assist her visitor by
procuring for her a disguise in the shape of a
convenient dress belonging to Katherine's military brother, Ivan, who happens to be 'just the
height' of Lola Montez, as he was naturally
bound to be in a play. She also agrees to
assume Zepherine's travelling attire, which likewise, in the play, is that of a theatre dancer.
With this costume alone she passes herself off as
the celebrated Lola, and as such she is, of course,

arrested by the myrmidons of justice and conducted to the Governor's citadel.

In the next scene we are introduced to the
Governor Muffenuff's state apartment, where that
high and mighty functionary is seen surrounded
by his admiring court. His Excellency has been
suffering for some time past from ennui, and his
courtiers have tried in vain to think of something
new to arouse him and divert his mind from the
troubles of the State.

'Can't any of you think of something to amuse
me?' he asks yawningly.

'Certainly, your Excellency,' promptly replies
Kyboshki, his Privy Councillor; 'I think I
could think, if I were to think; but it takes
some thought to think when we're not thinking.'
(*Meditates profoundly.*)

The treasurer and other attendants have also
grand ideas for entertainments of various impossible kinds. But the Russian Governor of
Neveraskwehr will have none of them, and after
another yawn or two, followed by a deep sigh, he
says he wishes it was bed-time again. At this
moment Grippenhoff, the chief of the police,
arrives post-haste with a piece of 'the most important and astounding intelligence.' In other
words, the runaway dancer has been caught, and
is at present in custody in the ante-chamber.

The Governor, of course, wakes up at these glad-
some tidings, and orders the foreign fugitive to
be brought before him, which is presently done,
and there trips lightly into the gorgeous apartment a young and attractive little lady, attired in
a black and amber Spanish dress.

'Bless me,' says this Spanish beauty upon
entering, 'what a lot of fine folks!'   Then,
addressing the chief of police, she goes on: 'I
say, old gentleman, which is the Governor?'

KYBOSHKI (*grandly*): Yonder, madame, is his
Excellency——

KATHERINE: Oh, that old chap with the
thingembobs at his buttonhole.   He don't look a
bit ferocious.   How d'ye do, Governor?

And so it goes on till Katherine, after describing the company as a 'set of stuck-up posts,'
asks: 'Can we have a little fun?'

GOVERNOR: Fun, eh?   What's that?   Kyboshki, what's fun?

KYBOSHKI: Fun?—a—a—I haven't the re-
motest idea.   What's fun, Count?

STIFFENBACK: Fun?   Don't know what it
means.

KATHERINE [Keeley] (*jumping up*): Not know
what fun means?   How I pity you poor creatures!
Ha! ha! ha!   How miserable you must all be!
Why, fun is—ha! ha! ha! ha!—rolling down a hill,

or riding on a donkey, or (*catches Kyboshki and forces him to waltz with her*) — there, that's fun !

The company again express their horror in various ways, with the exception of their chief, who now says to this enchanting lady :

' I hope you will not refuse delighting us with your celebrated *pas seul*,' and Mrs. Keeley's wonderfully expressive face was a complete study as Katherine replies :

' My celebrated *pas seul ?* What's that? Oh, very well ; it's all the same to me (*aside*). I haven't been so often to the Casino for nothing. Come, stand back, all of you ; let me have a clear stage and no favour. Keep out of the way. Baron, will you move on ? Stand back a little, madame ' (*pushing the company out of the way as she speaks*).

The music then strikes up, and Katherine Keeley proceeds to dance a wild cachuca, and at the end throws herself into a grotesque attitude, with one leg high in the air and so near the face of the Governor that I was told that every night the actor of the part was in mortal fear lest the energetic little lady should really kick him.

It need scarcely be mentioned that the gyrations, though a caricature of the genuine cachuca, were accomplished by the actress with excessive lightness, grace, and even elegance, and without the least show of vulgarity. Nor need it be told that the dance was received always with uproarious applause by the delighted spectators, followed by loud demands for its repetition.

The Governor is as enraptured as the audience, and after some talk with his attendants on official matters, he invites the 'distinguished foreigner' to come to a grand ball to be given in her honour, and, in order that she may appear with a title to her name, he presents her with a 'patent of nobility,' and insists that everyone shall address her for the future as the 'Countess of Katzenelenbogen.'

It is while acting in that capacity, and preparing for the ball, that the State barber is announced. Michael has come to dress 'her ladyship's' hair, and, of course, he recognises her, and she him. But neither one nor the other will acknowledge it till the barber, becoming again madly jealous, can no longer restrain himself, and charges his sweetheart with gross infidelity.

Matters are, however, satisfactorily explained, and the lovers are reconciled and made happy in each other's arms. But at this moment the Governor enters unperceived, and is naturally horrified to see the State prisoner in the arms

of the State barber.   Katherine, quite equal to
the occasion, then says :

‘ Bless me !   What are you staring at ?   It's
all very natural, ain't it ?’

At this point Grippenhoff enters to inform his
Excellency that there has been a serious mistake,
and that the real fugitive has just been captured
while endeavouring to pass the town gate dressed
in male attire.

GOVERNOR (*to Katherine*) : Then who the
devil are you ?

KATHERINE [curtseying in a manner that creates
roars of laughter in the house] : The Countess
Katzenelenbogen, your Excellency.

But this does not satisfy his Excellency, who,
fearing that he may be the laughing-stock of
the town, offers the clear-starcher five hundred
roubles on her wedding-day if she will give up
her ‘patent of nobility.’ This Katherine eventually does, and the curtain falls, though not
before Mrs. Keeley has addressed a few words
to the audience in accordance with custom in
those days.

It may be interesting to note that when ‘ Pas
de Fascination ’ was first produced, Mrs. Charles
Kean, who was among the audience, described it
as ‘ the most daring play she had ever witnessed,’
and afterwards congratulated Mrs. Keeley warmly

upon her new success. It is also worthy of record that, some nights after, Lola Montez herself was present in a stage-box, and that the celebrated danseuse was so genuinely pleased with Mrs. Keeley's acting that at the end of the performance she threw a magnificent bouquet at her feet.

CHAPTER IV.

An interval of nearly thirty years is, in theatrical parlance, 'supposed to have elapsed' between the last chapter and the present one, and the scene opens with the interior of a recently-built West-End theatre, not many yards distant from Leicester Square.

The stage and auditorium, constructed upon all the latest and most luxurious principles, are completely crowded by one of the most distinguished assemblies ever gathered together at a playhouse, for among the company are many leaders of the theatrical and musical professions, together with not a few representatives of art, literature, and journalism.

Upon the rising of the curtain (which is of double-plated iron and worked by hydraulic pressure) a number of persons are discovered on the stage, and, judging by the many notable star-performers, the 'cast' is the strongest on record.

But from my place in the stalls, it appears to be an odd kind of performance, and everyone seems to be speaking at once, so that only a general buzz of voices reaches my ear, and not a single word is distinguishable. As for the ' plot,' I can make neither head nor tail of it ; but the piece is apparently divided into about fifty acts, for the fire-proof curtain rises and falls at least once in every five minutes, disclosing much the same scene and with much the same performers in it.

The behaviour of the audience is just as eccentric as that of the curtain. For in the gallery overhead two gentlemen, attired in the evening dress of Lionel Brough and George Grossmith, are seen and heard trying conclusions with a well-conducted gentleman in the stalls, closely resembling Mr. Harry Paulton, and a highly respectable person in a private box, on the prompt side, exactly like Mr. J. L. Toole.

The conduct of those two occupants of the gallery is outrageous. But, singularly enough, it appears to amuse the rest of the audience, and even those upon the stage, for many of them roar with laughter. And yet there are present the *crême de la crême* of the theatrical world, among whom one easily recognises S. B. Bancroft, Henry Neville, W. Creswick, Edward Righton, G. W. Anson, Mr. and Mrs. John Billington, Edgar

Bruce, Mrs. Bernard Beere, Miss Lingard, Miss
Constance Loseby, Lotta, the American actress,
Lord Lonsdale, and last, not least, Mrs. Stirling.

Nearly all these good people are known to me
personally, and with not a few I shake hands and
converse. But there is one whom I think I
know intimately, and yet for the life of me I cannot
say where and when I have met her before, or
what is her name.

In appearance the lady was what the French
call *petite*, and from my place in the stalls she
seemed to be in her prime, or not far advanced in
the forties. For her figure, though well developed,
was decidedly graceful and slim, while the ease of
her movements, and gay, sprightly manner, as
she conversed with her friends, impressed me
more than ever with the feeling that she seemed
much younger than she was.

The object of my gaze was standing, when first
I saw her, in the very centre of the stage, and
when I went round to the wings to ask a theatrical friend who the lady might be, I found
her gesticulating with a letter in her hand to a
party of people in a box over that occupied by
Mr. Toole's double, as if wishing to attract their
attention. So I took occasion to inquire who was
the energetic little woman in the dark, close-fitting
dress and fashionable bonnet, and the friend I

consulted, who was Mr. Edgar Bruce, turning to me with an air of doubt as to the genuineness of my demand, said simply :

' Mrs. Keeley.'

He might have knocked me down with the proverbial feather, so great was my surprise at thus suddenly beholding a lady whom many persons confidently believed had been dead and buried ages ago. For it seemed ages since last we saw Mrs. Keeley at Sadler's Wells, and after that at the Adelphi, where, following close upon her fortnight's engagement with George Webster, she returned with her husband and daughter Mary to appear in the 'Camp at Chobham' and in ' Betty Martin.' To be strictly accurate, it was exactly nine-and-twenty years since I witnessed the Keeley performances, and then, somehow, I completely lost sight of the two favourites of the stage.

But there stood the Jack Sheppard of twenty-nine years ago, and she and I were presently standing together in the very centre of the stage, with her hand in mine, Mr. Bruce having just introduced us.

And the hand was the same that I had once — and more than once — seen from a distance, as it squeezed itself free of the highwayman's handcuffs, or, with the companion hand,

4

descended from the heights of Newgate by means
of a prison blanket. ' Now for an achievement
compared with which all I have yet done shall be
as nothing !' Those well-remembered words, and
many others of the kind, now came back to me as
I stood beside the original speaker of them, while
it occurred to me that the line just quoted might
not inaptly apply to myself in connection with my
recent presentation. But I had more reason still
for its adoption presently.

Meanwhile, I was content to contemplate my
new-found friend with the longing eyes of an
artist, and to converse with her with the appreciative feelings of an old playgoer. In doing so,
I noticed that, although Time had naturally set his
seal upon the actress's features, it was the same
bright, expressive face, the same merry eyes, the
same intelligent brow. When she laughed, the
laugh was as hearty and infectious as of old, and
when she talked the voice was as clear, articulate,
and varied in its tones as when last I heard her
saying with true dramatic force :

' Once more I breathe the pure air of heaven !
—once more am I on the outside of those terrible
walls.'

And now she spoke with scarcely less energy
and grace ; and in nearly the same language, too,
when expressing to me a wish that she might

inhale a purer atmosphere than was afforded by an overcrowded stage. There was, however, nothing very 'terrible' in those walls, for they belonged to Edgar Bruce, and formed a rather important part of his brand-new playhouse in Coventry Street, Piccadilly.

Mr. Bruce's recently-erected theatre was, as most persons know, called originally the Prince's, to be afterwards renamed the Prince of Wales's, and it was on the evening of January 16, 1884, that, at the proprietor's invitation, there were assembled within his handsome premises a large number of his personal friends, and every nook and corner was overrun by the guests. The stage was also open for their inspection, and though as yet divested of scenery, I was reminded very forcibly of the custom at some Spanish theatres that I had visited, of inviting the audience of the stalls and boxes to enter, between the long acts, the sacred precincts. So, altogether, the dream of my boyhood to go behind the scenes and know the players personally was, both abroad and at home, now sufficiently realized.

But of all my experiences as a playgoer and limner of faces, none could compare, in point of interest and pleasurable excitement, with that which happened not many days after the festivities at Mr. Bruce's theatre, when, in response to

my request, the Jack Sheppard, Smike, Nydia,
Little Nell, Audrey, Clemency Newcombe, Dot,
Topsy, Margot, Katherine Kloper, Rosina, Little
Pickle, Betsy Baker, and scores of characters of
the kind, consented to sit at my studio for a good-
sized portrait of herself.

By way of preliminary to this important undertaking, I went, by appointment, to my future
subject's home, in Pelham Crescent, where she
had lived for nearly forty years, either alone or
with her husband and daughters, and there secured
a small pencil sketch of her.

While waiting for my hostess to appear, I took
mental stock of some of the objects in the prettily-
furnished drawing-room into which I had been
shown by the servant Hunt, examining with care
the pictures on the walls of the front and back
apartments.   There were only a scattered few,
but nearly every one was of special interest, including some photographic presentments of the
owner and her theatrical friends, conspicuous
among whom were Mrs. Stirling and Miss Mary
Anderson, as the nurse and the heroine in ' Romeo
and Juliet.'   Close at hand was a large water-
colour drawing of Mrs. Keeley as Cinderella, in
the burlesque of that name, and as a pendant to
this hung a full-length figure of her late husband,
as Jacob Earwig in ' Boots at the Swan.'   On

MRS. KEELEY AS CINDERELLA.

To face p. 52.

the opposite wall was a coloured likeness of
the low comedian in one of his famous parts,
namely, Mrs. Caudle; while not far off was a
clever water-colour sketch of the Weir, Maiden-
head, from the brush of Charles Mathews, with
the following inscription written beneath it in his
own clear hand : ' To Mrs. Keeley, from her
youthful friend and old admirer, C. J. Mathews,
May 4, 1857.'

Similar souvenirs of Mrs. Keeley's son-in-law,
Albert Smith, were displayed upon side-tables, and
I took particular notice of some comic figures of
animals which the famous entertainer delighted in
collecting, among them being an intoxicated pig ;
a dog with a walking-stick in his paw and a straw
hat upon his head ; a fox smiling at a rooster who
has been caught in a trap intended for his wily
friend ; while near these curiosities was a quaintly-
bound volume, the covers of which were made
from a wooden log of oak saved from the fire of
Covent Garden in 1856, which I well remember
and was present at. The book was dedicated to
Charles Dickens, and on the fly-leaf was written,
' To Mr. and Mrs. Keeley, with Albert Smith's
kind regards.'

Upon another side-table was a glass case containing a pair of shapely hands in wax, beautifully
modelled from those of the Countess of Blessing-

ton, who wrote with one of them the autograph
letter placed near the wax effigy just described.

'I have only a very poor collection,' remarked
the proprietor, after a cordial, unaffected welcome
to her delightful home; 'my works of art are not
quite equal to those of the Royal Academy, you
know. That one you're looking at is a little
water-colour by Keeley Halswelle, which he was
kind enough to give me. I am a great admirer of
his work, and try to copy him sometimes in my
small way; but I can't manage the perspective.
I know it's all wrong, and do what I will it won't
come right. But I never had a lesson in my life,
and now I'm afraid I am too old to learn. It
amuses me, though, and helps to pass away the
time pleasantly. Yes, that is one of my daubs.
But don't look at it, for I'm sure you will be disgusted and say that it is horrible.'

I am sure that I said nothing of the kind, nor
did I think it; for the little landscape copy before
me, if not an exact facsimile of the original, was
very like it in composition and general tone. I
had no idea till now that the actress was an
amateur artist, so was naturally astonished to find
that she had dabbled in art; and still more, that
at the age of seventy-eight she was yet able to
handle the brush skilfully and without the aid of
glasses. But long after she had completed her

eighty-ninth year her sight was not more im-
paired, nor had her hand lost its cunning.

'No,' she answered in her emphatic way, as I
proceeded with my pencil sketch, 'I have never
sat to an artist for an oil-painting such as you
propose doing of me. But I once posed for a
little water-colour sketch to Mr. Lewis Wingfield,
though I don't think it was ever properly finished.
Nobody was allowed to see the picture while it
was in progress, so the artist hid it in a cupboard.
But an inquisitive brother of mine got a stolen
peep at it, and afterwards he came to me, and
said, "Well, my dear, if that's you, you must be
doosid ugly!" I also sketched myself,' she continued, after I had recovered from my laugh at
this amusing story; 'it was as Lucy Bertram in
the dramatized version of "Guy Mannering."
But that was a long time ago, when as a young
girl of sixteen and a half I made my very first
appearance upon any stage. It was only an experiment or trial of my powers; for, as I dare say
you know, my first professional engagement was
at the Lyceum in London.'

Yes, I knew that well, and I said so. But I
wanted to hear from her own lips the particulars
of that famous first appearance, as also of the other
coup d'essai, as it was called, at her native place.
These and many other things, however, would, I

trusted, be revealed in the course of the more important sittings at my studio. Meanwhile, the little anecdotes which had just escaped her, taken in conjunction with the small pencil sketch which I had secured, were regarded by myself as 'only an experiment or trial' of that which I hoped would follow when my sitter came to my studio.

And I was not disappointed, though it was some time before I could thoroughly realize that the lady quietly seated in a studio-chair before me was the same whom I had once beheld at a distance posing in fetters for her pretended likeness to Sir James Thornhill and William Hogarth, with Figg the prize-fighter and Gay the poet looking on.

Nor in my Sadler's Wells days was it easy to picture Jack Sheppard in petticoats, with a neat frilled collar round his neck, and a plain cat's-eye brooch fastened to it. Nor would it have been possible to imagine the impersonator of the 'notorious one' with iron-gray hair parted in the middle, with a natural fringe falling in loose curls over her forehead. As for predicting that the day would come when the bold highwayman would reveal the secrets of his prison-house, and out of his prison-house, as well might I have anticipated that in the coming by-and-by the actress would be posing for her likeness in my studio in Notting Hill for an unlimited number of matinées without a weekly salary.

But all these things, and many more besides, took place in that memorable year of 1884 ; and with regard to the posings, I may say that the retired housebreaker made the most tractable and patient of sitters, and that with only one regrettable exception (presently to be described) she played the part to perfection. But she did more than this, for, besides being an excellent sitter, Mrs. Keeley was also a most entertaining one, and it is to her pleasant chat while the sittings lasted that the reader of these pages is indebted for a series of what might be called 'interviews at the easel.'

My subject had, however, a poor opinion of her powers as a story-teller, declaring that she was a bad hand at repeating anecdotes ; while in respect of *bon-mots* and conundrums, she did not remember having told one correctly in her life. In touching upon these things at the first sitting, she remarked :

'Mr. Keeley used to swear at me for spoiling good stories and riddles. But I once repeated a riddle correctly, though I'm afraid it rather offended Shirley Brooks, as I asked him why he was unlike a donkey's tail. But my worst offence was in telling the pig story. It was always a standing joke against me, and my husband delighted in repeating it to his friends.'

Upon my asking Mrs. Keeley to repeat it for the benefit of the present friend, she was good enough to respond to my request by saying :

'Shirley Brooks had lately taken to farming in the country, and kept fowls, geese, pigs, and things of that kind. One day he killed a pig, and sent me as a present a good-sized piece cut from the hind-quarters. Enclosed in the parcel was a slip of paper, on which was written, " His end was peace, so I send you a piece of his end." Well, a day or two after I was trying to tell this to some friends at dinner, and I got on very well till I came to the part where the paper was found. I then said, " When we opened the parcel there was a slip of paper inside, and on it was written, " His end was peace, so I send you a bit of the pig." '

This story within a story seemed to belie the narrator's assertion that she was a bad hand at repeating good anecdotes. But there were plenty more behind that amusing specimen, and, memory serving, I shall do my best to reproduce them in print, leaving the reader to judge of their merits.

CHAPTER V.

DRAMATIC HISTORY REPEATS ITSELF.

IF I mistake not, the conversations at the easel began with the Jack Sheppard period of Mrs. Keeley's career, and it partly arose from my having incidentally stated that I remembered the actress vividly at the time that she was under the engagement with George Webster at Sadler's Wells. After briefly referring to that event, I recollect asking why, with such a fine soprano voice as Mrs. Keeley was said to have possessed when singing with Braham and Malibran in serious opera, she gave up her vocal accomplishments in favour of acting proper.

'It gave me up,' was her prompt answer. 'I lost my singing voice in playing Jack Sheppard. The part, as you know, requires great vocal as well as physical exertion, and it was altogether the most trying character of any that I attempted. But I never drank anything stronger than barley-water or jelly before going on. Nor did Mr.

Keeley. Not that we were total abstainers, but while at work we preferred not to take stimulants; and I don't think we required any.'

I asked Mrs. Keeley presently whether her studies for the part were effected with that degree of preparatory schooling which was reported of her, and from her answer I gathered that her preparatory studies were of the most elaborate description, and that they were pursued even in Newgate, where it seems she once went for inspiration, as the following interesting experience will show :

' I was once taken to Newgate,' she said; 'not as a prisoner, you know, but only as a visitor who wanted to watch the ways of criminals and pick up a wrinkle or two if possible. I was horrified' (with a shudder) 'by all I saw, and I pitied them from the bottom of my heart. I wondered why the poor creatures always turned their backs upon visitors as they entered, and why the governor of the gaol so severely reprimanded one unfortunate man for sitting upon his cap. In passing on to other parts of the building, I was shown some plaster casts of defunct malefactors, and I noticed how all the faces seemed to have the same placid, amiable expression. After looking at them attentively, I thought I should like to be a criminal myself; and for the moment I really

felt like one. Then, when they took me into
Jack Sheppard's cell and brought out the very
manacles that he had worn, while holding them
in my hands I tried to fancy I was the highwayman, and to bring him before me.'

While speaking in the above strain, I, too,
tried to bring before me the stage Jack Sheppard
of my youth. But it was not easier to do so than
when seeing the actress in 'Pas de Fascination,'
or as the maid-of-all-work in 'Furnished Apartments.' Mrs. Keeley herself was, however,
quickly recognised by all who had seen her on
the stage, an example being afforded by a little
incident at Manchester, where 'Jack Sheppard'
was at one time a great favourite.

'I once went over a cotton-mill, and as I
passed along the different departments the work-
men began to whistle "Nix my Dolly." In
Dublin I was also recognised everywhere I went.
It was there that the piece originally came out,
and the town was full of it. It so impressed some
of those who witnessed the new drama, that it
was generally believed that the crime committed
by the notorious murderer Courvoisier was insti-
gated or partly prompted by seeing it. At any
rate, the Dublin papers stated this in their reports
of the trial, saying that the criminal himself had
confessed as much. After that, when next I

appeared in the character, there was quite a commotion in the house, ending in a complete uproar.
So perhaps there was some truth in the printed
statement.   And this reminds me of what an
enthusiastic young lady once said to me after
seeing me in the part : " You have made a highwayman of me !"'

While engaged in sketching my sitter's small
hands, which were, in their way, as full of character as her face, I took pictorial note of their
slenderness across the wrists and knuckles, and
afterwards gave vocal expression to my observations.   This naturally led to further memories of
the Jack Sheppard days, in which the busy digits
of the housebreaker played an important part, not
only in pocket-picking and prison-clambering, but
in freeing themselves from the iron bracelets with
which the law-breaker's wrists are eventually
adorned.   Upon my asking whether it was true,
as reported, that they were the same handcuffs
as those worn by the real Jack Sheppard, she
replied :

' I think not.   But they were an exact copy of
them, and when I slipped them off it was no
stage slip, but a *bona-fide* operation.   And it hurt
me sometimes !' (with a comic *moue.*)   ' But I
contrived to squeeze my hands out by bringing
the broad part together — like this ' (doing it).

'It is not everybody that can do it. But I did it then, and can do it still. I came down to the front, in full blaze of the footlights, so that the audience might fairly judge, and I always got an extra round of applause, and' (with a comic nod) 'I think I deserved it. But while discussing my hands I have got them out of position. So, if you'll just tell me how you want them placed, I will put them right again.' Which she did.

I was always fond of painting the hands of my sitters; but after the account of those belonging to the lady before me the pleasure of depicting them was vastly increased. But they were without manacles now, and not even ordinary bracelets, as Mrs. Keeley never wore jewellery of any kind, the explanation being:

'I can't abide rings, bracelets, or anything else that clasps you tightly; and I never could. Neither do I care for tight-fitting clothes. I remember once having to put on shoes too small for my feet, and though they didn't pinch me much, I was in tortures all the evening. It was —wait now, let me see—yes, in 1826, when Weber's last opera, "Oberon," was produced at Covent Garden, and when it was said at the time that "none of the actors could sing, and but one singer could act." Madame Vestris was the Fatima, and I had a small part that was mostly dumb-show, except in the finale to the second act, when I had to warble the mermaid's song. It was some time before they would entrust me with it, and Weber, who was present at the rehearsals, had previously tried several vocalists. But none seemed to satisfy the fastidious composer. At last I was put on, and very nervous did I feel as I proceeded to try the song. But when it was over Weber came up to me, and, patting me on the head, he said, " My child, dat song vill do !" '

Later on she was called upon to enact Fatima at a moment's notice, Madame Vestris being suddenly indisposed. It was then that Miss Goward had to assume the close-fitting foot-coverings, having none of her own for the purpose; for, though histrionically walking in Madame's footsteps, it was found impracticable to do so in that lady's boots.

' So a lord—bless me, I forget his name !'—she continued, ' lent me his wife's shoes, which he took the trouble to send for ; and I shall never forget it—or them.'

If I mistake not, it was during a little gossip of this sort that an accident unfortunately took place. It happened at the third sitting in my studio ; though whether it was or was not at the precise moment that Mrs. Keeley was beginning to give me the particulars of her accident at the Adelphi in 1852, I cannot say. I remember distinctly, however, that we were still on the Jack Sheppard topic, when, as ill-luck would have it, a street-itinerant happened to be serenading exactly under my window.

'I fancy I know that man,' quickly says my subject, assuming a listening attitude. Then, after a pause, she continued : 'Yes, I'm sure I know his voice. I wonder, now, if it's the same beggar that sings in my street?' And before I could throw down palette and brushes and rush to the lady's assistance, she had tripped lightly, yet surely, from the raised platform or 'throne' of the studio, and, quite forgetful that it was two feet from the ground, she missed her footing and fell heavily on the floor.

My alarm at this sudden and most unexpected occurrence can be more easily imagined than described, and it may have been my look of extreme consternation, not to say bewilderment, combined by the actress's tendency always to see the humorous side of things, that caused her, even as she remained seated upon the ground, to explode with laughter.

But, as will be seen in more than one chapter, it was no subject for merriment, either with myself or with my sitter. However, it was some satis-

faction to find by the laughter that the damage
was not quite as serious as I had at first con-
jectured, and it was also a matter of rejoicing
when the lady had so far recovered from the shock
caused by the violence of the concussion as to rise
unaided.

Then I went for a doctor of my acquaintance,
who lived in the neighbourhood, leaving my injured sitter to the care of a lady, who by a singular
coincidence was related to the famous Lady
Boothby, and who remembered the Keeleys well
in their prime.

The kind medical friend who presently came to
our assistance was Mr. J. P. Hewby—better
known in whist circles as ' Pembridge '—and I
shall feel for ever grateful to him for his good
offices.   By his advice my sitter was shortly conveyed in a cab to her home in Pelham Crescent,
and having arrived there with Mr. Hewby and
myself, her own doctor, Mr. Pierce, was called in.
It was then found that in falling from the studio
throne Mrs. Keeley's ankle had become violently
twisted, and that it was no ordinary sprain, but
a distinct fracture of the thick ligament of the
heel.

However, her medical adviser appeared confident that with proper remedies and a good long
rest the injured parts would reunite in the course

of time, and happily this proved to be the case. But the healing process was terribly slow and wearisome, and meanwhile the invalid was confined for several long weeks to her room, though after the first day she was able to remain seated in an armchair, with the injured limb firmly bound up and placed upon a stool. Thanks to Mrs. Keeley's wondrously robust constitution and her ever-cheerful spirits, she bore up bravely throughout the whole of that tedious rest, while from first to last her general health left absolutely nothing to be desired.

Though she made light of the accident at the time, it was evident that the shock in falling had told upon the lady's nervous system, and exactly eight days elapsed before she was in a condition to receive me, or any other visitor. But at the expiration of that comparatively brief period my eyes were gladdened by the sight of a post-card, written in her own neat, clear, firm hand, to tell me that I might come, and, if I desired it, go on with the likeness.

It need scarcely be said that I responded at once to this invitation, though I had already called several times to make inquiries. I was, however, reluctant to resume the sittings, having strong misgivings as to the propriety of putting my subject to the fatigue. But with her usual good

nature and sympathy with the troubles of other
people, she smiled sweetly, and said gaily :

'Well, I shall have to sit in this old armchair
for days—perhaps weeks—whether I like it or
not. So I may as well sit for my " picter " as do
nothing. Besides, it will be something to divert
my mind and help to pass away the weary hours.
For I can't bear an armchair, and never sit in one
if I can possibly help it. But I can't help it now,
so pray begin whenever you please.'

The suggestion to continue my handiwork under
my sitter's hospitable roof was a temptation not
easy to resist. So the very next morning found
me and my pictorial belongings at Pelham Crescent, in a well-lighted upper room, which was
easily converted into a convenient atelier, and the
visit was repeated day by day till further notice.

The sittings usually lasted from 11 a.m. till four
o'clock, save for an interval devoted to lunch, and,
far from the lady experiencing any sense of fatigue
during those five mortal hours, she often remarked
when I was leaving, 'I shan't know what to do
with myself now.'

Our pleasant chats upon the drama, music, art,
and kindred subjects, were, of course, continued
at every sitting, and, finding that I was particularly interested in my first dramatic love—'Jack
Sheppard '—the actress of the title *rôle* took me

behind the scenes again, in fancy, and related all that had been left untold through the accident at my studio.

With that unfortunate occurrence still fresh in both our minds, we naturally touched upon the Adelphi accident, which happened more than thirty years before the last, and, by way of beginning, I asked whether it was true, as reported, that when Mrs. Keeley fell from the ladder at the rehearsal of the Flash Ken scene and found herself violently seated upon the stage, she called out, 'Oh, my prophetic soul—my ankle!' This she promptly and indignantly denied in her emphatic way, saying :

'I was much too alarmed to make that or any other observation. But our clever friends in front' (with an expressive grimace) 'are pleased to invent all kinds of stories about us poor, defenceless players. That is, I suppose, why so many untruthful or grossly exaggerated things are said of dear old Mrs. Swanborough and her Malaprop slips of the tongue. Byron was, I think, responsible for a vast number of her *lapsus linguæ ;* but, believe me, the majority were derived from his own fertile brain. There was one about a spiral staircase which the poor old soul was supposed to have spoken of as her "spinal staircase." I forget how the story went, but there was no truth in it.'

CHAPTER VI.

BEHIND THE CURTAIN.

Mrs. Swanborough and her fair-haired daughter
Ada were at that time close neighbours of Mrs.
Keeley's, as they resided at No. 5 in the same
street. Both ladies frequently dropped in to have
a chat and to see how the picture was getting on,
while in the intervals of the sittings the older lady
would sometimes play cribbage or bézique with
my subject. Later on, when Mrs. Keeley could
sit upright at table, I recollect that a little whist-
party was got up. Upon that occasion Miss Ada
was my partner, and we had as antagonists her
venerable mother and our hostess.

I mention these circumstances in order to show
that if Mrs. Swanborough was really guilty of
such orthographical blunders as were attributed
to the lady, I had every opportunity of judging
for myself. But I cannot truthfully say that I
ever heard her make such slips of the tongue as
report, assisted by Byron, gave her credit for.

Her chief social failing appeared to be chronic deafness.

One day, when on the card subject, Mrs. Keeley remarked :

'I delight in games of cards. But I never gamble—only twopence a dozen, and, you know, you can't lose or win much at that. Yes, I love " Nap," too ; but I am always so dreadfully un- lucky. Once I had ace, king of trumps, and three small cards of the same suit, and my opponent— who I think was Palgrave Simpson—had queen and four small ones. But one of his small cards was bigger than mine, and he won ! I often play " Nap " with Palgrave Simpson,' she went on, finding that I was interested ; 'and that reminds me of a little card-story which happened nearly fifty years ago, during a tour with my husband in America. We went for a trip from New York to New Orleans, and on the way we fell in with some card-sharpers—of course, without knowing it. Mr. Keeley wanted a game, as he was pas- sionately fond of a rubber. But the men declined to play, declaring what they were, and saying that they had far too much respect for such " eminent performers," as they called us, to gamble with us. But dad insisted, so one of the sharpers agreed to play cribbage with him fairly and upon condition that if Mr. Keeley lost the other was to pay.'

The story reminds me that I have got well on with the present chapter without having touched upon the Adelphi accident, as it was recorded *in propriâ personâ* by the chief sufferer. Upon resuming it, she remarked :

'The ladder which Jack Sheppard has to descend was hooked on loosely to the scene, and it was all right for those who went up it ; but it was different in coming down, and in my case the ladder got wobbly and for a moment detached, my foot slipped, and I fell heavily with one leg on the ground. The effect of the fall might have been much worse— and it was quite bad enough, I can tell you—had not Jack Saunders, a member of our stock company, rushed forward and half caught me in his strong arms. This somewhat checked the violence of the concussion. But I could not stand on my feet after that, and I did not appear again on the stage for two months, which was a dead loss to poor Webster, who had to pay my eight weeks' salary just the same and put on another piece in place of the long-promised revival. Yes, you are partly right,' she continued, when I had quoted from the published medical certificate of 1852, which I had had a peep at ; 'one of the doctors was Mr. Pollard. But, to the best of my recollection, the other was not Cahill. In fact, it couldn't have been, because I clearly recollect

that Sir James—something—I forget his name—
an eminent physician' (? Sir James Paget), 'attended me from first to last. Both feet and ankles
were bare when examined by the medical men,
and when at last they touched the injured spot—
ugh!' (with a shudder)—'I thought I should
have fainted. It was not a sprain, they said, but
one of the ankle-bones was completely broken.
When I returned to the stage I never felt as
secure as before on my feet, and I don't think I
was quite as light and nimble in my movements.'

The actress was light and nimble enough when
I saw her at Sadler's Wells three years after the
accident, and, judging from the printed reports of
the Haymarket revival referred to in a previous
chapter, if not as firm on her feet as before, the
circumstance apparently passed unnoticed.

Still harping on my favourite drama, I next
sounded the principal performer in it upon the
opening scene where Jack is discovered carving
his name upon the beam, and in order to make
doubly sure of what I had heard of the planing
business, I asked whether she really planed the
wood.

'Yes, I really did it,' was her answer ; 'and the
stage-carpenters used to help me by lending their
best tools and keeping the edges well sharpened
every night. They took a particular pleasure in

doing this, and the public liked to see the planing
on the stage, and gave me an extra round of
applause for it.   It was hard work, though !'

After this I took my subject to the opening of
Act ii., where Jack joins his pals in the Flash
Ken, and cross-examined her about her great
song, beginning, ' In a box of the stone jug.'
Happily, at the advanced age of seventy-eight
the little woman showed the same pluck as when
in the old days she was ascending prison chimneys
or letting herself down by a blanket from the
outer walls of Newgate.   As for her animal
spirits, at the bare mention of the cracksman's
song, the retired Jack at once began to warble the
first verse in her own sweet way, and having done
so, to my secret enjoyment, she remarked :

' The ditty was originally intended to be sung
only by the highwayman.   But I suggested to
Webster that it might be more effective if, after
the second line, ending " Of a hempen widow the
kid forlorn," Blueskin were to take up the refrain,
" Fake away !" and again, " Nix my dolly, pals,"
before the repetition by the chorus.   So my suggestion was adopted, and for the future Paul Bedford gave both refrains in his gruff, jovial voice
and hearty manner ' (with an excellent imitation,
using the lowest tones of her own varied compass).

This vocal souvenir of the old Adelphi favourite brought our curtain down upon the 'Jack Sheppard' experiences. Before leaving this interesting subject, I should mention that when the burlesque of 'Little Jack Sheppard' was produced at the Gaiety, with Miss Nelly Farren in the title *rôle*, the original Jack went more than once to see it, and though loud in her praise of the leading performers—notably Miss Farren and the late Fred Leslie, whom she profoundly admired, both as a graceful actor and a refined dancer and singer— she did not consider that the piece itself was altogether worthy as a clever travesty.

'There is, to my way of thinking,' she said, 'far too little of the original story and incidents, such as Planché or à Beckett would have introduced, and too much of the so-called "up-to-date" music-hall business. And why—oh, why! do some of 'em persist in painting their faces like clowns? They do it in serious drama, too, and I can't for the life of me make out why. It seems to take away from the human nature of the comedian. And' (with a good-natured grimace) 'it ain't pooty!'

While discussing the present fashions in grease, paint and burnt cork, the artist before me dwelt for a moment upon the palmy days of stage toilette, showing that in those days it was not found necessary for either a serious or a comic performer to lay much stress upon the artificial lines and hues of the features, but to trust mostly to nature, assisted by facial art. As for the Keeleys—husband, wife, and daughters—one of them assured me that their theatrical make-ups were so slight or well done as to be wholly un-noticeable from a distance, and scarcely perceptible when closely inspected. I myself am able to testify to these facts in respect of Mrs. Keeley's Jack Sheppard, while at the sitting about to be described the actress gave an amusing example of it by repeating the story of Leman Rede, the dramatist, who once ran against her behind the Adelphi scenes, at a time that she was waiting to go on as a maid-of-all-work, and mistaking her for a real 'cleaner' attached to the theatre, he ex-claimed with some enthusiasm :

' Ah ! why don't they dress like that ?'

Further evidence of the extreme care with which the actress studied and made up for parts was afforded by an interesting account of her prepara-tions for Nydia, the blind girl, in the dramatized version of Bulwer Lytton's 'Last Days of Pom-peii,' a character which Mrs. Keeley delighted in representing, and which showed off the pathetic side of her many histrionic resources. While preparing for this difficult *rôle* the industrious

artist went more than once to the blind asylum of
the Royal Normal College, to watch the ways of
the afflicted inmates and see what she could pick
up for stage purposes.

'I remember seeing a woman thread a needle
with her tongue,' she suddenly began, putting her
own tongue out and raising her hands to show
me how the feat was accomplished. 'But what
struck me most was their fixed, vacant stare'
(pausing for a moment to do it). I noticed one
poor girl in particular. She was a beautiful
creature, and it touched my heart to see her helpless condition. In walking along in my direction
she accidentally knocked against me, and she
seemed quite vexed and angry with herself for
her want of expertness. "Ah," I said to myself,
"I will remember that!" And I did. Then I
said to her, "Your eyes are wide open, and
round and blue, just like those who can see
clearly." "But I can't see you," she answered
softly; "I wish I could."

'I did the vacant stare for Nydia,' she went
on, after doing it again for me, 'and I always got
a round of applause for it. But it is a wonder
I didn't hurt my eyes doing it night after night'
(rubbing her eyes at the thought of it). 'The
most trying moment, though, was when I had to
go down to the footlights to warble two songs.

For I could never keep the tears from rolling down my cheeks, and the effort to maintain the rigid look of the eyes was often painful in the extreme.'

Mrs. Keeley was always remarkable for her powers of mimicry, as I could well understand from the many examples she unconsciously gave me from day to day in the course of conversation, and the gift, doubtless, was invaluable while trying to imitate the gesture or tone of her model. A striking instance was afforded quite early in the actress's career, at a time when she was singing in serious or light opera with Malibran.

' I got into sad disgrace over the cadences,' she remarked, while describing her performances in the ' Marriage of Figaro ' at Covent Garden. ' But my worst offence happened when I imitated the prima donna too closely to be agreeable to her ladyship. It was in the scene where the maid was to mimic her mistress, and I did it so well that Malibran was quite angry, and reprimanded me for it in the dressing-room. But she afterwards complimented me upon my powers of mimicry.'

It was imaginative rather than imitative art that was brought into requisition on behalf of one of Mrs. Keeley's greatest creations—Smike in ' Nicholas Nickleby.' In this case the artist went for her materials chiefly to Charles Dickens, and assisted by her own lively fancy, her intuitive perception of the picturesque and the published sketches by Cruikshank, she presented the most remarkable living picture of human misery and bodily suffering that the stage has ever known.

Dickens did not much approve of the adaptation, and when present at one of the rehearsals, he objected to some of the long-winded speeches put into the mouths of his characters by the adapter. He was particularly annoyed by Smike's gratuitous lines about 'the little robins in the fields,' and, turning abruptly to the prompter, he said, ' Damn the robins ; cut them out !'

The character formed, of course, a complete contrast to that of Nydia, the blind girl, both as regards the cause of the suffering and the actress's outward appearance. But, as already stated, the first-nighters of 1838 could not make up their minds whether to sympathize with or to roar with laughter at the pitiable object which met their gaze when the scene shifted to the dimly-lighted kitchen of Do-the-boys Hall, and Smike was discovered seated before the wretched fire. I now found that the actress was as much puzzled by the behaviour of her audience as they

were by her strange appearance, for, in referring
to the circumstance, she said :

'I couldn't make it out. I had to rise from
where I was and crawl my way down to the footlights without speaking. The gloom at the back
of the stage was so dense that I don't think the
audience had seen me at first. As I came
stealthily forward, they did not quite understand
the situation. My costume was certainly very
odd, and as I had recently been playing in many
comic parts, I suppose they expected something
funny from me. The house evidently thought
that the scene was intended to be comic rather
than pathetic, and there were roars of laughter.
But I had never before lost my presence of mind
on the stage, and I didn't mean to do it now.
So I stood it out. But it was the most difficult
task I ever had. However, when I spoke the
first lines of my part the laughter ceased, and there
was a dead silence. Then a stifled sob reached
my ear, and presently I could see there was
scarcely a dry eye in the house. After that
I felt the character !'

She must have felt the character quite as
acutely while enacting Little Nell in the 'Old
Curiosity Shop'—one of her most pathetic parts.
And outwardly the lady must have felt it, too ;
for she had as a Quilp no less an actor than

Yates, who, to use Mrs. Keeley's own words, was 'so horribly real that I thought every moment he was going to pinch me!'

'But I was always a big coward upon the stage,' she remarked. 'I was for ever fancying that something dreadful was going to happen. And something did happen, you know, while rehearsing "Jack Sheppard." As for traps— ugh!' (with a shudder)—'I can't abide 'em. They could never get me to go down or up one for love or money. Celeste often persuaded me to have a try, and once she went down a vampire trap to show me how easy it was. I said, "Yes, it looks very easy as you do it"; and she said, "Oh, it's nothing. However, you'll have to do it in the melodrama; and, remember, you will have three lovely dresses!" At last I promised to make an attempt. But when it came to the point I changed my mind, and, instead of standing bolt upright on the trap, I sat down ignominiously upon it.'

This was all the speaker said in explanation of the story's anti-climax. The ludicrous position of the actress as she remained seated in the circular aperture was left to the imagination, assisted by that wondrous by-play that was often quite as expressive as spoken words. Her merry laugh was—and I am glad to say still is—a

6

complete study in itself. It was a laugh as difficult to describe as it was impossible to depict by an artist. The phonograph alone could perpetuate it.

Once, when the present artist was striving to secure his subject's risible characteristics upon canvas, after a loud roar on her part at something funny that had tickled her fancy, she said :

'A Frenchman once warned me that if I grinned so much I should repent it when I got old. And I'm afraid he was right. But please don't put *all* my wrinkles in ' (with a comic look of entreaty).

But the lines in my sitter's face appeared to be the result of the professional uses to which the muscles were applied, rather than of old age. And apropos of her comparatively youthful appearance and neat figure, she was reminded of what was said to her by Palgrave Simpson, who also bore his years well : ' My dear, there's only one greater impostor than myself, and that's you !' And following closely upon this anecdote was :

' I remember Dickens telling me, in his rapid, earnest way, and with a slight lisp which he had ' (giving the lisp), ' " Ah ! when you're young you want to be old ; when you're getting old you want to be young ; and when you're really old you're proud of your years." '

The Dickens anecdote naturally led to a little reminiscence of the famous theatricals at Tavistock House, at which Mrs. Keeley was, of course, frequently present. After speaking in the highest terms of Dickens as an actor, she went on to say :

‘ I think the last time I went to the Tavistock House theatricals was at the coming of age of the eldest son, Charley. I sat in a nice place, and in front of me was Macready, with Lord Lyndhurst resting against the tragedian's legs. Edwin Landseer was also present among the audience, together with George Cruikshank, Augustus Egg, Stanfield (who painted the scenery), and, I think, John Forster. I recollect that Dickens “ gagged ” a good deal, as usual, in a piece called “ Uncle John,” and that Mac, who disapproved of such things, kept growling out, *sotto voce*, “ Oh, you shouldn't gag !” ’ (imitating him).

The mention of Macready's magic name brought to the mind of the speaker a little episode in connection with her performances at old Drury under his management, which was :

‘ I once had a part to play that required a certain kind of energy which I did not think myself capable of introducing, and Macready tried hard to persuade me to put the proper spirit into it. At last I got disgusted and threw the book down with, I fear, an oath. "Ah," grunted Mac, "you'll play it now!" And I did.'

The part referred to was Polly Pallmall in the 'Prisoner of War,' which, next to Nydia, was, she said, her favourite character, which she enacted with her husband as Peter Pallmall.

'Douglas Jerrold wrote the part for me,' she explained, 'and after the first night he came up and said, "You've topped your author!" That was something for him to say, was it not? But he was always saying good things. He could scarcely open his lips without something clever dropping from them. I remember once at the Haymarket the manager consulting him about the cast of a piece by Jerrold. They were both proposing different people for it, and the manager said, "There's Vining, too; he belongs to these boards." "Yes," says Jerrold, "and looks as if he was made out of them."'

While upon these highly - diverting topics, Mrs. Keeley told me that Macready first engaged her after seeing her Nydia in the 'Last Days of Pompeii.'

'It was really the part,' she said, 'that brought me prominently forward as an actress. On the first night Mrs. Yates came up to me, and said, "If you play the second act as well as the first,

your fortune's made." Mac was evidently much
struck by it, and engaged me there and then. So
I went direct from the Lyceum to Drury Lane,
where I appeared with the actor-manager in many
of his Shakespearian revivals—'As You Like It,'
for instance. Ah! that was something like a cast,
and it would be difficult to beat it, I think. Mrs.
Nisbett was the Rosalind; Mrs. Sterling the
Celia; I was the Audrey; Mr. Keeley was
Touchstone; Anderson, Orlando; John Ryder,
the banished duke; and, of course, Macready was
the Jaques. Phelps and Compton were also in
it. I worshipped Macready both as an actor and
a man. He was one of the kindest and most
courteous gentlemen I have ever known. I have
heard it said that Macready had no heart. I don't
believe it. Look what he did for Priscilla Horton,
afterwards Mrs. German Reed. But what I do
think and know is, that he disliked all people who
shirked or neglected their work.'

.

CHAPTER VII.

MARY ANNE GOWARD.

FROM William Shakespeare to Samuel Smiles much has been said and written respecting that desirable turning-point in one's precarious career known as the tide in the affairs of man. So, with a view to ascertain whether in Mrs. Keeley's case there had also been a tide in the affairs of woman, I began my examination-in-chief of her past history and professional struggles (if any) by asking if she could remember what was the particular turning-point in her own career that led to fame and possibly—though by no means necessarily— to fortune.

At this she smiled one of her wandering smiles, partly on account of the suddenness of the inquiry, partly in search of something like a Shakespearian 'tide.' But apparently she could find none, for, after a moment's reflection, she answered:

'No; I can't say I do. You see, in my case the success was gradual, and there was no luck or

chance about it when it came, as it did, with the
"Last Days of Pompeii," which led immediately
to my engagement with Macready. But I think
I owed the success more to hard work, with, I
suppose, some natural ability of my own, than to
anything else.'

At this point I ventured to ask whether she had
been brought up to one thing and took to quite
another by accident, which elicited the reply :

'No. I have been all my life mixed up with
the theatre, and was born and bred in the very
midst of it at Ipswich. It's true that at one time
my parents were in doubt whether drawing or
music would be best for me to study ; for I was
passionately fond of drawing, and I think I showed
some talent for it as a child.'

Upon my asking whether little Mary Anne
showed much talent for acting, the grown-up lady
answering to that name said :

' I was always very fond of acting, and the local
theatre being in Tacket Street, close to the house
in Orwell Place where I was born, I was in and
out of it all day, and at night helping the car-
penters and scene-shifters by fetching and carrying
things for them. You see, my father was a brazier
and tinman, and the stage-carpenters got their
nails, hammers, and things of that kind from his
shop. Yes, and some of the stage properties

came from our place, too, and from others in the
neighbourhood. For in those economical days
theatres kept no properties of their own, but borrowed them of people in the town. But all this
cannot be very interesting to you or to anybody
else, so I will say no more.'

Of course, I assured her that the child-history
of the future Jack Sheppard was immensely interesting to myself, as I doubt not it will be to my
readers. So she went on to say :

' I used to learn poetry by the square yard, and
once I clambered into a big plate-basket, and
recited, in presence of my dad and his friends,
" My Name is Norval." I distinctly remember
being taken one night on my father's shoulders
to the gallery of our theatre to see and hear the
celebrated actress, Miss O'Neill, in a stirring
drama, the name of which I have, of course, forgotten. I think I could appreciate her fine acting
even then, and I'm sure I did long afterwards.
She was a grand actress !'

Mrs. Keeley took occasion here to inform me
that she was one of a rather large family of eight
—three sisters and five brothers. Her youngest
brother, Fred, had a daughter on the stage, who
was married to Mr. William Faucitt, with whom
she appeared last at the Strand Theatre in the
successful farcical comedy of ' Our Flat.' Mrs.

Faucitt's stage-name was, and still is, I believe, Miss Annie Goward.

In answer to some further questions, my hostess said :

'At the age of thirteen my voice was being trained for operatic singing, and a friend having heard me, I was asked to sing at the Tower Church, in Ipswich, with a Mrs. Bland. After that experiment I was taken up by Mrs. Henry Smart, and my voice was by her further developed. It was she who brought me out as a public singer on the stage, and was also my dramatic tutor ; while D'Egville was my teacher of dancing and deportment, as it was called. One of the things I had to do was to walk about the room with a load of books on my head. That was to teach me how to walk. My critics were afterwards kind enough to say that I walked well. Those were the days, my friend, when a youthful aspirant had to learn his business before going on the stage. I really made my first bow in public as a concert-singer. I am a bad hand at dates, so can't say exactly when that was. But it was somewhere about the winter of 1823, when I was seventeen. I appeared at York, which was one of the principal towns of the old Norwich circuit, the others being Yarmouth, Ipswich, and Bath. It was Bellamy, of Bath, who brought me out as

an actress.   I did pretty well as a concert-singer ;
but I did better still as a singing actress.   It was
in that capacity that I went later on to Yarmouth
with my tutor, Mrs. Henry Smart, and fellow-
pupils, to appear for the first time on any stage as
Lucy Bertram in " Guy Mannering."   They said
I played the part well, and encouraged me to
continue.   But I felt a great fool in it, and, oh
lor ! such a guy, with a black gown and a huge
head-dress of black plumes.   I shall never forget
it ; and when I went home I sketched myself, as
I think I once told you.   Then I was taken to
Dublin to play Polly in the " Beggar's Opera."
And I shan't forget that, either ; for the Captain
Macheath was Harry Hunt, whose brother and
Thurtell and Probert were associated in the murder
of Weare, and the circumstance impressed me
much and made me rather nervous.'

The actress paused at this point, as if uncertain
what was her next experimental venture upon the
stage.   So I assisted her memory by taking her
back to Ipswich as a young girl of sweet seventeen and a half, and placing her upon the stage of
the local theatre there on June 15, 1824.

I should here mention that, in anticipation of
the gossip concerning my subject's very first
appearance in her native town, I had taken the
precaution to make myself sufficiently well in-

MISS GOWARD (MRS. KEELEY) AT THE AGE OF SEVENTEEN,
AS MARGARETTA IN 'NO SONG, NO SUPPER.'

To face p. 91.

formed respecting that event by referring to the journals and playbills of the period. I was, therefore, in a position to state upon the very best authority that the local manager announced Miss Goward for four nights only, and that she was to make her début in two pieces—namely, 'Rob Roy,' in which the young débutante was to represent Diana Vernon, and the musical farce 'No Song, no Supper,' in which she was to sing and act in the part of Margaretta.

Of course Mrs. Keeley remembered that important event perfectly well, and she also had a very vivid recollection of her benefit, which happened at the end of her four nights' engagement on June 19.

'It was my first benefit,' she remarked; 'and it took place about a year before my long-looked-for journey to the great Metropolis, where I was to make my first appearance upon a London stage. I never had a benefit in London in the whole course of my professional engagements here. Nor did Mr. Keeley. Once Macready proposed to my husband that we should take one at Drury Lane. But Mr. Keeley always disapproved of such things, and said that if the public wanted to see us they ought to pay in the usual way, and not be asked to purchase tickets specially. So no special announcements were issued and the tickets were sold in the ordinary manner. But the programme was extra attractive, and completely filled the big house, and the next morning Macready presented my husband with a hundred pounds—quite a little fortune in those days.'

This digression in connection with the Ipswich benefit looked like bringing in the Macready experiences again. So, in order to insure against any such anachronism, I conducted the speaker gently back to Miss Goward's benefit by asking what she did in particular upon that memorable occasion.

'I spoke an address,' was her prompt reply, while her bright eyes twinkled with pleasure at the very thought of it. I tried to catch that twinkle for the benefit of her portrait, and while so engaged my sitter went on to say, 'The address was specially written for the occasion by my devoted friend and benefactress, Mrs. John Cobbold. She was the good lady who at one time took me under her protecting wing, and to whom I am indebted for many an act of kindness. I shall never forget the dear creature.'

The actress had not forgotten, either, Mrs. Cobbold's verses which she had delivered in 1824 at the footlights of the Ipswich theatre, in evidence of which she repeated them, word for word, from memory. Later on she wrote them down in

her clear, firm hand, and as the address may possibly
interest the present reader, I here reproduce it :

'Should I attempt in language to reveal
The force, the tenderness of all I feel,
The mix'd emotions utterance would subdue,
And tears be all that I could give to you.
Yet something I would say:—would fain express
Such thoughts as grateful hearts alone can guess ;
To speak *their powers* I feel my own unable,
Allow me, then, to temper them with fable.

'The new-fledged nightingale, when first she leaves
The thorn on which a parent's bosom heaves,
Her flutt'ring wing essay'd, speeds back to rest,
Trembling and panting on the well-known nest.
There cherish'd with renew'd and strengthen'd wing,
Again she takes her flight, and tries to sing,
Then seeks the skies—on ether dares to float—
Visits each clime, improves each thrilling note ;
But still returns with gratitude and love
To wake the echoes of her native grove.

'Though not like Philomel's my song be heard,
Can you not fancy me that trembling bird ?
Who, having tried my early song and flight,
Seek on the sheltering nest again to light ;
To meet those fostering smiles, for ever dear,
And grow in strength from growing kindness *here*.

' If, through that kindness, it be mine to claim,
By persevering wing, the heights of fame ;
Should I again to those lov'd scenes belong,
Matured in mind and perfected in song,
O ! with what transport would that song be given
In notes of grateful praise to you and Heaven !

Hope waves me on, presenting to my view
Such blissful hour—till then, Adieu, Adieu.'

As in all human probability there does not exist among us a single person who could adequately describe from the eye-witness point that first night of a little over seventy years ago, it has occurred to me to quote from the opinions of the local press of 1824, in respect of Miss Goward's performances.

In noticing Miss Goward's début the local newspaper, published at Ipswich, says :

' Miss Goward, a native of our town, was received with marked applause, and returned the salutations of her friends in a very graceful and respectful manner. This young lady possesses a voice of great sweetness, variety and compass, and appears to have profited much from the instructions of her late excellent preceptor [Mrs. Smart]. The style of Miss Goward's singing is peculiarly chaste and pathetic ; the ornaments she introduces are well chosen, and calculated to embellish the taste of the composer, but not (as is too often the case) to overload and almost obliterate the melodies which they should only decorate.

' Miss Goward has given the greatest satisfaction in all the songs she has introduced in the several characters she has impersonated during the week [the notice was written on June 19], and it would also be great injustice to this young *aspi-*

rante's merit were we to pass unnoticed the very correct and pleasing style of her acting. We are very often compelled to compound for good singing with bad acting, but Miss Goward certainly unites the correct actress with the talented singer, and we have no doubt but her benefit, which is fixed for this evening, when she will appear in Rosetta ("Love in a Village") and Virginia ("Paul and Virginia") will be well attended, and that in these characters, so well suited to the display of her talents, she will fully justify the encomiums which we have felt it our duty to pass upon her previous performances.'

Mrs. Keeley's recitation of Mrs. Cobbold's well-remembered verses brought our curtain down for the day. But it was raised again next morning upon much the same scene. This time, however, the studio talk was devoted to Mary Anne Goward's début at the London Lyceum, called in that young lady's days the Royal English Opera House, then under the management of Walter Arnold.

' I was much too nervous,' she said, ' to take particular note of anything or anybody. So horribly nervous was I, that if it had not been for Miss Kelly, who urged me to go on, I think I should have run away.'

The mention of Miss Kelly's name in this

matter-of-course way left me for the moment in doubt whether the lady named was the Miss Kelly whose theatre in Dean Street, Soho—now the Royalty—I remembered well. So to make sure that it was the same Miss Kelly, I put the question clearly.

' Yes,' was the reply, ' it was that wondrously-gifted actress. And it was Miss Kelly who really brought me out in London and taught me so much by example and precept, though, of course, she was not actually my tutor. But she couldn't put courage into me on that dreadful first night. You see, I had been only a twelvemonth upon the provincial stage. Besides, I had to come on in the opening trio for Rosina, William and Phœbe, which began appropriately enough, "When the rosy morn appearing." I dare say I was quite as rosy as the morn. And like a deadly-white rose, as well as a red one. But I managed to get through the business somehow, and when the piece was over and I again appeared as Little Pickle in the " Spoiled Child," in which I had to sing and dance a hornpipe, I felt rather more at home on the stage.'

As Little Pickle, in the ' Spoiled Child,' Miss Goward appeared for the first time in a boy's part, and it, of course, formed a complete contrast with the timid, blushing Rosina, for Little Pickle

is the boldest and most unblushing young imp on
record ; and one can well imagine that the character must have fitted either Miss Goward or
Mrs. Keeley like the proverbial glove. Those
who can remember the actress in boy parts may,
perhaps, easily picture her, attired first in a pair
of nankeen trousers, a white waistcoat, a smart
green jacket, a frilled shirt-collar, open over the
shoulders, and with white stockings and pumps.
In her second dress of the sailor-lad she had to
assume white trousers and a white waistcoat,
together with a navy-blue jacket, trimmed with
white braid and buttons.

Readers unfamiliar with this ancient musical
farce, which was first produced at Drury Lane
exactly one hundred and five years ago, will,
perhaps, be interested to hear that it was originally written for the famous actress Mrs. Jordan,
who is said to have been the authoress, though
it has been attributed also to Isaac Bickerstaff.
The principal part appears to have been a great
favourite with many actresses of note besides
Mrs. Jordan, chief among whom were Madame
Vestris and Mrs. Charles Kemble (Miss de
Camp). But from all accounts Mrs. Jordan took
the palm, and after her Mrs. Keeley, who was
unapproachable in the character.

According to one writer, ' those who remember

7

Mrs. Jordan have often said that Mrs. Keeley was at least her equal,' and the same authority goes on to say : ' There is but one performer, in the writer's recollection, who could be said to surpass Mrs. Keeley in humour and pathos, namely, the French comedian, Bouffe—a great actor un-rivalled for the variety and scope of his remark-able genius. It is between him and the late Mr. Robson—if we can compare an actress with actors—that one might place Mrs. Keeley, not very far from either. . . . Mrs. Keeley, arch, pointed, epigrammatic, and full of buoyant spirits, can hardly be associated with anything dismal ; but when she had to say anything with feeling it was done with exquisite touches of most won-derful nature.'

All this, and much more, was, of course, written of the actress long after she appeared as Rosina and Little Pickle. But doubtless some of it might have been applied to her impersonation of the young scapegrace, who certainly required an actress full of buoyant spirits to represent him, and something besides. For Little Pickle is, from beginning to end, a perfect demon of mis-chief, and his pranks, frolics, and practical jokes, are of such a nature as to drive his fond father and his maiden aunt nearly frantic. At last they can stand it and him no longer ; so, with a view

to bring the young reprobate to his senses, they
conspire with the old nurse to represent to Little
Pickle that he is his nurse's child, and that she had
changed him at birth for her master's son, who
is now to be installed in his place. In this way
they propose to get rid of the urchin, and they
so far succeed in their plan as to cause Little
Pickle to abandon the parental home. But not
for long, for the young scamp has got an inkling
of their scheme, and means to give as good as he
has received.

With this in view, Little Pickle returns to his
home disguised as Nurse Margery's sailor-boy
son, and in that character he leads them all such
a life that they begin to wish either that they
never were born or that the rightful heir would
return and ask for forgiveness. But the rightful
heir, of course, does nothing of the kind, except
by being actually present without the knowledge
of his relatives. And so it goes on, till the
broken-hearted father and badly-used aunt have
been taught a lesson which the young scamp
confidently hopes will last them a lifetime.

The very last lesson taught by Little Pickle
refers to his fiendish behaviour in respect of the
maiden aunt and Mr. Tagg, a penniless poet
whom she has taken up with amorously, greatly
to the disgust of her brother. There is an

amusing scene at the fag-end of the farce, in
which the love-sick spinster and her money-
seeking lover meet by moonlight alone in the
garden.   It is during the action of this scene that
Little Pickle, who has overheard some of their
amorous talk, creeps softly behind the well-shaded
arbour, where the lovers are lost in one another's
embraces, and securely sews them together with
needle and thread.

This final piece of pleasantry on the part of
Little Pickle is attended by the most disastrous
consequences ; for when the lovers eventually
rise in great alarm at the approach of Old Pickle's
footsteps, they are practically unable to part, and
when at last they tear themselves asunder, by
the most violent efforts on both sides, it is a
veritable tear, as regards the tail of Tagg's
coat, which remains firmly fixed upon his lady
love's best satin dress.

'One last adieu,' sighs Miss Pickle, before she
is aware of what has happened.   'Think you we
shall ever meet again ?'

'Tagg (*finding himself sewn for life to his
loved one*) : Damme if I think we shall ever part !

' Miss P. (*tenderly*) : 'Don't detain me. Won't
you let me go ?

'Tagg (*still struggling hard to get away*) :
'Zounds, madame, I wish you were gone !'

Though occasionally referred to in the piece, Tagg is not actually seen till the encounter just described, so that it was a comparatively small part. All the same, it was a great favourite with many star-performers, among whom were Liston, Mathews the elder, Elliston, John Reeve, Tayleure, and Wrench. Little Pickle and his frolics formed, however, the backbone of the 'Spoiled Child,' and as enacted by Miss Goward, and afterwards by Mrs. Keeley, the character was the life and soul of the farce. But a much greater success awaited the young actress, as will be presently seen.

CHAPTER VIII.

ALONE AND TOGETHER.

WHILE Miss Goward was being made desperate love to at the Lyceum by Captain Beleville and his brother, Mr. Keeley was round the corner, so to speak, at Covent Garden, courting the widow Ramsbottom, sublimely indifferent to, and perhaps wholly unconscious of, what was going on at the Strand-end of Wellington Street.

But the fates decreed that the young couple should not be 'thrown together' just yet, either upon the stage or in private life; so Philander Postscript continued to pay his addresses every night to the widow in the new 'local sketch' called the 'Ramsbottoms of Rheims,' while Rosina, the maid, allowed herself to be made up to till 'Rosina,' the play, was taken off, as it was after three nights, and 'Presumption; or, The Fate of Frankenstein' was put in its place. While that piece was in rehearsal, however, Miss Goward continued to enact her boy's part of Little Pickle in the 'Spoiled Child,' which, now that the first night's nervousness was a thing of the past, the new acquisition to the boards made quite a speciality of, as the famous Mrs. Jordan had done before her, when the little musical farce was first produced at Drury Lane in 1790.

Then began what might be called a perfect Babel of plays, old and new, in most of which the young lady from Ipswich took part. For after a run of a couple of nights, 'Presumption' was withdrawn to give place to the 'Castle of Andalusia,' in which Miss Goward was put on as Catalina, with the song 'There's nae luck about the house,' and there being apparently nae luck about that play, it was soon taken off, and 'Der Freischütz' substituted. In this Miss Goward appeared as Ann, and after that as Effie in the 'Vampire; or, The Bride of the Isles,' and again as Elamir in a new opera oddly named 'Tarrare; or, The Tartar Chief'—a piece that completely beat the record of long runs in those days, as it was played for no less than fifteen consecutive nights, being three nights 'better' than another new operatic drama entitled the 'Shepherd Boy,' and five nights better than the 'Spoiled Child,' which enjoyed uninterrupted prosperity for an entire week and four days.

I have not the faintest idea of what 'Tarrare' was about, so I am unable to tell the reader whether or not it contained anything in common with the modern music-hall ditty of nearly that same name ; but it appears to have been a huge success, with Braham as Tarrare ; and next to it the 'Shepherd Boy.' This last piece was followed by the 'Stout Gentleman,' 'Where Shall I Dine?' 'Hit or Miss,' 'Inkle and Yarico,' and so on to the end of the season, which began on July 2 and terminated on October 5, or eighty-two playing nights. Of course the majority of these pieces were tried for a single night, or at the utmost three, except in the case of the new musical farce of the 'Stout Gentleman,' which, when first presented, was very nearly brought to an end before it was half over.

This not very strange circumstance was, of course, due to the demerits of the piece. At any rate, we are told that it met with 'great hostility from the audience, and was heartily condemned by the press,' while upon its repetition, two nights after, the audience created such a disturbance in the house that the manager was obliged to come forward and announce its entire withdrawal. All the same, Miss Goward appears to have made a great hit in it as Sally, a chambermaid with a mania for novel-reading, the papers saying at the time, 'We anticipate a harvest of future comedy from this young lady.'

The press also spoke well of Mr. Keeley in the ill-fated piece, observing that he was most diverting as a bookseller's assistant. And in connection with this subject it is worthy of note that this was the second time the popular low comedian and Miss Goward played together, the first being on the preceding night (September 7, 1825), when they appeared in the 'Shepherd Boy,' with Miss Kelly and Messrs. Cooper, Baker, and Bartley. The papers also spoke highly of Mr. Keeley in the last-named play, describing his acting as 'piquant and amusing,' while in reference to Miss Goward's Lucetta, in the same opera, they said that she 'sang and acted with great spirit.' But something had apparently gone wrong with the young lady, as the *Times* took her rather severely to task for over-acting her part. Could it have been that Miss Goward, and not Lucetta, had lost her heart while playing for the first time with her future lord?

Miss Goward and Mr. Keeley's next engagement was at Covent Garden in the winter season of that year, which began not long after the close of the English Opera House, and the actress then made her London début as Margaretta in 'No Song, no Supper,' which she had previously tried with success in her native place. The press generally spoke well of her performance, but the severe critic of the *Times* still took exception to her over-acting, and said: ' She will begin, perhaps, to act a great deal better when she leaves off taking such very obvious pains to act well.'

But the leading organ was harder still upon the young actress when, five days before her nineteenth birthday, its dramatic critic presented her with his publicly-expressed opinion that she was not fit to act Sophia in the ' Road to Ruin,' and was surprised that the management had cast her for the part. In all probability, however, the character did not suit the actress. Nor was a sea-nymph in ' Oberon ; or, The Elf-King's Oath,' which she appeared in next season at Covent Garden, exactly to her liking, though she seems to have scored even in that small part.

Weber's famous opera was produced on April 12, 1826, and personally conducted by the composer. The cast was a strong one, with Madame Vestris as Fatima, Braham as Sir Heron of Bordeaux, Fawcett as Sherasmin, and Mrs. Davenport as Fatima's grandmother. In the same year Mr. Keeley and Miss Goward were both playing at the English Opera House in a wonderful ' operatic romance' called the 'Death Fetch; or, The Student of Gottingen,' described by the press as ' a regular

churchyard horrific,' in which the two comedians figured as servants who are haunted by
ghosts. Keeley enacted Ebert's timorous foot-
man—a fellow who fancies that he is a wizard's
factotum—and he 'excited a good deal of well-
deserved laughter by his tremors and terrors,' in
which the actor was unapproachable on the stage.

The popular 'Tarrare' was also played at the
Opera House that year, together with 'Free
and Easy'; a new melodrama called the 'Last
Guerilla'; a serio-comic opera entitled the 'Oracle;
or, The Interrupted Sacrifice,' besides innumerable
musical farces, of which 'Lock and Key' and
'Before Breakfast' appear to have been the more
successful.

The season of 1827 was, with one notable exception to be spoken of presently, pretty much
the same as the last just described. Mr. Keeley
and the young lady from Ipswich continued to
perform together in a variety of pieces, old and
new, both at the English Opera House and at
Covent Garden, and during the season of 1828
the united couple were still appearing in double
harness, or alone, at the same theatres. At
Covent Garden the first piece of importance was
the 'Somnambulist' in which Keeley was highly
amusing as the unhappy M. de Trop, who wants
to marry everybody and is refused by all. Miss

Goward also scored in this piece, though in spite
of her three years' continued appearances upon
the London stage, and at least one big hit, she is
merely referred to as 'a remarkably promising
and clever actress, by the way,' and as having
'played a very disagreeable part, not only with
extreme archness and spirit, but with exceeding
good taste also.'

The pair were next seen in a new farce called
the 'Point of Honour,' which, in spite of its
powerful cast, as represented by Fawcett, Bartley,
Wrench, O. Smith, Mrs. Davenport, and the two
favourites just referred to, was a complete failure,
owing, no doubt, to its questionable morality.

Then came an opportunity for Miss Goward,
of which that enterprising little lady was not slow
to avail herself. On March 10, 1828, Madame
Vestris was to have appeared at Covent Garden
in a sort of fairy extravaganza, called 'Cymon,'
announced to follow Shakespeare's 'King Lear,'
in which Charles Kean took the lead and was
supported by Fawcett, Warde and other notabilities of the day. But Madame being 'seriously
indisposed,' her part was offered to, and readily
undertaken by, Miss Goward at a moment's notice.
Some disorder and hooting, however, took place
in the house when it was announced that Vestris
would not appear, and someone in the pit was

MRS. KEELEY AT THE AGE OF TWENTY.

To face p. 108.

heard to declare that he had seen the actress that day in the street. Then Mr. Fawcett, who was one of the managers, came forward, and, addressing the audience, said :

'A gentleman has said that he saw Madame Vestris this morning. I can take it upon me to say that it is false. That the disappointment may be felt as little as possible, Miss Goward will undertake Madame Vestris's part. Although she is a volunteer, I beg leave to remark that she is a very young recruit, and must trust a little to your generosity, having undertaken the part at so short a notice.' He then retired and led Miss Goward forward on the stage. She was well received ; and on leaving her the veteran gave her a hearty shake by the hand, as much as to say, 'I wish you success,' and his good wishes were verified, as, in spite of the very short notice and the unfavourable circumstances, Miss Goward acquitted herself more than creditably.

This was, of course, another feather in the cap of the future Mrs. Keeley, the last having been secured when the young actress made her first big hit as Margot in the 'Sergeant's Wife.' This new triumph was one of many in which the actress was so closely associated with Mr. Keeley that the audience seemed to regard them already as man and wife. Indeed, it was said at the time of the real event, 'the public married them.' But, of course, they were wedded over and over again, upon the stage, as the following scrap of dialogue, culled from Act ii. of the 'Sergeant's Wife,' will show :

Enter Miss Goward.

Mr. Keeley (*coming forward from his hiding-place*) : Oh, Margot, my own beautiful Margot, you can't think how your coming rejoices my poor little heart!

Miss G. : Does it, Robin ?

Mr. K. : Does it ?   I believe it does, indeed ; Margot, will you oblige your tender, loving husband with one kiss?

Miss G. : Kind, simple Robin, you shall have one.   (*Kisses him rapturously.*)

In noticing this piece after the first night of its representation at the English Opera House, the press was, as usual, full of predictions and prophecies concerning the future success of the inseparable couple whom the public had long since married, in their minds ; and it is amusing to note how, up to a certain point, the newspapers of the day were always most guarded in passing judgment upon the pair in any new play in which they appeared.   They did not say decidedly whether they were good, bad, or indifferent, but that they

'showed great promise,' or that the writer 'predicted,' and so on.   Thus, in reviewing the 'Merchant's Wedding,' in which Keeley appeared to
advantage as Timothy, in conjunction with Charles
Kemble and W. Farren, the *Athenæum* said : 'We
are convinced Mr. Keeley is destined to fulfil our
prophecy of rising to the very top of his branch
of the profession ;' and in noticing the 'Sergeant's
Wife,' the *Examiner*, following suit, remarked :
' Miss Goward made quite a character of the little
humane shrew Margot, and evinced that tact and
intelligence which led us in the first instance to
prophesy that she would prove an acquisition to
the stage.   Keeley's simple Lubber is well known,
and to be cowardly and henpecked only adds in
this instance to its piquancy.'   But the *Morning
Advertiser* was content with : ' The efforts of Mr.
Keeley as the frightened-to-death Robin, and of
Miss Goward as his wife and Lisette's guardian
angel, were of the most effective kind.'

More to the purpose, perhaps, was Mr. Montagu
Williams' account of Keeley in this piece, when
he says : ' I shall never forget him in the "Sergeant's Wife," in which he played Robin to Mrs.
Keeley's Margot.   There is one situation in the
piece that lives especially in my memory.   Robin
finds out that he is the servant of a band of
robbers, that they have been committing no end

of murders, and that the bodies of the victims have been buried in the wood-house. He comes and relates the discovery to his wife, and tells her how, on going to the wood-house to get some wood, "I saw his heels, Margot—I saw his heels." Then again I well remember how, in describing a conversation that he had had with his master, the captain of the band, he states what his feelings were when the robber patted him on the head, with the words, " Robin, Robin, how plump you are !" '

Charles Dickens also says in his delightfully graphic way, in reference to Mr. Keeley in this piece : ' In the melodrama of the " Sergeant's Wife," where he and Mrs. Keeley played two innocent fellow-servants in a murdering household most delightfully, his terrors were of the very finest order of acting. We can see him now, when the principal murderer, his master, patted him on the head, and praised him for a good lad, sinking and sinking under the bloodstained hand until the hand stopped, finding nothing to touch.'

In reverting to this play Mrs. Keeley herself remarked, in answer to a question from me :

' Yes, that was the first piece in which I made something like a big hit. It was really the piece that brought me prominently forward as an actress.

But nobody thought it would, and least of all the author, John Banim ; for when he heard who had been cast for Margot, he said, " If Miss Goward plays it, the piece will be damned !" But he was mistaken, as you have heard. The papers were full of my success, and I'm afraid they spoke more of me than they did of Miss Kelly, who was the Lisette. One of them—I think it was the *Examiner*—said, " There are now two stars in the theatrical firmament." That was a feather in my cap, was it not ? Fortunately, my patron did not see the notices till long after they appeared, or it might have been injurious to our great friendship and my future prospects. I think I told you once that Miss Kelly practically brought me out as an actress. Dear Miss Kelly !' (with a sigh). ' I was very fond of her, and she of me. I admired her style, and tried very hard to follow it. Poor soul ! she died only two years ago at the marvellous age of ninety-two.'

But to return to Miss Goward's marriage off the stage. The Keeleys were united in the holy bonds of matrimony in June, 1829, shortly before the season of that year, while engaged to play in the 'Sister of Charity' and the 'Middle Temple ; or, Which is my Son ?' at the old theatre in Wellington Street. From that day forward the happy and gifted pair prospered in a

8

manner that caused the press to speak of them with more critical certainty than before, and without a single prediction or prophecy, and when the bridegroom eventually appeared at Covent Garden in the famous *rôle* of Verges in ' Much Ado about Nothing,' all critics were unanimous in their praises of him as an actor of the highest rank, the *Times* saying : ' Mr. Blanchard and Mr. Keeley, as the immortal Dogberry and Verges, were so good and so true to nature that it is difficult to conceive they have ever been surpassed in those parts.'

As for the blushing bride, she was extolled up to the skies for everything she did, including the male part of William in her début-play of ' Rosina,' when it was revived in 1830 at the Adelphi. But when, much later on, the wife of Robert Keeley took the whole dramatic world by storm with her excellent performance in Searle's drama, ' The Shadow on the Wall,' this is what was said of her :

' If Mrs. Keeley continues to act so admirably in parts like this of domestic pathos, there will be a sad struggle for her between the tragic and comic muses of humble life. To those who know how clever she is in low comedy, we cannot pay her a greater compliment than we do in saying that, as far as the public is concerned, it matters little which gets her.'

In going over this old ground with the lady so deservedly extolled, she gave me two amusing stories relating to her husband. The first of these refers to the beginning of Mr. Keeley's career.

'You know,' said his widow, 'he ran away from Hansard's printing-office, where he was an apprentice, and joined a company of strollers. He got on pretty well after a time, and gave some promise of making his mark in the future. But his family were opposed to his play-acting, and his sister remarked, "Yes, I hear Bob is making something of a name ; but what a pity he is not a respectable tradesman !"'

The other story relates to a private letter which Mr. Keeley wrote to a friend after 'popping the question.'

'My future husband had been for some time in correspondence with a man named Jim Thorn, and he had often spoken of me to his friend. So one day he wrote Thorn a long letter ; I forget what it was all about, but I remember that he began by saying, "I've done it! I have proposed! And I'm d——d if she hasn't accepted me !"'

CHAPTER IX.

WITH the account of Miss Goward's last performances as a spinster my own performances at the easel came to an end; or, rather, they were suspended, to be resumed when my pictorial services were again required for an entirely new production at the same popular house. Before referring to this, I propose to devote a chapter to the account of some interesting ' business '—to speak still in theatrical parlance—which took place at Pelham Crescent shortly after my first portrait of Mrs. Keeley was finished, framed, and otherwise ready for public inspection.

The business in question consisted of a private view of the picture at my sitter's house, previous to sending it for exhibition to the Institute of Painters in Oil-colours, from which place it was purchased for the Garrick Club, the purchaser ordering a similar likeness of Mrs. Stirling, by way of pendant.

Among the many personal friends and theatrical

comrades of Mrs. Keeley who came to view her portrait were old Mrs. Swanborough and her daughter Ada, who had previously seen it while in progress, which is much more than can be said of the original ; for from first to last my sitter never once saw the painted side of the canvas, and if she occasionally peeped at it from behind when the canvas was still transparent, that was all she saw till the picture was fairly completed. It was, however, Mrs. Keeley's own wish that the likeness should not be shown to her during its progress, and whenever invited to inspect it she would give as a reason for declining with thanks :

'I hate myself on canvas or in a photograph at the best of times, so, if you please, I won't look at myself till I am quite done. They nearly always make a monster of me in a photograph, and as for the newspaper atrocities, or the majority of 'em—well, I know I ain't pooty, and never was a Venus ; but I'm not quite the hideous wretch they often represent me to be. There is one that makes me look as if I was suffering from some horrible cutaneous disorder, and there are several that give me a frightful squint. I may not be a fashionable beauty, but I don't squint like that ; now, do I ?' (showing me one of the printed caricatures).

My sitter's eyes were straight enough, as I
took occasion there and then to assure her.
And they were also keen enough ; for, without
seeing the picture, she could often tell, by reference to my palette, which part I was engaged
upon.   Thus, while preparing some pinky colours
with the brush, she would remark in her quick
way :

'I know what you're doing now.   You are
painting my lovely complexion.   I can see the
red tints on your palette ; rose madder, you call
it, don't you ?'   Or when a dark mixture was
being concocted she would say, ' Now you're
doing the dress '—or ' the hair,' as the case might
be, and she was invariably right.

But with these private views in paint, I am
forgetting my private viewers.   One of the first
to enter the ' early doors ' of that ' professional
matinée ' was our old friend Mr. J. L. Toole,
who, accompanied by his daughter Florence, had
' just popped in, don't yer know, to have a look
at the picter and the old gal.'

' And the artist, too,' added the cheery comedian, extending his warm hand in my direction ;
' how are you ?   And how's the club getting on—
flourishing as usual, eh ?   Haven't been there
much for some time.   You see '—in a confidential
whisper—' I've been so busy lately at my theatre

—impossible to get away, especially with these Saturday matinées going on. But we mustn't forget the picture. Where is it?' After a contemplative pause : 'Ah! wonderful old lady, isn't she? Yes, I think you've just caught the Betsy Baker look. She played it for my benefit—bless her!—only two years ago. And she could play it again now, and till further notice.' To our hostess : 'Thank you, I think I will. But draw it mild—plenty of water for me, please.'

Among other private viewers were those excellent comedians, Mr. and Mrs. Arthur Stirling, the former looking more than ever like an ancestral picture just stepped out of an 'old master'; Mrs. Lyons, the married daughter of Mrs. Swanborough, and at one time a clever actress ; Mrs. Pennington, an old friend of Mrs. Keeley's, who looked in at odd moments to play bézique or cribbage with her ; Miss Hogarth, a notable member of the Charles Dickens family ; Mr. Fred Burgess, of Moore and Burgess renown, who limped in to see the picture-show accompanied by his good lady; Mr. R. H. Wyndham, the scarcely less famous lessee of the Edinburgh Theatre Royal, where, in their touring days, the Keeleys had played many a time and oft ; Mr. Montagu Williams, the famous Q.C. and police magistrate ; Major Richardson, of Stonyhurst,

husband of Mrs. Keeley's grand-daughter Jessie,
who had previously looked in ; Miss Alexander,
a niece of Mr. Keeley, and many others whose
names I have forgotten.

Mrs. Keeley was carried down to the drawing-
room floor ; for, though still in the best of general
health, she had by no means recovered from the
effects of her accident of two short weeks, and
was not likely to do so till the injury to the heel
was a thing of the past. However, with another
twelve days' complete rest the patient was so
much better in this respect as to be able to preside at her own festive board upon the occasion
of a little luncheon given by her in honour of the
much younger American actress known in her
own country and in this as Lotta.

I had the pleasure of witnessing the first performances of that clever comedian when she
appeared upon the stage of our Opéra Comique,
and though I cannot say that I was better impressed by the piece selected for her début than
were more critical first-nighters, I could not help
admiring the actress, and I admired her still more
when I saw her afterwards as Little Nell and the
Marchioness, and in pieces suited to her peculiar
style of acting. Mrs. Keeley also thought highly
of Lotta, whom she had seen before her accident,
and one day she remarked :

'She is a genuine artist. But I like her best as the Marchioness, and I laughed immoderately at it. Her Little Nell was also fairly good. But I don't approve of "doubles" or "dual" parts in plays. They never answer on the stage.'

At this memorable lunch-party there were also present Miss Lotta's mother, Mrs. Crabtree, together with a bright and clever actress once known to the stage as Rosina Vokes, afterwards Mrs. Cecil Clay, wife of the famous English composer of that name. Mr. R. H. Wyndham likewise looked in after lunch, so altogether we were a merry and a congenial party.

Naturally, the lion, or lioness, of the afternoon was the American actress, so we all did our best to entertain her and to 'draw her out'; while our hostess, who was as curious as the rest of us to learn how certain things undertaken by Lotta on the stage were prepared by her off it, assisted in the general cross-examination. The Opéra Comique being then closed for Passion Week, there was no hurry for our honoured guest to go away after lunch, or even when afternoon tea was disposed of. But the actress had been rehearsing that day in the English version of the French piece 'La Cigale,' known here as the 'Grasshopper,' so that she was just a little fatigued, even after a refreshing drive from the Strand.

If I am not mistaken, the general conversation began with a brief reference to the 'Grasshopper,' and Miss Lotta said that she was very anxious to appear in this piece, to show the English public what she could do, and that she would have done so before, but that she feared invidious comparisons with Miss Nelly Farren, who had already made a great hit in it at the Gaiety. Some-one then raised the subject of Lotta's ill-advised début in ' Musette,' but she seemed reluctant to dwell upon that unpleasant event, and when some-one informed her he had been present, she re-marked rather bitterly, ' I hope you do not belong to the first-night claquers?' while she declared that, with the exception of that unfortunate evening, she had never in her life played to more appreciative audiences even in the States. She, however, much regretted the absence of a pit, and thought it was greatly against her at the opening per-formances.

'We can't get on without our pit,' she said, and Mrs. Keeley cordially agreed with her, and took occasion also to compliment her in high terms upon the Marchioness, saying that it was 'the best piece of low-comedy acting that she had seen for some time.'

Then we asked the lady how she contrived to make such rapid changes during the action of the piece, from Little Nell to the Marchioness, and from the latter back again to Little Nell, Mrs. Keeley inquiring whether the dresses were 'prepared.'

'Oh dear no!' said Lotta, quite proudly. 'I use no "trick" dresses, but just take them off and put them on in the usual way. Formerly I changed my stockings as well, but I found that too much exertion. Besides, black stockings go well with anything nowadays, and I therefore wear black ones in both characters.'

At this point her amiable mother chimed in by saying that, although she (Mrs. Crabtree) was never seen by the audience, she had 'plenty to do behind the curtain.'

'I work pretty hard every night,' she said, 'in the dressing-room as well as out of it, I can tell you ; and I never get any credit for it, either in front or anywhere else.'

She smiled good-naturedly at her own odd notion of a theatrical dresser requiring applause for her unseen services, and we all laughed heartily at the suggestion. But we were still more amused when Lotta presently recorded her experiences as a boy-actress with a mania for putting her hands in her pockets.

'To cure me of this habit,' she explained, 'they once sewed up my pockets, and when I played

the part at night, of course I couldn't find them.
But such is the force of habit, that I felt utterly
lost without the pockets, and had great difficulty
in repeating my lines. At last I broke down
altogether, and was quite unable to go on with the
part.'

When lunch was over, we took Lotta round to
the Swanboroughs' to see Miss Ada's wonderful
talking bird—a wee paroquet, with bright green
feathers and beady eyes. This remarkable bird
could pronounce clearly many phrases in English
and French, among them being ' Baisez moi, mon
petit '; ' Bon soir '; ' Keeley—kiss Keeley, Betsy
Baker !' ' Bravo! "Our Boys!" Bravo,' "Madame
Favart "!' So its manifold accomplishments were
now trotted out for the benefit of the new visitor,
and when it had gone through most of its vocabulary, Ada Swanborough proceeded to introduce
her guest, saying to her little pet :

' This lady is Miss Lotta, the great American
actress. So remember—Lotta—Lotta !' But the
facetious bird instantly squeaked out as distinctly
as any human being :

' Minnie Palmer—" My Sweetheart !" ' as if well
aware that there existed a sort of rivalry between
the one American actress, who was then playing
at the Strand Theatre, and the other, who was
appearing the same night at the Opéra Comique,

exactly opposite. The situation was, therefore, an embarrassing one, to say the least of it. But all present laughed heartily at the bird's harmless joke, including Lotta herself, who could, of course, see that the remark was the result of previous training and much practice.

It is sad to reflect that the proud owner of that parrot prodigy, and the feathered thing itself, are no longer in the land of the living. But the little bird ceased to talk and to exist long before its loving mistress did so, and Miss Swanborough felt her loss acutely at the time and for many months after, as did also her tender-hearted neighbour, Mrs. Keeley, who was devoted to her feathered friend of No. 5, Pelham Crescent.

Sad also is it to remember that not a few of those visitors, old and young, to the pictorial private view at No. 10 have gone to that undiscovered country from whose bourn no traveller returns !

Chief among those who have left us since that day is Mrs. Keeley's distinguished son-in-law, the late Montagu Williams, of whom I shall have occasion presently to speak more particularly. Mr. Williams had looked in once or twice to see the picture while it was in progress, and his opinion and advice were as valuable in their way as when the Q.C. was consulted professionally by his numerous clients.

Though he himself has passed away, there still
remains a living and speaking representative of
Montagu Williams's household, in the shape of
his favourite parrot—now in the possession of his
mother-in-law—and I remember going to Pelham
Crescent, not long after the arrival of the intelligent bird, when its power of speech was for the
first time strangely exemplified in my hearing.
The servant had, as usual, shown me into Mrs.
Keeley's cosy parlour on the ground-floor, while
she went to announce my arrival to her mistress.
When she was gone, I took up a newspaper,
which lay on the table, and, with the supposition
that no other person was in the apartment, I began
to peruse its pages. But I had scarcely glanced
at the theatrical column, when a voice was heard
distinctly to say in a tone of marked inquiry :

'Well?'

This most unexpected remark naturally startled
me for the moment, and being uttered in the tone
of a person asking, 'Well, what do you want
here?' I was inclined to resent it as rather rude.
However, when the word was repeated, as it was
presently, in precisely the same tone, I saw that it
came from the pet parrot of the late Queen's
Counsel, who was apparently cross-examining me
upon the purpose of my visit.

CHAPTER X.

LOUISA MILLER.

It may be noted as a rather singular example of the irony of Fate that an actress who had been remarkable for her realistic impersonation of a housebreaker and a companion of thieves should be destined to one day become the mother-in-law of a metropolitan police magistrate. Such was, however, the case, as it is pretty generally known that Mrs. Keeley's younger daughter, Louise, was married to Mr. Montagu Williams, Q.C.

So far no mention has been made in these pages of that charming young actress, who, unfortunately, died on January 24, 1877, at the comparatively youthful age of forty-one. But her début upon the stage took place some years later than that of her elder sister, Mary, who was married to Albert Smith, her first appearance having been at Drury Lane on July 12, 1856, when she enacted Gertrude in the 'Loan of a Lover,' originally played by Madame Vestris, with Mr. Keeley as Peter Spyk. In referring to the printed records of that event, I find that the occasion was an amateur performance given in aid of the establishment of the ' Fielding Fund,' for the immediate relief of emergencies in the literary or theatrical world ; the title ' Fielding ' having reference to an amateur dramatic club of that name. The young débutante, who was then scarcely twenty, appears to have made a very successful *coup d'essai*, and I can well ·believe it, for I had the pleasure of seeing her in the same part much later on, as I also did when, in 1859, she appeared as Love in Planché's ' Love and Fortune,' produced at the Princess's under the late Augustus Harris's management. Miss Keeley's professional name was then Louisa Miller, and the *Times*, in noticing her début at Drury Lane, said :

' Particular interest attached on this occasion to Mr. Planché's farce, " The Loan of a Lover," which preceded the pantomime. The leading patrons of amateur performances are usually acquainted with the secrets of the coulisses, and it was well known to a large portion of the audience that the young lady who, under the name of Louisa Miller, made her " first appearance on any stage " in the character of Gertrude, was a member

MARY KEELEY
(MRS. ALBERT SMITH).

LOUISE KEELEY
(MRS. MONTAGU WILLIAMS).

From photographs by Adolphe Beau.

To face p. 127.

of one of the most esteemed theatrical families in London. A storm of applause greeted her as she first came forward, accoutred in a smart Netherland costume, in which the gold helmet, celebrated by Mr. Albert Smith, played a conspicuous part— the beau-idéal of a Flemish beauty. Sanguine as the expectations were, they were more than justified by the performance of the interesting young débutante. The character of Gertrude admits the greatest delicacy of interpretation. . . . All the rapid changes of emotion that pass through the mind of the young beauty were expressed by Miss Miller in the easiest and at the same time most piquant manner. So perfectly was she at ease in the delivery of her dialogue and in all her gestures, that nothing in her performance, except her extremely youthful appearance, marked the débutante. The favourite song, " I've no Money," sung with the nicest feeling, revealed the possession of a sweet soprano voice, and was enthusiastically encored. Peter Spyk, played originally by Mr. Keeley, was sustained by Mrs. Keeley on this occasion, and admirably did she give all the phases of indifference and passion through which the thick-skinned swain is forced to pass till he acquires the highest degree of sensibility.'

The song just referred to began :

'I've no money, so you see
Peter never thinks of me—
    I own it to my sorrow;
Oh, could *I* grow rich, and he
Be reduced to poverty,
What sweet revenge 'twould be for me
    To marry him to-morrow!'

Another of Miss Keeley's songs began :

'I don't think I'm ugly! I'm only just twenty!
    I know I should make a most excellent wife;
The girls all around me have lovers in plenty,
    But I not a sweetheart can get for my life!'

Louisa Miller's appearance at Drury Lane with the amateur company was, of course, only a tentative performance, as she was not seen again upon the London stage till Saturday, September 24, 1859, when J. R. Planché's 'Love and Fortune' (which the author called 'a dramatic tableau in Watteau - colours') was first produced.

The cast was a strong one, with Louise Keeley as Love ; Carlotta Leclercq, Fortune ; Rose Leclercq, Nicholas ; and Frank Matthews, G. J. Shore, Saker, R. Cathcart, Kate Laidlaw, Grace Darley, and others, in the rest of the characters.

Before the act-drop rises there is some introductory business between Louise Keeley and Carlotta Leclercq, relative to the production of

a new piece, each suggesting a new idea, together
with some old ones and adaptations, of which
Miss Keeley says :

> ' But then, you know, one man may steal a horse,
> And t'other not look over a French leaf
> Without some critic crying out "Stop thief !"
> What does it signify ?   Pooh ! let 'em bawl !
> " Tantararara !" Cupid cries, "thieves all !"
> It saves a deal of smoky midnight oil ;
> All my advice is, if you steal, don't spoil.
> " Chacun reprend son bien en il le trouve ;"
> Shakespeare himself could prig, as I could prove.'

Still speaking of adaptations and what Cupid
has done in that way, she says :

> ' And though he may take something from the French,
> It is a field on which so many trench.
> To act no piece that had a smack of Paris in,
> Poor Mr. Harris would find very harassing.'

Of course the Mr. Harris just mentioned was
the father of the present lessee of Drury Lane
and Covent Garden, who was then a little boy of
about seven or eight, at school in the French
capital.

Then, after a duet between Love and Fortune,
in which they propose to dress 'après Watteau,'
the curtain rises upon the gardens of Cassandre's
(Frank Matthews) country-house, and the play
begins.

As usual with all Planché's pieces, it is full to
the brim of good things and clever rhymes with
a reason, one of the most notable songs being
Crispin's (G. J. Shore) beginning :

> 'Threescore and ten, by common calculation,
>   The years of man amount to; but we'll say
> He turns fourscore, yet in my estimation
>   In all those years he has not lived a day.'

It was just a month and five days after 'Miss
Miller's' essay at the National Theatre that she
went on a provincial tour with her parents, beginning at Edinburgh—then under the management
of Mr. Robert Wyndham—and the local papers
announced 'the Keeleys and Miss Louisa Miller,
from Drury Lane,' for a week beginning August 17.
The programme for those six nights included the
'Governor's Wife,' 'That Blessed Baby,' 'Betsy
Baker,' and the 'Loan of a Lover,' in which
Louise Keeley, of course, sustained her original
part, and her mother that of Peter Spyk.

The engagement was a very great success in
every way, and the local press spoke in high
praise of the new actress, as was also the case
when the company went to Glasgow, which
was their next town, and where, in addition to
the pieces just named, they played the 'Little
Treasure,' 'Valentine and Orson,' and 'Gilderoy.'
The Glasgow papers spoke in glowing terms of

Miss Miller, saying that 'special praise was due to the young actress for her sweet singing and unaffected simplicity of manner' (which, I well remember, were among the many histrionic charms of Louise Keeley), and the same writer predicted for the actress a brilliant career. He had also more than a good word to say of Mrs. Keeley, whose 'vivacity kept them quite on the *qui vive*'; while the writer spoke also of 'Mr. Keeley, who with his grave, quaint humour and statue-like face, threw the audience into convulsions of mirth.'

It is worth a passing note that the year 1856 marks the period when all four Keeleys were for the first time in 'full swing' on the stage, for Mary Keeley was then fulfilling an important engagement at the Adelphi under Celeste's management. Among the many pieces she appeared in were 'Good - night, Signor Pantalon,' an adaptation, if I mistake not, of the Spanish musical farce of 'Buenas noches, Señor Don Simon,' which I have often seen on the Spanish stage, in which Paul Bedford, J. Bland, Miss Arden, and Miss Kate Kelly took part; the 'Flying Dutchman,' with Webster, Wright, Paul Bedford, Madame Celeste, Kate Kelly, and Mary Keeley; 'Urgent Private Affairs,' 'Media,' 'Paul Pry,' and last and best of all, 'Born to Good

Luck,' in which Mary Keeley, in a soubrette part, sang a pretty ballad and danced an Irish jig with the famous American actress, Mrs. Barney Williams, who in that year acted at the Adelphi.

Returning to the touring members of the Keeley family, I should mention that it was in Edinburgh that Louise, under her proper name, appeared on her own account next season, which opened at the Theatre Royal on July 21, 1857, with a burlesque founded on the 'Winter's Tale,' called 'Perdita.' At that time Henry Irving and his bosom friend, J. L. Toole, were playing at the same theatre, so that the cast of 'Perdita' was a strong one, with Miss Lydia Foote in the title-*rôle*, Miss Louise Keeley as Florizel, Toole as Autolycus, and Irving as Camillo. For Miss Keeley's benefit on July 27 'Paul Pry' was announced among other attractions, with, of course, Mr. Toole in his favourite part, and Mr. Irving as Harry Stanley ; and after that 'London Assurance' was played, with Mr. Irving as Dazzle, Toole as Dolly Spanker, Sir William Don as Mark Meddle, and Miss Keeley as Grace Harkaway.

It was in Edinburgh that Mr. Montagu Williams first encountered his future wife, and when he and his friend, Mr. Disney Roebuck, were acting in the provinces. The strollers had been performing at Manchester, Birmingham, and other big towns in the Midlands, and after that they obtained engagements at Edinburgh and Glasgow for the same dates on which Louise Keeley was about to terminate her own season there. Upon their arrival in Edinburgh, the companions went to the theatre to arrange matters with Mrs. Wyndham, who was virtually the manager, and in the words of one of them this is what happened :

' I was on the stage, leaning against one of the boxes, and my eyes were, I presume, wandering toward the talented little lady who was to become so great a blessing to a portion of my future. Mrs. Wyndham, calling me over, said, "I have much pleasure in introducing you to Miss Keeley." We at once commenced a conversation, and very quickly became friends. The next day I, not being quite perfect in the part I was to play on the Monday night, was wandering in the neighbourhood of Arthur's Seat, studying my lines, when whom should I meet but the lady to whom I had been introduced on the previous morning ! We walked together for a considerable time, and in the end I asked her to hear me my part, a favour that was at once granted.'

At the suggestion of Mrs. Wyndham it was

arranged that 'London Assurance' should be
played on Thursday for the last night of Miss
Keeley's engagement, with Mr. Roebuck as Dazzle,
Mr. Montagu Williams as Charles Courtley, and
Miss Keeley in her original part of Grace Harkaway.   Mr. Williams mentions that the piece was
a great success, and that Mrs. Wyndham told him
more than once that in 'all her experience she
had never known Charles Courtley make love
to Grace as naturally as he did on that occasion.'

The lovers parted after this performance, Mr.
Williams and his friend betaking themselves to
Glasgow, Perth and Newcastle, besides Hanley,
and other towns in the Potteries where the pair
secured engagements, and Miss Keeley going to
Dublin to play at the Queen's Theatre, then
under the management of Harry Webb.   Learn-
ing through the pages of the *Era* that the young
actress was in the Irish capital, Mr. Williams made
the best of his way thither, partly with a view to
obtain a theatrical engagement.   But his visit
ended with a matrimonial one.   Mr. Williams
proposed and was accepted, and he and his
fiancée were shortly afterwards married without
the consent or the knowledge of their respective
parents, and without possessing any settled in-
come.

The newly - wedded couple then went to London, where they took a small house in Pelham Street, close to the young bride's parental home ; and while it was being prepared for their occupation, they went on tour again, beginning with Edinburgh, where they both obtained a month's engagement with the Wyndhams. There they met Mr. Irving, and when going afterwards to Belfast they encountered also ' Johnny' Toole, and performed with him at the local theatre in ' Perdita,' Mr. Toole playing Autolycus as before, and Mrs. Montagu Williams Florizel. From Belfast Mr. and Mrs. Williams went to Sunderland, South Shields and Nottingham, accepting engagements of about a fortnight in each town, and then returned to their home at Brompton.

' This was the end of my experiences as an actor,' remarks the future Q.C. and police magistrate, after recording in print all these things, ' for on our return to Pelham Street, as the result of a long conversation with my father-in-law, I determined to leave the stage and enter myself as a student at one of the Inns of Court.'

That wise step was assuredly the turning-point in the career of the late Montagu Williams, who, as everyone knows, was one of the most

successful and prosperous barristers of his time.
Their daughter Jessie married Major (now Colonel)
Richardson, of Sandhurst, by whom she had
four children—three girls and one boy. The
eldest, now fourteen, promises to resemble her
father in point of stature, her height being five
feet six inches, and his a little over six feet;
while the youngest girl is not unlike, in appearance, her great-grandmother. She also inherits
some of Mrs. Keeley's powers of mimicry. Not
less bright and intelligent is the only son, Bob,
named, of course, after Mr. Keeley.

Shortly after the completion of Mrs. Keeley's
picture, she was good enough to commission me
to paint a posthumous likeness of her lamented
daughter Louise. The new work was intended
as a surprise-gift to her son-in-law, and it was
begun in my studio from various photographs and
coloured miniatures, together with a silky lock of
fair auburn hair slightly tinged with red and gold.
With these things, and my own rather vivid
remembrance of my subject, I endeavoured to
bring before me the somewhat dreamy yet spark-
ling bluish-gray eyes, with their well-defined
arched eyebrows, the perfectly oval face, the
pale complexion, varied by a delicate crimson
in the cheeks, and the bright expression, which,
when smiling broadly, as in one of the photo-

graphs, reminded one not a little of her mother.

When the portrait was sufficiently advanced, the canvas was transferred to Pelham Crescent for some finishing touches under the useful guidance of Mrs. Keeley.

CHAPTER XI.

POSTHUMOUS PRODUCTIONS.

IT need scarcely be said that, while engaged in putting the finishing touches to the portrait of Mrs. Montagu Williams, my patron and I conversed, as before, upon many interesting subjects, more or less connected with her daughters and their father. But with her triple bereavement still fresh in the mind of the veteran survivor, she was not always inclined to speak of her loved ones.

Now and again, however, her eyes would sparkle while recalling some pleasant incident in her daughter's career, as was the case when, after contemplating with a loving smile one of the photographs before us, she turned to me and said :

' I recollect Louise coming to me one day after some recent triumph on the stage, and saying, " Mother, my salary is raised to £15 a week !" " Fifteen pounds !" I exclaimed ;

"why, bless me! if they give you all that you
must indeed be somebody." Fifteen pounds
were high wages in those days, I can tell you.
Why, Mr. Keeley and I never got more than
£30 between us, though they always gave me
more than my husband; and when acting alone
I sometimes received £20 weekly. But Mrs.
Glover once told me that she played for £12.'

These particulars of the pay of comedians in
earlier days reminded the speaker of a story about
Fawcett, who was at one time stage-manager at
Covent Garden.

'He was a first-class actor, as I dare say you
know,' she said; 'but a bit of a martinet, as
perhaps you don't know. If anyone happened
to be late at rehearsal, he called him to account
at once, and threatened to fine him; and if the
late-comer pulled out his watch to show he
was punctual—by his own time-keeper—Fawcett
would say, "Don't bring me any of your broken-
winded watches, but be in time." Once he said
to me in his pompous way, "We have thought
it well to raise your salary to £8 a week—£8 a
week! But you must not expect all this money
for looking on."'

This story led to one about her daughter
Mary:

'Mary was quite old enough to see and understand Smike when I played the part at the Adelphi.   Upon our return home from the theatre one night, we found her sobbing as if her young heart would break.   "What's the matter, child?" we asked, wondering what it could be.   "Oh, mother dear!" she cried, "do you think there is such a place as Do-the-*Girls*-Hall?"'

Quite a string of anecdotes of Mrs. Keeley's husband was once the result of some touches of flesh-colour I had been putting to the complexion of his daughter Louise, which impressed me as being not unlike that of the famous low comedian.

After speaking of an unsuccessful attempt which her husband once made to grow a moustache, Mrs. Keeley referred to the early married days when she and he were in lodgings in Long Acre.   Happening to take a stroll through Covent Garden Market, the young wife saw a robin for sale, and expressed a wish to have it, for she loved feathered creatures of all kinds.

'Always ready to oblige me,' said Mrs. Keeley, 'he went at once to the owner of the bird and asked the price.   "A guinea," said the man; and my husband was in the act of taking out the coin, when a stranger, who had overheard us, exclaimed: "Oh, lor!—a guinea for a cock-robin!" That settled it; for Mr. Keeley was so ashamed that he wouldn't buy it, and so I never got my bird.'

This story was followed by another relating to the same period, when the actor and his colleagues, John Reeve, Frank Matthews, and other congenial spirits, occasionally met at Kilpack's, a cigar-shop and bowling-alley next door to Evans's. On Saturday, which was pay-day at the theatre, the friends would sometimes remain at Kilpack's till the small hours of the morning, playing cards in a room over the shop, and once they stopped out later than usual.

'I was, of course, fast asleep in bed,' Mrs. Keeley explained, when telling this story; 'and it seems that, before retiring for the night, my husband placed our united salaries, which he had brought home safely, in one of his boots. Next morning, or, rather, that morning, I got up early, as usual, letting Mr. Keeley sleep on, as I knew he had come home very late; and after breakfast Frank Matthews looked in, as he often did on Sundays, to go for a walk with my husband to Hampstead, or some such place. Finding "Mary mother," as he called me, in the dumps, he asked what was the matter, and where was Bob. "Why, fast asleep in bed, of course," I said. "Pretty hours for you and him to keep, coming home at five in the morning! But the worst of it is that all our hard earnings of the week are gone. Yes, Frank, gone! For I looked in all his pockets, and not a sou could I find." "That's strange," said Matthews. 'Why, I was with him all the evening and saw him home." "Then you're as bad as he," I said; "however, our hard earnings have gone, so there's an end to it." But it was not the end, for presently Matthews went into the next room to wake up Mr. Keeley. My husband was already wide awake and roaring with laughter. "What's this about the salaries being lost?" asked his friend. "Hush!" said the other; "she thought I was asleep when she ransacked my clothes this morning, but I wasn't. It's all right, Frank; the money's in my boot!"'

This led to some other interesting records of Robert Keeley's social and domestic habits.

'My husband was not always as dissipated as I have described,' his widow remarked. 'He loved his home and its belongings, and, as a rule, would never show himself in "society" if he could possibly help it. That is, perhaps, why I have never been to the Henley Regatta; and I should so much like to go there too: not for the boating, no, no—I don't think they could persuade me to go into a boat; I should be afraid of its capsizing

or something—but I should like just to contemplate from a distance the general effect of the
scene. But Mr. Keeley never went there, or
to the Derby, or anywhere else after we were
married. You see, he had sown his wild oats—
and he had plenty to sow, I can tell you—for he
didn't marry till he was thirty-six.'

While speaking of the early days of their happy
union, Mrs. Keeley incidentally informed me that
they began married life by working out on the
stage the large sum of £400 to pay a bill that
her good-hearted husband had put his name to,
to oblige a friend.

Upon another occasion Mrs. Keeley related a
couple of provincial stories, the first of which
referred to a time when the Keeleys were on tour
and went to Glasgow. But as the story required
a little acting to give proper effect to the sequel,
its narrator stood up, as she not unfrequently did
upon similar occasions, and said :

'Wallack was playing at Glasgow in some
Shakespearian piece—I think it was " Macbeth "
or " Richard III."—and the manager, Alexander
—a third-rate actor, with first-rate opinions of himself—called Wallack to account for his acting, and
found all sorts of fault with it. Then he had the
effrontery to offer to show him how to play the
part. Wallack said nothing ; but after leaning with

10

folded arms against the wing—like this—he
looked hard at the other, and said very calmly :
" Well, Mr. Alexander, *show* me." And Alexander
did so, in the broadest possible Scotch.'

The other story was :

' We were playing at Sheffield in a farce called
the " Young Tiger." After the performances, a
native of the town came up to my husband and
said : " Yes, it was certainly very good ; but it
would have been better still if you had kept your
promise and shown us the tiger. You should
never deceive the public by announcing things
that you don't intend to do. It looks bad, you
know." '

While the portrait of Mrs. Montagu Williams
was in progress, a friend told me an amusing story
in connection with her gifted husband, whom I
knew slightly in private life, and very well indeed
in his public capacity, first as Queen's Counsel,
and afterwards as Police Magistrate.

This story had reference to an odd mistake
once made by Stirling Coyne, the author and
dramatic critic, who was noted for his polished
manners, especially towards ladies, and who
was, moreover, very handsome, with beautiful
silver-gray hair and moustache. This gentleman had had occasion, one broiling hot day
in August, to look in at the Bow Street police

court, and there he saw Montagu Williams engaged in some important case and struggling manfully against the stifling heat. On leaving that oppressive atmosphere, Mr. Coyne went to the Crystal Palace, where whom should he meet, almost at the entrance, but one of the Keeley sisters! With his accustomed courtliness of manner, he raised his hat and bowed gracefully, while the lady remarked :

'Ah, Mr. Coyne, I am so pleased to see you. How hot it is to-day, is it not ?'

'It is indeed,' was his unfortunate reply ; 'but not so hot as where your poor husband is !' Then, with a look of horror in his face, he saw that he had made a terrible mistake. For the lady before him was not Mrs. Montagu Williams, as he had thought, but the widow of Albert Smith.

CHAPTER XII.

ROBERT KEELEY.

My recollection of the personality of the famous low-comedian, familiarly known as 'Bob' Keeley, was far more vivid than of his daughters, or even of his wife, when the latter was on the stage. But, then, a man's face is, as a general rule, much easier to remember than a young woman's or a child's, more particularly a man of middle age, or one close upon threescore, as Keeley was when first I saw him at the Haymarket in 'Box and Cox.'

Keeley's features were not only well marked, but comparatively without expression when in a condition of complete repose, and, taken in conjunction with his clean-shaved face and perfectly white hair, he presented an appearance which reminded one not a little of a marble bust. It was this stolid look which assisted in giving such point and unconscious humour to the comedian's

ROBERT KEELEY.

To face p. 149.

utterances upon the stage, and off it also, as I am told that he was quite as funny in private life.

His widow tells me that her husband was, when in his thirties, a handsome man, and I can well believe it ; for when I saw the actor in '52 he was decidedly good-looking, with finely-cut features and an aristocratic bearing. We usually saw him with his own face, and not one disfigured by extravagant eyebrows, a preposterous false nose and ' comic ' lines. In fact, the more Keeley was himself, the funnier he appeared ; and much the same may be said of his voice and manner, which all mimics of the day closely imitated. I remember there was a story current at the time, to the effect that some imitator of actors once ' took off ' Keeley in his presence, and that when he had done so the comedian said, in his slow, jerky way, ' Well, if I'm like that, dem'd if I like it !'

The actor was never more like himself than when playing in a little piece called ' Keeley Worried by Buckstone,' which its authors, Mark Lemon and Benjamin Webster, described as ' a most personal extravaganza in one act, freely adapted from the French.' In this dramatic trifle, which I saw half a dozen times at least, Bob Keeley was to be seen much as he was at his home in Pelham Crescent in the early part of the day, attired in his dressing-gown and slippers ;

and once, when I witnessed the farce from a stage-box, it was almost like being in his company.

There was, of course, not much 'plot' in this farce, while the fun was of the fast and furious kind. The main purpose, however, was to bring forward the best-known mannerisms and characteristics of the two low-comedians named in the title, and with this in view the authors had represented Keeley as having made up his mind to retire from the stage. He has had enough of it, he thinks, so he means to 'indulge his natural disposition, which is sentimental melancholy,' and says, as only that actor could say, 'Ha! ha! my laugh is perfectly hollow and O. Smithish. My face, no longer disguised with rouge, has assumed an interesting pallor. I can now say what I please, no longer compelled to utter the bosh of authors. I can give the rein to my imagination and set my eye "with a fine frenzy rolling!"' In any case he is a free man, and seriously contemplates retiring into the country, perhaps to 'keep a turnpike.'

Unfortunately his friend, Buckstone, has had an inkling of Keeley's contemplated retirement, and being of opinion that it will be a great loss to the stage, does his best to force him to desist from his purpose. With this object in view

he invades Keeley's peaceful home at Pelham
Crescent, and behaves so badly—first by making
desperate love from the window to some imaginary
female over the way, thereby endangering Keeley's
domestic happiness ; next by throwing plates and
flower-pots out of the window to attract his lady-
love's attention, which compromises Keeley with
the police ; and, lastly, by converting the neatly-
arranged apartment into a perfect bear-garden—
that altogether its owner is driven nearly dis-
tracted, and after trying in vain to get rid of his
unwelcome visitor, he eventually determines to
accept an engagement from Webster, which comes
opportunely through the old stock Haymarket
actor, Clark. With this the curtain falls, leaving
Keeley alone on the outside.

A favourite piece in which the humorous characteristics of both Keeleys were strongly developed was Tom Taylor's farce 'Our Clerks,'
which, when revived at the Gaiety Theatre, was
enacted with success by Mr. Toole and Miss
Nelly Farren. When originally produced, in
March, 1852, the Keeleys were, of course, the two
clerks, John Puddicombe and Edward Sharpus.

In my Keeley researches I tried to meet with
some odd volume or scrap-album that would enlighten me concerning the departed actor's early
history and theatrical career, or that gave such

particulars as I was not yet acquainted with ;
but all that could be gathered from these inves-
tigations was that which was already known,
namely, that he was born in 1793, at No. 3,
Grange Court, Carey Street, Lincoln's Inn Fields,
and was one of a rather large family of fifteen
children ; that he had a slight limp in his walk ;
that his hair was red till it turned gray, and
that he was very much below the 'middle
height,' his precise measurement being five feet
two inches.

As for the comedian's first appearance on the
stage, there did not appear to be any record of it
in print ; nor could his widow much enlighten me.
She only knew that after running away from
Hansard's printing-office, where he was an apprentice, the lad joined a company at the Richmond
Theatre and went on the stage as a super or
'banner-bearer.'   Thence, curiously enough, he
betook himself to his future wife's birthplace, at a
time when little Mary Anne was exhibiting some
precocity as a child of eight, and after remaining
four years on the Norwich circuit, he returned to
town and appeared at the obscure Queen's Theatre,
in Tottenham Street.

'My husband,' said Mrs. Keeley, 'really made
his first appearance at a barn, in John Home's
"Douglas."   He used to tell the story something

in this way : " In the scene where young Norval
delivers the well-known lines beginning, 'My
name is Norval,' he has to say, ' I left my father's
house and took with me a chosen servant to conduct my steps—yon trembling coward who for-
sook his master.' I was that trembling coward,"
added my husband in a way that always excited
roars of laughter.

' He made another début at Birmingham in the
" Forty Thieves,"' she continued ; ' Mr. Keeley
was one of the forty, and hadn't a word to say.
He only came on with the others on horseback.
There were six horses and six men, but by re-
appearing several times they made up the right
number. My husband came on half a dozen times
in this way, till at last he was recognised, and
someone in the gallery shouted out, " There he
be again ! I know'd 'im by his 'at." '

In 1818 Elliston offered young Keeley an engagement at the Olympic, where he played Lepo-
rello in ' Don Giovanni,' and the success which he
met with encouraged the manager to take him
next year to Drury Lane, where, however, the
young man did not much improve his position as
an actor. So he went to try his fortunes at the
Adelphi, and there he remained for two entire
seasons, making a hit as Jemmy Green in Pierce
Egan's ' Tom and Jerry.' On April 22, 1822,

he was at Sadler's Wells, playing Jerry in the
same author's version of ' Life in London,' and
shortly after at Covent Garden, where he was
engaged by Charles Kemble to enact Darby in
the ' Poor Soldier.'

Though steadily coming to the front, it is evident that the comedian had not yet found the
much-coveted turning-point in his career, perhaps
because he had not made the acquaintance of the
young lady from Ipswich who the Fates decreed
would be instrumental in improving the stroller's
fortunes.   Meanwhile, he did pretty well on his
own account, and among the almost endless parts
which the actor assumed, with more or less success, were Marcel, a country bumpkin, in ' 'Twas
I '; Abel, in ' Honest Thieves '; Spado, in the
' Castle of Andalusia '; Peter, in ' Romeo and
Juliet '; the Clown, in the ' Winter's Tale '; Bob
Barnacle, in the 'Wife's Stratagem'; Jerry Sneake,
in the ' Mayor of Garratt '; King Arthur, in ' Tom
Thumb '; Scrub, in the ' Beaux' Stratagem ';
Wamba, in Lacy's ' Maid of Judah,' and Nicko-
demus Crowquill, in ' Peter Wilkins ; or, The
Flying Indian.'

But the young actor was evidently making
headway in the opinion of the public and the
press, for in a general notice of the stage published
in the twenties by the *Athenæum* the writer says :

' We have singled out Keeley for exactly the converse reason to that which caused us to speak of Liston. This actor is a growing favourite with the town, and will, we doubt not, in a few years, stand where Liston does now. And he well deserves it a great deal more, for he is an artist as well as a mere farceur ; he has, we are convinced, a reason for everything he does, and yet there is throughout an unvarying ease, nature and simplicity which throw study completely out of view. The chief fault he has to guard against is a tendency to monotony of delivery ; but this is much less than it was, and we doubt not ere long will be eradicated. Keeley's Shakespearian comedy is as admirable as Liston's is the reverse. It was seeing him in the little part of Verges that stamped our opinion of his merits. We prophesy that this gentleman will be the first low-comedian of his day.'

It was in the beginning of the forties that Keeley boldly attempted to enact Shylock in orthodox style, and not as a burlesque, at the Strand Theatre ; but the performance appears to have been a failure on the whole, though his widow assures me that there were many good points in his acting, that he had an excellent conception of the character, and looked it well. But the comedian was more at home in such Shakespearian parts

as have been previously noted, and in most of
these he appeared with his wife in the early forties,
when the pair were under an engagement with
Macready at Drury Lane. It was then that 'As
You Like It' was revived, with the wonderful
cast already described by the impersonator of
Audrey, of whom Phelps, who then enacted Anti-
gonus, once wrote, 'That imp of mischief, Mrs.
Keeley, the best Audrey and about the best all-
round actress I have ever seen.' Macready also
considered her Audrey by far the best that had
been seen upon the stage.

No person was better qualified to pass judgment upon Robert Keeley as an actor and a man
than the Keeleys' warm admirer and personal
friend, Charles Dickens, who was himself an actor
of no small pretensions. Shortly after Keeley's
death, in 1869, Dickens wrote anonymously a
graceful tribute to the old low-comedian's memory,
and as it has never been reprinted from the journal
in which it originally appeared, I propose to make
some extracts from it, having obtained the permission of the novelist's eldest son.

Mr. Dillon Croker, who was good enough to
send me a copy of the article, tells me that Macready had a hand in the composition. But Mr.
Dickens thinks that his father was not so aided.

After dwelling for some length upon Charles

Lamb's admirable description of the low-comedian, Dodd, whom Keeley was said to closely resemble in manner and look, more particularly in parts of the Sir Andrew Aguecheek kind, the writer goes on to say :

' Low-comedy is no limited sphere ; it ranges over many and various degrees of art and acting, from the comedy of Touchstone and Dogberry, to the broad humour or no-humour of modern farce. Through all these various degrees Keeley was equally admirable. Harley was an excellent artist in his way ; but he was always full of his own humour, and showed it, as much as to say, " See how funny I am !" His audiences were willing enough to admit that he was, and, indeed, who could help it ? but Keeley's was the truer art. In their respective performances of Dogberry, the difference was remarkable. The blunders of the old constable fell from Harley's lips as if he felt their absurdity, and enjoyed it ; from Keeley's, with the most immovable and pompous stolidity, as from one who believed that the whole weight of Messina was on his shoulders, and that he was well worthy to bear it, and well able to bear it. If anybody had told the one Dogberry that he was a funny fellow, tempted thereto by the merry twinkle in his eye, he would have been treated to a glass of liquor at the nearest wine-shop ; if he had so far forgotten himself as to offer such an insult to the dignity of the other, he would have been incontinently " moved on," or comprehended as a vagrom man of the most dangerous sort.

' No doubt, in some characters, Harley's face and style, expressing mirthfulness in activity, gave him an advantage ; as in Launcelot Gobbo, who is eminently a " wag," or believes himself one, and of whom it may be true that the total want of point betrayed by many of his utterances was intentional—a satirical comment on the funny man who, because he is very amusing sometimes, " will always be flouting," and often fails in being anything but silly. But the majority of Shakespeare's " clowns " are unconscious or saddened humorists ; and their jokes are far more in keeping with the grave face than the gay. Sometimes we meet with two of them placed side by side in sharp contrast ; and that contrast can never have been better realized than by Keeley and Harley in the same play ; as when the former played Sir Andrew to the Clown of the latter, in that very comedy of " Twelfth Night," about which Charles Lamb gossips so delightfully. The contrast was even more effectively shown in Sheridan's " Rivals," when Harley was the Acres, and Keeley the David. His more ambitious successors of the present day would scarcely submit to the degrada-

tion of playing David to the Acres of a fellow-
comedian of even equal standing in the salary-list
of their theatre, however much nature may have
fitted them for the one part, and unfitted them for
the other. Keeley knew better ; and what a delicious David he was! Though forced, by the false
though most attractive art which inspired that
school of comedy, to talk in a succession of epi-
grams, as rounded and brilliant as the wittiest
fashionable of them all, Keeley made David a
miracle of stolid rusticity—a man of one idea, very
much in earnest, both in his disgust with his
master's follies and in his anxiety for him—which
in Keeley's hands acquired a touch of pathos from
the devotion of the man.

' For Keeley was a master of pathos in his way,
and many of our most delightful memories of him
are connected with characters into which, by a
few words or a little touch, he threw a certain
homely tenderness quite his own. He never
strained that chord too far, but struck it, as it
were, in passing, relying upon delicate ears to
catch the sound as it fell. By the general public,
perhaps, this power of his was not as fully recognised as it might have been. Poor Robson could
make his audience laugh and cry alternately, at
his will ; and that he could do so was due to what
was really an artistic defect in his acting. He

was an actor of genius ; but of subtlety he had little or none. He did not hint himself to his audience ; he threw himself broadly at them ; and he could bound at once, without preparation or gradation, from pathos to fun. Not so Keeley ; subtle his acting was, in the highest degree ; and his light and shade were most delicately and beautifully blended. He must have suffered sometimes from the misplaced laughter of gods and groundlings (stalls not always excepted), at moments when his own eyes were filled with tears. For he was too sensitive an artist not to feel, when his part gave scope for feeling. All audiences, however, contain some delicate perception ; and it is not only by critics and constant playgoers that Keeley is remembered as among the most touching, as well as the drollest, of actors.

'Of the personal regard of the public he had an extraordinary share. One great difference between French and English audiences is, that the former have the higher feeling for the art, the latter for the artist. The noisy "receptions" which a favourite actor obtains with us, whenever he appears on the stage, are sometimes rather excessive in their demonstration ; but they are very infectious, withal, in their enthusiasm, and are, doubtless, most inspiriting to the performer. At a French theatre, an actor, however established

his reputation and great his popularity, often has
no " reception"; the tribute is confined to special
occasions, as when he appears in some part which
he has "created." It is the part, as it were, that
is applauded in advance, and not the artist. There
is something pleasant in the personal affection of
a British audience, who make no such nice dis-
tinctions. Of that personal regard which unites
us with our theatrical favourites Keeley had a
lion's share, and it followed him in his retirement so faithfully, that when the town heard
of his death the other day, it regretted him as
much as if he had left the world and the stage
together.

 ' In one sense, indeed, he did so ; for, though
it was to all intents and purposes certain for some
time past that he would never act again, he took
no formal farewell of the theatre—a device which
is painful when it is real, as too rude and material
a severing of the link between actor and public ;
but which of late years has been too often a
fiction, a prelude to a succession of "last appearances" which provoke laughter and extinguish
regret. We have no drawbacks of that nature
in our recollections of Keeley ; and we have still
the consolation of hoping that his other half, the
partner of his name and popularity—so closely
united with him that we can never think of the

one without the other—may not be entirely lost to the stage.

'We saw Keeley act on the occasion which proved to be his last appearance, when he played his old part of Dolly Spanker—one of the most finished figures in his portrait-gallery. The little trot across the stage—the " Here I am, Gay "—the grotesque devotion and not unmanly weakness of the doting husband—made up a picture whose colours time had not in the least blurred or faded when he played for the last time. The stage was as elastic under his feet as it ever was in his best days ; and he never allowed us to feel that he had outstayed his time. Ah, the *laudatores temporis acti* have reason on their side when they talk of the theatrical companies of old days, if there were many like him !

'We do not profess in this little paper to attempt anything like an exhaustive criticism on Keeley's acting, or, indeed, anything that can properly be called criticism. Our purpose does not extend beyond a few words of admiring remembrance and regret—a momentary lingering on lost intellectual delights. We have mentioned his Dogberry. As we write, we hear again the very inflexions of his voice, and see again the wonderful expression of his face at the supreme moment when he was called an ass ! No other catastrophe on earth, or in the waters under it, could have aroused in living man such an amazing exposition of stupendous astonishment, indignation, and incredulity, as that insult wrung from Dogberry as Keeley drew him. But his Verges was even finer. By the force of his profound belief in Dogberry, one may say that he absorbed that Jackass into himself, sublimated and enhanced the drollery of the character, and made it all his own. The more preposterous Dogberry, the more steeped and lost in admiration he. When Dogberry was most ridiculous, Verges wandered away through the broadest realms of speculation how the heavens ever came to make a man so wondrous wise. It was a true triumph of art. Considered with a reference to the very few words set down for Verges, it was certainly the most finished and thoughtful piece of suggestive comic acting that one can easily imagine possible. And it culminated when his asinine chief patted him on the head, and he first bent under the honour, and then became the taller for it, gazing into his patron's face with an expression of fatuous contentment perfectly marvellous.

'In the "Loan of a Lover," his Peter Spyk had no approach to a parallel that ever we have seen on the English, French or Italian stage. Its immovable stolidity, and apparent insensibility to

everything but a big pipe, until he made the
tender discovery that he loved the little woman
who had grown up about him from a child—and
its pathos when that truth burst upon him con-
currently with the information that she was
going to be married to someone else—were
simply beyond praise.

'For the richest humour, his reading of a letter
in " Betsy Baker" may be quoted ; or his extraordinary devices for getting out of the room in
"Your Life's in Danger," where he had to pass
a man at breakfast, who, he thought, might stop
him by the way.   Foremost among the pleasantest
laughing faces we have ever seen at a theatre is
our recollection of the Queen's face and its natural,
unrestrained abandonment to the humour of the
scene, when, in " A Thumping Legacy "—at
Drury Lane, in Macready's time, years ago—
Keeley received the intelligence that he had
come to Corsica not so much to inherit a property
as to inherit a vendetta, and, in supreme vexation
of spirit, suddenly and surprisingly hit out at his
informant after the British manner.   There was
once an unsuccessful piece at the Lyceum, founded
on a charming tale by Washington Irving.   We
do not recall a single point in Keeley's part,
except that he had seen a ghost before the curtain
rose.   That he had indubitably seen it, and that

he went about ever afterwards expecting to see it again, the audience knew as well as he did from the moment of his first entrance.

'We are not thankful enough to great actors for the relief they give us, and the good they do us. These are but a few untwined forget-me-nots scattered on a great actor's grave. In private, he had the heart of a child and the integrity of the noblest man.'

CHAPTER XIII.

THE proverb which tells us that a man's character is indicated by the company he keeps, has been sometimes applied in respect of his books. In the case of Robert Keeley, his small but select library was sufficiently suggestive of his calling and his literary tastes. So, in the intervals of my own pursuits at Pelham Crescent, or when my kind hostess had left me to my cigarette, I looked at her husband's books with a view to ascertain what was his favourite reading.

I found that he was not less fond of collecting old plays by the standard English and French dramatists than were many other students and bookworms of his kind, and that he was also partial to rare prints ; odd volumes of obsolete magazines ; choice editions of the poets, bound in calf ; old-fashioned family medical works ; theatrical biographies, some of which had been presented to the actor, and popular books on the stage. Intermingled with these things were a few standard novels and some stray modern romances whose bright covers showed that they belonged to Mr. Keeley's novel-devouring widow, who passed most of her spare time in reading the very latest from the circulating library of her preference.

Mrs. Keeley's critical opinion of the novels of the day was always worth having, and her estimation of their merits was, as a rule, sound and correct. Anything dramatic, or with touches of humour and pathos combined, at once took her fancy ; but she showed only a passing interest in sensational stories, pure and simple, and for those going by the general name of 'shockers,' she cared not at all.   As for books written up to one main idea of a startling or a repulsive description, the actress would never read one if she could possibly help it. But she raved about stories like 'King Solomon's Mines.'

One day, when I happened to be glancing over a thick volume of Hone's ' Every-day Book,' which had once belonged to Albert Smith, and bore his autograph and address on the fly-leaf, Mrs. Keeley remarked :

' My husband loved his books and his literary pursuits ; he was a scholar, and could write well upon many subjects.   At one time Mr. Keeley contributed to *Colburn's Magazine*, and used to

get five guineas for an article. But he was too
lazy to continue.   His criticisms of books of the
day were often sound and worth listening to.
When "Adam Bede" came out, I remember our
asking him for his opinion.   "What do you think
of it, dad?" I said.   But he was silent.   "Come,
say something," I went on, finding he remained
mute ; " tell us what you really think of the book."
" Well," said he, in his slow but sure way, " what
I think of it is this : it's like driving through a
beautiful country in a mourning-coach." '.

It was easy to perceive by reference to the well-
stocked bookcases that their late owner was a
student ; while in an interesting letter, which Mrs.
Keeley was good enough to show me, it was not
difficult to tell that the comedian was on intimate
terms with most of the literary notabilities of the
day.   The letter in question is as follows :

                           ' Athenæum,
                              ' *Saturday* [no date].

' DEAR SIR,

        ' I am not altogether conscious of the criti-
cism, or were you before. But I well remember
forming an opinion the first night I had the pleasure of seeing you act, which your future triumphant success fully justified.   I am much obliged
for your MS., which, if not used this month, shall

be brought forward next month. I am much obliged, also, for the American *announce*. The character is quite suitable, and I dare say I shall do wonders.

' Believe me, dear sir,

' Yours very faithfully,

' THEODORE HOOK.'

Here is another document which Mrs. Keeley also kindly placed in my hands. It was written by the well-known dramatist, Pierce Egan, author of ' Tom and Jerry,' in which Mr. Keeley enacted with such marked success the part of Jemmy Green. Mr. Egan is apparently asking for a contribution to a biographical book that he has in hand ; for, writing under date of September 15, 1831, from 4, Paget Place, Waterloo Road, he says :

' DEAR SIR,

    ' Having been employed for upwards of the last two months on a forthcoming work, some time since announced, " Recollections of the late Robert William Elliston," and having received the promises of anecdotes, etc., from several per-formers in addition to my own exertions, you can, if you please, render me considerable assistance by imparting to me those which you are in pos-

session of respecting that brilliant actor. If you
will have the kindness just to note them down in
as concise a manner as possible, in order to save
you time and trouble ; or, if you will give me an
hour's conversation, any time you think proper, I
will attend to it. I do not intend it shall be a
work of scissors and paste. I shall return from
Doncaster Races after the 27th inst., and if you
will oblige me, I shall say you are a trump.

' I remain, dear sir,

' Yours truly,

' PIERCE EGAN.'

A printed scrap was from the pen of the
famous Planché, who, in describing the opening
performance of Weber's opera of ' Oberon ; or,
The Elf-King's Oath,' of which Planché wrote the
libretto, says :

' A young lady, who subsequently became one of
the most popular actresses in my recollection, was
certainly included in the cast ; but she had not a
line to speak, and was pressed into the service in
consequence of the paucity of vocalists, as she had
a sweet, though not very powerful voice, and was
even then artist enough to be entrusted with anything. That young lady was Miss Goward, now
Mrs. Keeley, and to her was assigned the exquisite mermaid song in the finale to the second act.

It was of this song that in rehearsal Fawcett did not approve. " That must come out ! It won't go !" he said. Weber, who was standing in the pit, leaning on the back of the orchestra, so feeble that he could scarcely stand without such support, shouted : "Wherefore shall it not go ?" and leaping over the partition like a boy, snatched the baton from the conductor and saved from excision one of the most delicious morceaux in the opera.'

It is to this event that Mrs. Keeley's story of Weber, told in another chapter, refers.

The Keeleys were never in the habit of preserving their press notices ; indeed, Mrs. Keeley informed me that she seldom saw any in her acting days ; but in Mr. G. H. Lewes' excellent volume on ' Actors and Acting ' both Keeleys are so well described that I am tempted to note the following passage :

' Mrs. Keeley,' the writer says, ' had little or none of the unctuousness of her husband, but she was also remarkably endowed. She was as intense and pointed as he was easy and fluent. She concentrated into her repartees an amount of intellectual *vis* and " devil " which gave such a feather to the shaft, that authors must often have been surprised at the revelation to themselves of the force of their own wit. Eye, voice, gesture sparkled and chuckled. You could see that she enjoyed

the joke, but enjoyed it rather as an intellectual
triumph over others, than (as in Keeley's case)
from an impersonal delight in the joke itself.
Keeley was like a fat, self-satisfied puppy, taking
life easily, ready to get sniffing and enjoyment out
of everything.   Mrs. Keeley was like a sprightly
kitten, eager to make a mouse of every moving
thing.   The humorous predominated in Keeley ;
in his wife the predominant mood was self-asser-
tion ; so that the one was naturally the comic
servant, the other the pert soubrette.

' It was not said of Mrs. Keeley that she was
" always Mrs. Keeley," although in truth her
strongly-marked peculiarities were quite incapable
of disguise ; but she laid hold of some characteristic in the part she was playing, and rendered it
with such sharpness of outline and such force of
effect that her own individuality was lost sight of
to the critical eye.   Her physique was also more
flexible than that of her husband, and she could
" make up " better.   Her perception of characteristics (within a certain range) was very acute, and
sometimes she presented a character with extraordinary felicity.   Did the reader happen to see
her play the maid-of-all-work in " Furnished
Apartments "?   He will not easily forget such a
picture of the London " slavey," a stupid, wearied,
slatternly, good-natured drab, her brain confused

by incessant bells, her vitality ebbing under over-
work.   He will not forget the dazed expression,
the limp exhaustion of her limbs, or the wonderful
assemblage of rags which passed for her costume.
There was something at once inexpressibly droll
and pathetic in this picture.   It was so grotesque,
yet so real, that laughter ended in a sigh. . . .
Mrs. Keeley was an excellent melodramatic actress,
and her pathos drew tears. . . . She was great in
farce, low comedy, and melodrama, pathetic and
humorous, and always closely imitative of daily
life.   Their career was one uninterrupted triumph,
and they live in the memory of playgoers with a
halo of personal affection round their heads.'

The Keeley book-cases, of course, contained
Montagu Williams's 'Reminiscences,' of which
there were three or four big volumes.   In one
of them some amusing stories of the Keeleys are
repeated ; but from all accounts, I am inclined to
think that a few are only *ben trovato*.   There
is, however, one sufficiently characteristic to be
referred to here.

Mr. Keeley was in the habit of going nearly
every afternoon to the Garrick Club to play whist.
One day the actor had for his partner Henry
James (afterwards Sir Henry James, Q.C., M.P.,
and now Lord James), and when the rubber was
over he happened to say to the eminent barrister,

'Why didn't you lead spades?'—perhaps in reference to a particular discard of Keeley's—and his partner replied, 'Because I didn't think it was the game.' 'Well, then,' says the actor, 'you're a fool!' and petulantly shuffled out of the room.

Some days after, as the future Attorney-General was mounting the Garrick staircase on his way to the card-room, Keeley's four-wheeled cab drove up, and its occupant got out, and catching sight of the distinguished barrister, he called out, 'Hi!' and made a noise with his stick upon the marble pavement of the hall to attract his attention. Seeing who it was. Mr. James at once descended, thinking that perhaps the old actor wanted to apologize for what had lately happened. But with that grave, stolid look, for which Keeley was as remarkable as Dr. Johnson, he said:

'I have been thinking over that little matter of the spades, James, and I find that I was right—you *are* a fool.'

Though occasionally rough or plain-spoken in his manner, the old comedian was the most generous, kind-hearted man living, and a most loving and indulgent husband and father. His generosity showed itself in various ways, and not least in his readiness to respond to the many

KEELEY AS JACOB EARWIG IN 'BOOTS AT THE SWAN.'

To face p. 175.

applications from brother actors and others in need of pecuniary help. It is sad to reflect that there should have been men of acknowledged repute and absolute genius requiring such assistance. But this was undoubtedly the case, as I have seen with my own eyes letters addressed to Mr. Keeley from persons of high distinction in literature and the drama, asking the comedian for a few pounds to enable them to go on with work begun, and in some notable instances the work, when completed, was worth untold gold.

Once, after a pleasant half-hour passed in fancy with the old comedian at his book - case, I remember Mrs. Keeley entering the apartment with her usual sniff of enjoyment at the fumes of tobacco, which she loved to inhale when the perfume was pleasant, and in answer to a question from myself concerning some plays I had just run through, she said :

' Yes, he was very good in the pieces you have named. But his greatest creation was undoubtedly Sairey Gamp, and nothing like it was ever done before, or has been since. As my husband played it, there was no indication of the man, either in dress, speech or look. It was the character drawn by Dickens, though without caricature or the least sign of exaggeration.'

'I learnt much from Mr. Keeley on the stage,' she remarked upon another occasion ; 'imperceptibly I borrowed from his manner, and felt that I was doing so.   What made his acting so irresistibly droll, was his stolidity ; the perfectly placid, un-ruffled look and utter unconsciousness of being funny.   He never asked his audience to laugh, and if they did, it was because they discovered the fun for themselves.   Yes ; smoke another cigarette, by all means.   I like it.'

Then she produced for my inspection one of the most curious documents that I had yet seen in that place.   It was an entire newspaper in manu-script, written from beginning to end by her gifted spouse.   This singular composition, which was of the size and form of the *Family Herald*, was neatly penned by Mr. Keeley on board ship during the voyage homewards from America, where the inseparable couple had been for a long professional tour, and it was 'published' for pri-vate circulation among the passengers and officers of the vessel.   The journal bore the title, in red letters, of the 'Sunday Shakespeare Gazette,' in compliment to the name of the ship, which was called after the bard ; and it was intended to be issued weekly.   But I am inclined to think that the proprietor and sole contributor of the paper never got further than 'No. 1,' which is dated

August 13, 1837, and contains over the heading an imitation penny stamp of the period, together with a sketch in blue pencil of a ship in full sail, with the following motto :

> ' Life's like a ship in constant motion.'
>
> *Old Song.*

The good ship *Shakespeare* must have been very much in motion when the actor-editor came to the last page of his journal, this being a blank save for the following parting announcement in an ominously shaky hand :

' *Sunday morning.*—The state of the weather forces us to publish in an unfinished state. Press of sail, nor Press of any other sort, can flourish in such a sea !'

CHAPTER XIV.

THE KEELEY SCRAP-BOOK.

WHILE overhauling again the Keeley bookcases in quest of hidden treasures, the present owner of them was good enough to place in my hands a large-sized scrap-book containing many interesting souvenirs of the past. Among these were several water-colour drawings contributed from time to time by friends of more or less public notoriety; old and recent letters from members of the theatrical profession; rough sketches from various sources, and complimentary verses.

Among the most interesting and best executed of the sketches was one by a lady representing the house at Ipswich where Mrs. Keeley was born and passed most of her girlhood. As it is my intention to reproduce in facsimile the drawing itself, I will say nothing further about it, except to explain that the primitive window over the iron-monger's shop, to the left of the spectator, indicates the room where the future Jack Sheppard made her first appearance in the world.

Next in point of interest was a similar sketch

THE HOUSE IN ORWELL PLACE, IPSWICH,

Where Mrs. Keeley was born on November 22, 1805.

of the local theatre in Tacket Street, where Mary Anne Goward made her first appearance upon the stage. It was at this same old-fashioned building that nearly all the notable actors and actresses of the day, and long after that, were from time to time seen, not forgetting Mr. J. L. Toole, who, I am told, made his very first bow before an audience at the Ipswich theatre, where he played under the name of John Lawrence. The late Charles Dillon was acting there at the same time.

The next item is an autograph letter and a pen-and-ink illustration by Charles Mathews. The document is undated, and addressed from the Haymarket Theatre, where he was then playing :

'My dear Keeley,

'Presuming that you have not yet fashionables enough in town to fill all your private boxes, will you, if we put on our best clothes, let us come and do duty in one to-morrow evening? We do not at present play in the after-piece, and are therefore anxious to come while we can. We can send a detachment at seven, and join our forces at about a quarter to ten, which, I hope, will just catch the curtain down before the last piece. With our best regards to yourself and Mrs. Keeley,

'Yours faithfully,

'C. J. Mathews.'

The sketch on the fly-leaf of the letter is headed 'A Sunday's Ride,' and is evidently intended as a

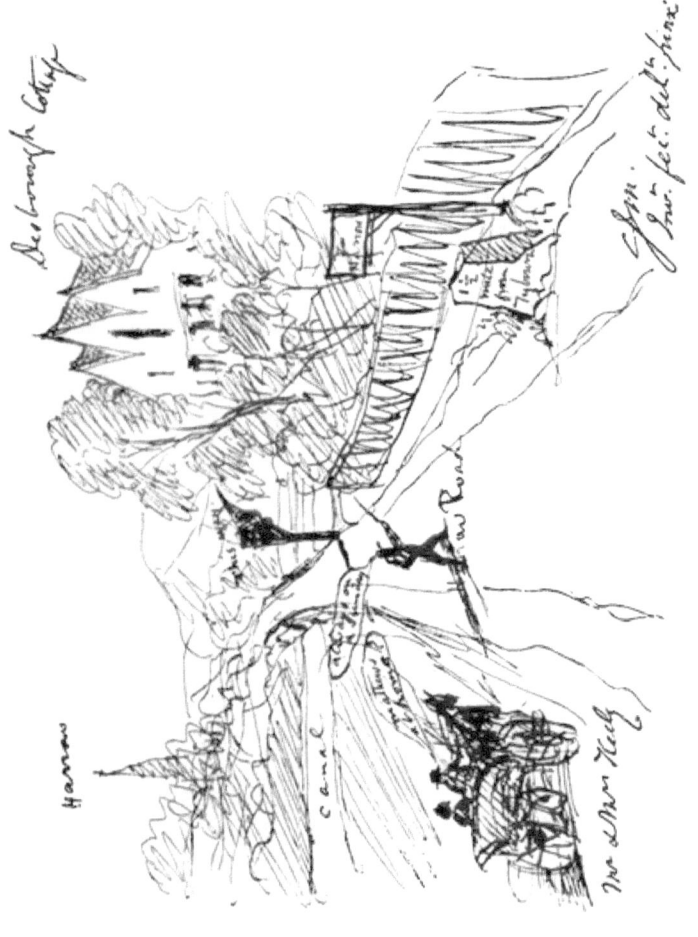

pictorial hint to the Keeleys to pay a visit to Mr. and Mrs. Mathews at their pretty home near Harrow, called Desborough Cottage. Mr. and Mrs. Keeley are shown in the act of driving there in an open carriage, and inquiring on the way, 'Is Mathews at home?' to which a man in the Harrow Road replies, 'Always on Sunday,' and points with his stick to the cottage. A milestone to the right of the travellers informs them that it is one mile and a half to Tyburn, while a tall finger-post, further up the road, opposite the canal, points aggressively to the cottage.

On another page is a pencil sketch of Mr. Charles Peake, by Forrester (Alfred Crowquill); and further on is another clever sketch by that celebrated caricaturist, introducing a letter, in which the writer asks for the autographs of Mr. and Mrs. Keeley in the following terms:

' MY DEAR KEELEY AND WIFE,

' I desire a joint autograph from you. Send me one, then, that I may place you in my curious " Book of Records" of the celebrities of my life. Keeley and wife.

'ALFRED CROWQUILL.'

This curious record is dated March 6, 1852, and addressed from 3, Portland Place, North Clapham Road. The sketch represents a Shake-

spearian jester seated upon a stage, with his back
to a table, upon the cloth of which the letter is
inscribed.

Not far from the Crowquill sketch is a quaint
design for an 'Ancient Playing Card, used by the
Monks at the Convent of the Great St. Bernard.'
It is signed by Albert Smith, and addressed to the
Keeleys 'from the Clavandier, August 30, 1840.'

Two interesting souvenirs of the Keeleys' visit
to the United States take the form of a couple of
programmes neatly and handsomely printed in
black and gold. The popular comedians were
giving their last performances at the Park Theatre,
New York, before returning to England, and
these programmes were specially printed for their
respective farewell benefits, of which Mrs. Keeley's
took place on July 17, 1837, and her husband's on
July 26 of the same year. On the first of these
occasions the attractions were 'Julie ; or, The
Forced Marriage,' with Mr. Keeley as Morisseau,
and his wife in the title-*rôle*. This was followed
by Planché's 'Loan of a Lover,' in which Mr.
Keeley appeared in his original character of Peter
Spyk, and Mrs. Keeley as Gertrude, and the performances concluded with 'The Invincibles,' with
the beneficiary as Victoire. A triple bill was also
provided for Mr. Keeley's benefit, consisting of
'The Sergeant's Wife,' in which his better-half was

PEN AND INK SKETCH

BY

ALFRED CROWQUILL.

To face p. 182.

the Lisette, and he himself played his old part of
Robin ; ‘ Weathercock,’ with Keeley as Briefwit,
his wife as Variella, and Mr. Abbott as Young
Pickle ; and ‘The Swiss Cottage,’ with Keeley as
Natz Teick, Mrs. Keeley as Lisette, and Mr.
Richings as Corporal Max.

Here is a poetic tribute from a Frenchman,
after witnessing Mrs. Keeley in ‘ Jack Sheppard,’
produced after her return to England :

‘À Mrs. Keeley (*pour son album*).

‘ Toi, que l’on voit dans Jack Sheppard
 Si mauvais sujet, si perfide,
 Dans ta famille, sa, sans fard,
À la mère, a l’épousse, on peut t’offrir pour guide.
 C’est donc un singulier hazard
Dans ce monde ou le vice assez souvent se cache
 Sous le masque de la vertu
 Que l’on t’ait impose pour tache
La rôle d’un bandit ? . . . Mais Keeley, que veux tu ?
 Du destin tel est le caprice.
Dans Jack Sheppard fais donc le garnement ;
 Car, chacun dit, en ta voyant :
L’est vertus ont, ce soir, pris le masque du vice.’

Mrs. G. H. Gilbert, the American actress from
the Daly Company, was born in 1821, and in
commemoration of that event, seventy years after
its occurrence, on October 21, 1891, a lunch was
given at the Savoy Hotel by the actress’s many
friends. Among the honoured guests was Mrs.
Keeley, and the menu card was carefully preserved

by that lady.   Upon the back of it most of the
company had written their names, beginning with
Mary Anne Keeley, who headed the list, followed
by Augustin Daly, Mrs. G. H. Gilbert, Joseph
Knight, Genevieve Ward, Edward Ledger, Louisa
Hatton, Justin McCarthy, Charles LeClerc, Justin
Huntley McCarthy, Margaret J. Farjeon (Mrs.
B. L. Farjeon), James Lewis, Ada Rehan, S. B.
Bancroft, Marie E. Bancroft, Harold Frederic,
Henrietta Labouchere, and Clement Scott.   On
the other side was the menu, the principal items
of which were :

Royal Natives à la Keeley.   Œufs Savoy.
Filets de Soles à la Mellon.   Noisette d'Agneau Provençale.
Pommes Gilbert, Faisans escortes d'Ortolans en Cocotte.
Salad Nicoise.   Terrine de foie gras à l'Alsacienne.
Pêches Impératrice.   Mousse d'ananas à la Rehan, etc.

Carefully preserved, also, is a little note, dated
February 9, 1887, from Mr. Henry Irving, in reply
to one written by Mrs. Keeley congratulating the
actor upon his forty-ninth birthday.   Writing from
Grafton Street, Mr. Irving says :

'God bless you, my dear Mrs. Keeley.   I value
your sweet remembrance more than I can tell.
That I shall see you soon is the hope of yours ever,
'Hy. Irving.'

The next epistolatory treasure follows naturally
upon the last, as it comes from Miss Ellen Terry,

and is an answer to a letter from Mrs. Keeley wishing Miss Terry a happy New Year. This characteristic document bears the date of January 1, 1889, and is addressed from Barkston Gardens, Earl's Court. The style is so delightfully natural and unaffected that I cannot help quoting it:

'Why, what a kind, nice, dear little New Year's letter you have written about me, the last day of the poor old year! It is so sweet of you that I am compelled to write "thank you," and send "a good wish to you" for the new year—" I wish you your heart's desire."

'I can't play Lady Macbeth, of course, properly, but I hope to play her much better than on Saturday before the next few hundred nights have passed. I have never had the passion of ambition, but watching my own mother, and some few friends of mine, all good women, I have wondered at the lengths to which ambition—generally for some son or husband—drove them, and long ago I concluded that the Thane of Cawdor's wife was a much be-blackened person. She was pretty bad, I think, but by no means abnormally bad. What fogs! You seemed so splendidly well the other night, I envied you. Again, thank you, and farewell in every place. With much respect,

'Affectionately yours,

'Ellen Terry.'

The following birthday letter is from another
prominent member of the Lyceum company, Mrs.
Stirling (now Lady Gregory) :

' DEAR MRS. KEELEY,

        ' I hope I have not mistaken the date you
named to me, and that this is really the day on
which you begin another year of life ; may it be
followed by ever so many happy birthdays and
happy years of life. You have given so many
such great pleasure that I am sure many must
strive to make life pleasant to you, and that you
will be overwhelmed with letters and congratula-
tions. So I'll not bore you with more words than
the heartiest good wishes of,

                        ' Yours ever,

                            ' FANNY STIRLING.'

Upon the occasion of Mrs. Keeley's eighty-
eighth birthday, Mr. W. Beatty-Kingston sent
her these impromptu verses, and they have, of
course, found a prominent place in her album :

> ' Friend of my storm-tossed youth,
>   Friend of my riper age,
> These lines in faith and sooth,
>   Are true affection's gage.
>
> ' Rough are they—rugged—rude—
>   What then? They symbolize
> Old pledges, now renewed,
>   Of that which never dies.

'Pure, honest friendship. This
  Be my poor off'ring, dear;
Prognosticate of bliss
  To thee, for many a year!'

A place of honour is also awarded to a neatly-
written note from Mrs. Keeley's old and stanch
friend, Mr. J. Ashby Sterry, and refers to the
writer's charming verses which the actress delivered at the Hospital for Sick Children, Great
Ormond Street, in 1888, and to others by the
same pen which she had previously recited. He
writes :

'MY DEAR MRS. KEELEY,

   'He who has written two pieces in which
Mrs. Keeley has sustained the principal part,
"with tremendous success and unbounded applause," ought to be a very proud man. I have
written those two pieces. I am a very proud
man. Till I heard you deliver my lines I had no
idea I could write so well. Now I am becoming
so vain that I shall become a nuisance to all my
friends. But my vanity receives a check when I
remember that the great success of yesterday was
entirely due to the admirable way the lines were
delivered—the feeling you conveyed in every
word—the heartiness you put into my fun, and
the reality with which you invested my pathos.
Pray accept my most sincere thanks for giving

such life and such vigour to my ideas, and for all the trouble you have taken over the whole matter. I sincerely trust you are none the worse for all your exertions of yesterday.'

On the opposite page is pasted in a lengthy document, dated November 22, 1888, from the Hospital for Sick Children, wishing Mrs. Keeley many happy returns, and signed by seventeen of the little ones, with a footnote from the lady superintendent, Mrs. Hicks, to say that 'the remainder of the hundred and twenty-seven children are too young, or too ill, to sign their names.'

The last letter of interest in the scrap-book is one dated February 4, 1894, from the editor of *Punch*, who, writing from Royal Crescent, Ramsgate, where Wilkie Collins often lived and worked for a time, says :

'MY DEAR MRS. KEELEY,

'Did your ladyship receive a copy of *Punch*—there are many copies of *Punch*, but this was one of Mr. Punch's very own numbers—with a paragraph in it about yourself at the Lyceum ? I hope you did, as I wrote it, directed it, paid it, and posted it all myself.   But never a word have I heard from your ladyship anent the same.   Let

me see your handwriting, and relieve the burden
now oppressing the mind of

' Yours very truly,

' F. C. BURNAND.'

An actor's album would, of course, be incomplete without some rare old playbills, and here
are three curiosities of the kind. One of them
dates as far back as November 17, 1763, when,
'By desire of the Norwich Company of Comedians,
at the Town Hall, Colchester, there will be presented a comedy called "The Busy Body,"' together with 'Singing by Mr. Kear,' and 'a farce
(never acted here) called "The Author," written
by Mr. Foote.' The next is a Drury Lane bill
of April 21, 1820, and is interesting chiefly from
the fact that Mr. Keeley figures in it as Third
Justice in a 'broad farcical pantomimical drama
in two acts, entitled "Shakespeare versus Harlequin, or Harlequin's Invasion,"' and that Edmund
Kean was announced to make his first appearance
in 'King Lear.' The third curiosity is a lengthy
programme of an equestrian circus at Constanti-
nople, printed in Italian, Turkish, and Armenian,
and dated September 11, 1849.

CHAPTER XV.

A COMPLETE list of all the plays in which the two Keeleys—to say nothing of their accomplished daughters—took part either singly, or in double harness, would form quite a volume in itself. But a mere catalogue of pieces and casts would have no interest to the general reader, though doubtless the old playgoer's memory might be pleasantly awakened by the mention of their magic names.

Had the subject of this biography and her husband existed professionally in these days of long runs, it might not be difficult to enumerate their various triumphs in a page or two of their history.

In those fastidious days, however, and long before, when the 'season' lasted only three months, a programme, unless overwhelmingly attractive, as in the case of 'Jack Sheppard,' 'The Green Bushes,' 'Janet Pride,' and similar pieces, was changed at least once every two weeks, and not unfrequently every night. Even when a big success enjoyed some consecutive prosperity, it was found necessary to strengthen the bill by a new curtain-raiser and an after-piece, with perhaps some music and dancing, or an interlude (as it was called in the time of Vestris) thrown in.

I remember Mrs. Keeley saying to Mr. Charles Warner, on the first night of a modern melodrama which was not over till long past midnight :

'The whole evening, and only one play! Why, I recollect when Mr. Keeley and I were engaged at the Princess's to appear in a couple of farces when the main piece was over and half-price began.'

For this reason there remains for the biographer of the Keeleys such a vast accumulation of plays in which they appeared as to be perfectly bewildering. It is, besides, not always easy to 'get at' the Keeleys, either singly or in twos and threes, unless one or other, or both, or all four—for we must not forget the daughters—were performing for a long time at the Adelphi (which was, of course, the headquarters of the leading lady) or at the Haymarket, which at one time was the histrionic home of the low-comedian.

The Keeleys were together from the latter end
of the twenties till nearly the end of the thirties,
when they parted, professionally, for awhile, Mr.
Keeley to fulfil a long engagement at the Haymarket, and his wife an equally long engagement
at the Adelphi. Early in the forties the couple
were united again upon the stage, and after that
an important event in their history took place,
namely, the opening of the Lyceum (late the
English Opera House) under Mrs. Keeley's sole
management, assisted by her husband and a
lawyer named Strutt.

The theatre in Wellington Street was formally
opened on the evening of April 14, 1844, under
this new *régime*, and in addition to the Keeleys,
the company included Mr. and Mrs. Alfred
Wigan, Miss Woolgar, Miss Mary Keeley, Mrs.
Woollidge (mother of Mrs. Honey), Miss Fairbrother (afterwards Mrs. Fitz-George), Frank
Matthews, Sam Emery, and F. Vining. The
opening performances began with an entirely
new two-act comedy entitled ' Hasty Conclusions,' followed by a new drama, ' The Post of
Honour,' and concluding with a new 'grand
burlesque, fairy extravaganza' by Gilbert à
Beckett and Mark Lemon, called ' Open
Sesame ; or, A Night with the Forty Thieves,'
which Mr. Arthur à Beckett tells me was cast

with Mrs. Keeley as Morgiana and Mr. Keeley
as Hassarac. Miss Sally Turner, whom he
believes is still among us, was also in the cast,
together with Miss Fairbrother and old Jarnold.
The piece ran for three months, which was considered a rather long spell of continuous prosperity
in those days, and upon the first night of its production Mrs. Keeley spoke an address specially
written by Albert Smith as follows :

'When a new minister assumes the reins
  His policy 'tis right that he explains.
  I. having taken office, don't refuse
  To make the house acquainted with my views.
  Some may conceive I owe an explanation
  For having headed the administration ;
  Upon that point a motion I will make,
  The opinion of the house at once to take—
  That ladies can't good managers be reckoned—
  Is that a motion anyone will second ?   (*Great cheering.*)
  I thank the house for its polite decision :
  The motion is thrown out without division.
  To look on idly ne'er could be my choice.
  A woman always likes to have a voice ;
  Silent indifference could never suit her,
  The grammar tells us woman can't be neuter.
  'Tis true, I might have filled a humble station
  In our theatrical administration,
  But female influence soon gains the ascendant,
  When it begins no one can see the end on't.
  Instead of coming to it by degrees,
  I thought at once the Premiership I'd seize.
  To keep the place I very much incline,
  Unless this house calls on me to resign.

13

Now for the measures I shall introduce—
I mean to do away with one abuse.
The scheme on innovation somewhat borders,
But I propose to drop the standing orders.

   (*'Hear, hear !' from the pit and gallery.*)

My policy may probably be hinted
In a short bill I've ordered to be printed ;
That bill I see already in your hands ;
I trust that you will pass it as it stands. (*Cheers.*)
'Tis not the least remarkable of facts,
That if you pass that bill, you can five acts.
If Parliament as fast could use its powers,
It wouldn't be complaining of late hours.
My views with brevity I now will state,
Upon the principle legitimate.
The drama, called legitimate, may thrive
As well in two or three acts as in five.
Were length legitimacy's standard—then
What would become of all the little men ?
Heirs to a throne, if short, would lose a crown,
Which must be given up, not handed down.
Man by his mind, not by the height, we rate.
Talent, not length, makes plays legitimate.
But here am I. Don't practise what I teach,
Making a long and perhaps empty speech ;

   (' *No ! no !*')

So I'll be brief in coming to a close ;
We've several measures ready to propose.
But if you deem them wrong, they shall be stopp'd ;
Amendments we are anxious to adopt.
The confidence I feel there's one thing clenches,
As yet I see no opposition benches.
Before I bring my statement to an end,
One thing most earnestly I recommend :
Throw out our bills, object or criticise,
But never think of stopping the supplies.'

It need scarcely be said that this cleverly-written and admirably - recited prologue was received with the most tumultuous applause by the close-packed audience, or that the papers next day spoke in high praise of it, and of the first night's performances.

The ' Forty Thieves ' was withdrawn to give place to a new burlesque by Albert Smith called ' Aladdin ; or, The Wonderful Lamp,' in which the manageress took the lead in the boy part, and I think it was in reference to this part that the actress spoke of a letter which she once received from Mr. Edmund Yates after her retirement from the stage.

'It was in answer to one I had written to him,' she explained, ' asking if he remembered me, as I had not the pleasure of his acquaintance, and wanted to consult him about something. In his reply he said : " If you are the same Mrs. Keeley who had such shapely legs and dainty feet on the stage, I remember you well." '

At the period to which Mr. Yates refers ' Martin Chuzzlewit ' was produced with a strong cast, and it was then that Mr. Keeley appeared for the first time as Sairey Gamp, to the Master Bailey of his better-half.

Among other new plays produced at the Lyceum in the course of this first Keeley season were 'My Wife's Out,' 'The Wise Wives of Madrid,' 'Polkamania' (a topical farce), 'The Love Birds,' 'The White Feather,' 'Two Heads Better than One,' 'The Three Fra Diavolos,' and 'The Momentous Question,' most of which are by this time quite obsolete. The 'season' appears to have extended to the end of the year, as we find that on December 26 another Dickens adaptation was announced, under the title of 'The Chimes,' with Keeley as Trotty Veck, and Mrs. Keeley as Margaret. A dramatic edition of the 'Caudle Lectures' was also tried, with, of course, Keeley as Caudle, and in addition to this the public were favoured with 'The Seven Castles of the Passions,' 'Home Again,' 'A Trip to Kissingen,' 'Watch and Ward,' 'To Persons about to Marry,' and 'The Swiss Cottage.'

'The Cricket on the Hearth,' dramatised as before by the future husband of Mary Keeley, was the next Dickens adaptation, and it was then that young lady made her first public bow as Bertha, the blind girl, her mother appearing as Dot. The papers spoke well of the débutante, one of them saying that the young actress played 'in the most unpretending manner, assuming with skill the appearance of blindness, and touching her audience by the unaffected nature of her delivery. Her voice is as yet thin and juvenile, but remark-

KEELEY AS MRS. CAUDLE.

To face p. 196.

ably clear, so that not a word is uttered unheard.
. . . The greeting to Mrs. Keeley, who has
recently been indisposed, was so enthusiastic that
it almost overpowered her, especially when a voice
from the gallery cried out, " Glad to see you well
again !" '

Encouraged by the success of her first venture,
Mrs. Keeley took the same theatre next year for
a long season, and the year after that for a shorter
one, when, as before, several new and old pieces
were presented, notably ' The Battle of Life,' in
which the manageress scored one of her greatest
triumphs on the stage, namely, Clemency Newcombe. The critics of the day spoke in high
praise of this remarkable performance, the
Athenæum saying :

' The whole stage interest is in truth centred in
Clemency Newcombe (Mrs. Keeley) and Benjamin Britain (Mr. Keeley). The acting of the
former is one of those admirable examples of
histrionic art which almost reconcile an audience
to every possible fault in the scenes that give
occasion for their exhibition. The part of
Clemency Newcombe was the life, the soul, the
salvation of the new drama. The actress was
unwearied in her exertions. Her costume was
picturesque, her action and by-play were everywhere appropriate, her tones were full of feeling,

honesty, and earnestness.   There was the eccentric, hard-working, faithful little body, an unmistakable identity !   The part of Benjamin
Britain is of inferior calibre, but nevertheless
served to set off its companion, and was cleverly
supported by Mr. Keeley.'

The *Times* said : ' " The Battle of Life " has
gained a most unequivocal success ; but the cause
of success is not to be mistaken.   The triumphant
reception of last night was owing wholly and
solely to the admirable acting of Mrs. Keeley, who
has put forth even more than her usual strength in
the character of the clumsy, good-humoured servant, Clemency Newcombe.   The awkwardness
of the attire alone produced a perfect picture ; the
ungainly movement, rendered interesting by the
strong bearing of native amiability, the rich
colouring given to the minutest details, such as
the strange smiles and self-satisfied hugging of
the arms, are inimitable.   The motion of the hand
and head, when signing her name in huge characters, is the perfection of clumsiness ; the pathos of
the third act was brought up with great power, a
part of the drama that, without it, would have
fallen as flat as possible.   Mr. Smith, with the
eye of a practised dramatist, has evidently seen
the use to be made of this one character, for he
has put into Clemency's mouth not only the

SCENE FROM 'THE BATTLE OF LIFE,' AT THE LYCEUM THEATRE, 1846.

MRS. KEELEY (CLEMENCY).   MR. KEELEY (BRITAIN).

By kind permission of the Proprietors of 'The Illustrated London News.'

To face p. 198.

dialogue assigned to her in the tale, but also such bits of the narrative as might be worked in effectively. . . . The Atlas of the piece is Mrs. Keeley, who supports it by her own individual strength, and an observation which we overheard in the theatre is worth repeating—that the drama ought not to be called "The Battle of Life," but "Clemency Newcombe."'

In 1850 the Keeleys and the Charles Keans went into partnership and took the Princess's for a long season, beginning on September 28 of that year and ending on October 17, 1851—the year of the Great Exhibition in Hyde Park, and of Macready's retirement from the stage.

It was partly on account of the Great Exhibition that the Kean-Keeley season was a very prosperous one, the net profits having been £7,000. But the managers and their company had to work for it, as we find that in the course of their thirteen months they produced several Shakespearian pieces, dramas and farces, all of which were well mounted and splendidly cast, with such notable performers as Mr. and Mrs. Charles Kean, Mr. and Mrs. Keeley, Mr. and Mrs. Alfred Wigan, Mary Keeley, Carlotta Leclercq, Agnes Robertson, Miss Murray, Miss Desborough, John Harley, John Ryder, and Messrs. Bartley, Meadows, Fisher, King, Cathcart, Bolton, Addison and Flexmore, the famous pantomimist.

The pieces included 'Hamlet,' 'Twelfth Night,' 'As You Like It,' 'The Merchant of Venice,' 'Henry IV.,' 'The Wife's Secret,' 'The Gamester,' 'The Prisoner of War,' 'The Stranger,' 'Town and Country,' 'The Templar,' 'The Duke's Wager,' Boucicault's charming play of 'Love in a Maze,' 'Pauline,' an adaptation from the French, by John Oxenford; the farces of 'Platonic Attachments,' 'A Model Wife,' 'Sent to the Tower,' 'Apartments to Let' (apropos of the Great Exhibition), 'To Parents and Guardians' (one of Keeley's crack pieces), and the scarcely less popular 'Betsy Baker.'

In addition to the attractions just enumerated, there were produced at Christmas the pantomime of 'Alonzo the Brave,' and at the following Easter a new burlesque extravaganza by Albert Smith. Think of it! single-handed Mr. W. S. Penley, with your one farcical comedy running uninterruptedly for more than three years, with no present prospect of its withdrawal, while the gross receipts from the forty different quarters of the globe where the piece has been played have already reached half a million sterling!

And think of it, Mr. Weedon Grossmith, with your 'New Boy' and yourself as a two-year attraction! Think of it, also, present manager of the Lyceum, where, if your solitary Shakespearian revival does not draw crowded houses for at least a year, you consider that you have been hardly used by the public! We will say nothing of many other successful actor-managers; and nothing of 'Our Boys,' 'Two Roses,' 'The Private Secretary,' and similar running wonders of our time.

Yet in the old days there were not so many playhouses—no Vaudeville or Gaiety; no Terry's or Toole's; no Comedy, Savoy, Trafalgar, Avenue, Shaftesbury, Criterion, Court, Lyric, Prince of Wales's, Daly's; no theatres of variety, and not a sign of an Olympia or an Earl's Court. Still the public craving for change was not to be appeased even with a first-class drama beautifully mounted, and with at least four star performers in it, as was the case when 'The Wife's Secret' was offered by Charles Kean in 1850, or when it was originally produced in the January of 1848 at the Haymarket, and the audience of that time saw in it Mrs. Charles Kean, Benjamin Webster, and Mrs. Keeley; besides the usual stock company, which included Rogers, Clark, Coe, Braid, and *our* Mr. Henry Howe, who was then six-and-thirty. That excellent actor, now in his eighty-third year, was cast for the fugitive cavalier, Lord Arden, and I have very little doubt that if Mr. Howe's manager, Sir Henry Irving, were to revive 'The Wife's Secret' to-day, the veteran of the old Haymarket would be quite equal to undertake his original part.

But perhaps no cast that was offered at the time of the Kean-Keeley management could in the least compare with the one provided for the Royal audience at Windsor Castle on Thursday, December 12, 1850, when the 'First Part of Henry IV.' was played.   For here is a copy of the bill :

Henry IV.	Mr. Cooper.
Henry, Prince of Wales ...	Mr. Anderson.
Prince John, of Lancaster	Miss Daly.
Earl of Westmoreland	C. Fisher.
Sir Walter Blunt	Mr. Belton.
Thomas Percy, Earl of Worcester ...	John Ryder.
Henry Percy, Earl of Northumberland ...	Mr. King.
Henry Percy, surnamed Hotspur (his son)...	Charles Kean.
Archibald, Earl of Douglas	F. Cooke.
Sir Richard Vernon	J. F. Cathcart.
Sir John Falstaff	Mr. Bartley.
Poins	J. Vining.
Gadshill	R. Cathcart.
Peto	J. Binge.
Bardolph	Mr. Addison.
Francis	Mr. Meadows.
Carriers	{ Mr. Harley, Mr. Keeley.
Sheriff	Mr. Paulo.
Raley	Mr. Stacey.
Travellers	{ Messrs. Wynn, Daly, Stokes, and Harries.
Lady Percy (wife to Hotspur)	{ Mrs. Charles Kean.

and

Dame Quickly	Mrs. Keeley.

The theatre was arranged by Thomas Grieve, who was also the painter of the scenery, and the piece was produced under the direction of Charles Kean, who received from the Queen a beautiful diamond ring in commemoration of the occasion.

CHAPTER XVI.

RECOLLECTIONS OF OLD PLAYGOERS.

As I have been lately favoured with a few interesting documents having reference to the palmy
days of the Keeley performances by living members of their old audiences, I propose to devote a
chapter to a selection from them.

Some of these souvenirs take the form of letters
which have from time to time been addressed to
Mrs. Keeley from all parts of the world, while
others are brief notes, anecdotes, or more lengthy
records sent to me direct from various quarters.
In referring to the list I find that the earliest recollection comes from one of the oldest inhabitants
of Ipswich, who appears to have a distinct remembrance of the Keeleys, when, in the June of 1830,
they were announced to appear at the local theatre
for four nights only.

' It was the first time,' writes this veteran playgoer, ' that the pair were seen together at Mrs.
Keeley's birthplace, and there was naturally great

interest taken in the event. The house was crowded in every part, and their reception was most enthusiastic and delayed the performances on each night. On the opening night " She Stoops to Conquer " was played, with Mrs. Keeley as Miss Hardcastle and Mr. Keeley as Tony Lumpkin, and after that a farce, acted here for the first time, called " The Master's Rival," was played. On the following night " The Beaux' Stratagem " and " Paul and Virginia " were given, and for the other two nights we had " Love and Reason," " Wives by Advertisement," " The Sergeant's Wife," " Home, Sweet Home," " The Master's Rival " again, and " The £100 Note." In my possession is a memorandum, made at the time, showing that for the four performances the Keeleys received, including the share of their benefit, thirty-six pounds one shilling and nine-pence.'

The same writer informs me that three years previous to the Keeleys' visit to Ipswich Mrs. Keeley, who was then Miss Goward, took a run down from London to take part in a morning and evening concert of sacred music at the Tower Church and the Theatre Royal respectively, for the benefit of the public charities in Ipswich, and that she sang the solo parts in the ' Creation,' together with ' Cara adorata,' ' Follow, follow

over the Mountains,' besides taking part in some
duets with Mr. C. Fisher and Mr. Taylor in turn.
For this the young actress received £26 5s., so
that she must have had a share in the receipts,
which amounted to the (in those days) very respectable sum of £216 6s.

In writing to Mrs. Keeley to congratulate her
upon her eighty-fifth birthday, an ' Old Admirer'
says :

' I am a perfect stranger to you, yet you gave
me much pleasure fifty years ago, for which I
thank you.   The remembrance of many pleasant
evenings at the old Adelphi—your sympathetic,
cheerful voice—your genial manner in light farces
and comedy, and your pathetic elucidation of more
serious plays like " Oliver Twist," still ring in my
ears, and afford pleasant meditation in my old age.
I am glad you still enjoy life, and have no doubt live
much in the past.   Long may you continue to do
so.   I suppose there are not many who enjoyed
your successes more than fifty years ago.   I only
wish they would form a society and ask you to be
present and give you an annual welcome to a
dinner.'

Another veteran playgoer, who was inspired to
write to the actress after reading Lester Wallack's
' Reminiscences,' says :

' James Wallack, when stage-manager at the

Haymarket, took me behind the scenes. The play was " The Rent Day." The cast was : Martin Heywood, Mr. Wallack ; Rachel Heywood, Mrs. Keeley ; Polly Briggs, Mrs. Humby. I was standing at one of the wings beside Mrs. Humby, and the acting of you and Mr. Wallack was so excellent and realistic that we were both affected by it. It had such an effect on Mrs. Humby— old stager as she was—that she repeatedly ex- claimed to me. " Isn't it beautiful ! Isn't it splen- did !" and then rushed on to the stage to play her part. It is difficult to imagine higher appreciation of good acting. Please accept my grateful thanks for the great pleasure you and your dear husband have so often afforded me.'

From New South Wales a ' constant visitor to the Lyceum in 1844-5-6, during Mrs. Keeley's management,' writes :

' Of course I do not remember all the plays I saw you in, but I do not forget " The Dustman's Belle," in which Mr. Keeley played Ned Windfall, and you his sweetheart Sally. When he came into his fortune of £16,000 he promised to hire a coach and drive all over London to buy things for Sally, and also give all the dustmen a great dinner. I also saw you both in " To Parents and Guardians," and many other dramas ; but I remember you best in the English operas staged

under your management, such as "The Forty
Thieves" and "Robin Hood," in which you took
the part of Robin Hood; Miss Helen Fairbrother, of Little John; and Mr. Keeley, Friar
Tuck and the Old Man of the Mountains. I
also saw you in "The Magic Horn," and in
"The Enchanted Forest; or the Bear, Eagle
and Dolphin." I saw this so often that I could
repeat a great part of it, and can now, after
so many years. I saw, likewise, "The Wood
Demon; or, One o'Clock," which, I think, was
the last. I was present on the night you bade
the audience farewell on retiring from management. I remember quite well the names of
many of your company, of which your daughter,
Miss Mary Keeley, Miss Fairbrother, Miss
Howard and Miss Daly formed a part, together
with Frank Matthews, Leigh Murray, Meadows,
Bellingham, Collier, Kinloch and others.'

A similar letter is addressed to the actress from
an old friend living in New Zealand, while from
Redfern, Sydney, a lady, aged sixty-five, writes:
'Honoured Madame," and, after a few preliminary
remarks, goes on to say:

'When a city belle in my teens, a great treat
was to go to the Adelphi to see the Keeleys.
It was a treat indeed! I remember well "The
Moustache Movement," and Nettles in "To

Parents and Guardians." What an impression
that piece made on me! I can recall it vividly.
I was at the Adelphi on the occasion of Webster
becoming lessee, when Madame Celeste presented the keys on a cushion. She was dressed
in ruby velvet, and Mr. Keeley held a spirited
dialogue from the stage-box. My future wavered
between the stage and the palette; Mrs. R.
Honor's advice decided it, and I became an
artist, and have now earned money by my brush
for nearly fifty years. . . . I worked once for
Jenny Lind, so had the honour of four interviews
with her. One of my pupils was a Mrs. Arm-
strong, who married Charles Stuart at Chelsea.
You were at the wedding. I should have had
the pleasure of meeting you, but an elaborate
costume was an extravagance I dared not indulge
in, being then a widow, and children depending
on my earnings. Since then my daughter has
entered the profession and has been constantly
rising in opera. Even this may be a new trifle
in your life : to receive a letter from a stranger in
Australia, whose admiration of half a century since
dares to express itself.'

Not a few of Mrs. Keeley's correspondents,
while recalling the past for her benefit, take
occasion to ask for her autograph. Among the
last to do so was the Rev. J. C. Westley, of

14

British Guiana, in South America, who, not knowing her address, sent his letter under cover to the editor of the *Daily News,* London, with a request that he would forward it to 'The Aged Mrs. Keeley.'

'I am in my ninetieth year,' remarked that lady upon receipt of this document; 'but I am not quite so old as aged!'

Here is an interesting souvenir from an old playgoer, who afterwards took the front rank as a comedian of the highest order. The name of that old playgoer is Henry Neville, and in giving me his experience as a youth at the play, he says :

'My mother remembers her (Mrs. Keeley) when she was eighteen. She used to be called the "Little Pet Goward." When a boy, after being put to bed, on two occasions I slipped down the water-pipe to go to the Adelphi to see her in "Jack Sheppard," and as Topsy. She made a very great impression on my young imagination, and I keenly appreciated the honour of acting with her later on. I have a letter of hers to Sam Emery, in which she writes : " Keeley says I am to drop you a line. I make it a strong cord—here !"' (with a sketch of a musical chord).

Mr. Neville has since informed me that, as

quite a young man, he often played *jeune première* parts in the Keeley farces when they went on tour, one of these being Crummy in 'Betsy Baker' when the Keeleys enacted it at the Theatre Royal, Liverpool.

Another popular comedian, Mr. Tom Thorne, who was not on the stage till after the Keeleys had retired, remembers seeing them in many of their favourite pieces, and contributes this interesting experience of his playgoing days when 'Jack Sheppard' was performed for a limited number of nights at the Surrey Theatre:

'It was in the fifties, and Mrs. Keeley was starring at different theatres. I was then a lad in my teens and had the entrée at the Surrey, where I sometimes went behind the scenes. Once, when standing at the wing during the performance of "Jack Sheppard," Mrs. Keeley staggered off completely exhausted after the escape from Newgate, or some such scene. In coming off there was usually a man in readiness to catch the actress as she threw herself exhausted into his arms. But on this occasion he was not at his post, so I came forward and she fell into my arms instead. I don't suppose Mrs. Keeley would remember the circumstance, but I myself was much impressed by it at the time, and I have never forgotten it.'

Mr. Henry Howe, the actor, has some very
vivid remembrances of all the Keeleys, in spite
of his fourscore and three years. He had seen
them in most of their favourite pieces before and
after his own début on the stage, which happened
in the days of Edmund Kean, who gave Mr.
Howe his first engagement.

Mr. Howe played without a pause at the Haymarket for forty years and nine months, and it
was there that he became acquainted with the
subjects of these memoirs, and often acted with
them in their favourite pieces, and in farces such
as 'Twice Killed,' in which Mr. Howe was the
Tubal Cain. While speaking of this farce he
remarked :

'I remember playing in it with the Keeleys at
a theatre, where the stage was so scanty at the
back that we had great difficulty in throwing the
basket out of the window, there being scarcely
room between the scene and the wall behind. In
my own opinion, one of the pieces in which Mrs.
Keeley showed to the best advantage was "The
Prisoner of War," and her husband was also
good in it. In 1844, or '45, they were starring
for six weeks at the Marylebone under Watts's
management; I was in the same company, and
"The Prisoner of War" was often in the bills.
Our manager afterwards hung himself in Newgate.'

' Yes '—in answer to my question—' I recollect
the royal performances well, for I took part in
some of them. One of the pieces presented
before the Queen was " Used Up," in which I
played the blacksmith, and I remember Colonel
Phipps coming round to say that he did not think
I ought to appear with bare arms. However,
when the matter was referred to Her Majesty, she
graciously expressed a desire that the part should
be played in the ordinary way. Talking of arms
reminds me of old Keeley's advice to me as a
young actor : "Never throw up your arms," throwing up his own to show me what he meant. He
was always ready to help me with hints and sug-
gestions of the kind, and when the Keeleys were
living for a time at Isleworth, I was often their
guest. When the Duke of Wellington died, I
myself was near death's door with a bad attack of
typhoid, and I remember on the day of the funeral
Keeley and Hudson coming to see me. Upon
leaving, I heard Keeley say to his friend, " We
shall never see him again !" That was more than
forty years ago, and I have not yet retired from
the world, or from the profession either.'

Mr. Arthur à Beckett, to whom I am indebted
for a few useful notes concerning his father's
pieces in which the Keeleys appeared, remembers
the Keeleys chiefly in farces, and has a rather

vivid recollection of a topical skit on the licensing
question called ' Bonâ Fide Travellers.'   Mr. à
Beckett says he has a special reason for remembering this little piece, because at the time it was
produced his father was one of the principal
magistrates engaged in deciding the all-important
topic of the day upon which the Keeley farce was
founded.   As for Mrs. Keeley, Mr. à Beckett
cannot remember her upon the stage, but he and
his two boys once heard her recite from memory
some lines out of his father's burlesque of ' The
Forty Thieves,' one of these being where Mr.
Keeley says :

> ' I've found the spot without a guide or leader ;
> This is the place, and there's the blasted cedar.'

The recitation in question took place quite
recently in a private box at the Lyceum between
the acts of ' King Arthur,' which the veteran
actress went to witness in the character of a
modern playgoer.

A very much older playgoer than Mrs. Keeley
now is—for of course the actress has only become
one since her retirement from the stage—can
remember the Keeleys in most of their leading
pieces.   And he not only saw them before and
after their marriage, but once took a rather active
part in their performances.   This event occurred
at a time when the Keeleys were starring in

the provinces. They were then at Brighton, where my friend lived with his parents near the local theatre. The piece presented was 'The Bottle Imp,' a two-act melodramatic romance by R. B. Peake, with an overture and incidental music by Rodwell.

The piece was specially written for Mr. Keeley, who enacted Willibald, a terrified German servant, and O. Smith, who played the Bottle Imp in a tight-fitting skin dress, sea-green in hue, with horns on his head and a demon's face and wings. J. Vining and the sisters Cawse were also in the cast. The play was first produced at the English Opera House in 1828, and afterwards went on tour, and on August 20, 1832, found its way to the queen of watering-places. Much the same cast was offered there, but as travelling was in those days a rather costly undertaking, only the principals went down, while the supers figuring in the piece were of local extraction. Chief among these were six children who had to come on in an important scene in which Willibald (Mr. Keeley) invokes the demon with the enchanted bottle, by means of which all his wishes may be instantly gratified. So he wishes that his 'six lovely little brothers and sisters,' whom he has not seen since he left his home at Slauchenhausenberg, were present, saying :

' I wish, pretty creatures, I could hear all their little voices singing, as I did the night I left them, just as I was going to bed, the night I came away!'

Then voices of children are heard at the wings, singing :

> ' Boys and girls come out to play,
> The moon doth shine as bright as day.'

After this, six children are seen to run through some panels in the scene, attired in their night-dresses, and while overpowering the poor man with their caresses and frolics, they shout out : 'Willibald! Willibald! Brother Willibald!' till at last their relative wishes them all in bed again, upon which, of course, the children instantly vanish.

' I was one of those children,' remarked my friend, who is now a respected stockbroker, in recalling this story of sixty-three years ago, 'and my age was then about ten.'

My brother, E. J. Goodman, who can remember the Keeleys well in their prime, contributes the following note on the favourite farce by Tom Taylor, ' Our Clerks ':

' Mrs. Keeley was the smart, bright, impudent office-boy, and her husband was the slow, dull, stolid one, and they made an amusing contrast. The scene in which the heavy little clerk tried to emulate the sharp lad, and came to signal grief, always provoked roars of laughter. Keeley's gradually paling face and sudden rush to the window after smoking a cigar were irresistible, and he never overdid the business. His agony, also, at the thought that the babies he and his accomplice had to hide in a cupboard were being smothered was intensely funny. And no one who witnessed the performance can ever forget the exquisite grave drollery with which Keeley drawled out these lines :

' " What's the use of being in an 'urry ? Great men and great things never is in an 'urry—the law's never in an 'urry—Government's never in an 'urry—and I'm never in an 'urry."

' Keeley had, perhaps, the better part of the two, but his wife was equally good. She was a perfect London boy, full of " cheek " and chaff, and the life and soul of the whole performance.'

Mrs. Keeley tells me that these two characters were taken from a couple of real boys in the employ of the author of the piece and his friend, at a time when they had chambers as barristers in the Temple.

My mother, who is numbered among octogenarian playgoers, was in her thirteenth year when Miss Goward made her first bow upon the London stage, seventy years ago. She recollects all the Keeleys in most of their favourite pieces, and once she had the pleasure of meeting them at the studio of Abraham Solomon, painter of 'Waiting for the Verdict,' when the artist was engaged in painting Louise Keeley. Mr. Gilbert à Beckett, one of the authors of the Keeley burlesque, 'A Night with the Forty Thieves,' sat to my mother, who has been herself an artist for more than sixty years, for the only portrait that exists of the dramatist and police-magistrate. It is now in possession of his son, Mr. Arthur W. à Beckett.

Mr. John Ryder, who saw the Keeleys from the front times out of number, and also acted with them on the stage, once said of the female partner in the firm :

'Mrs. Keeley was as full of mischief as an egg is full of meat, but, by Jove! she could act any mortal thing. I believe she'd have tackled Lady Macbeth, or even Richard III., in an emergency.'

An old habitué of the theatres, and associate of actors in the Keeley days, has an amusing story to tell in connection with Mark Lemon's famous farce of 'The Camp at Chobham,' in which Mr. Keeley played old Cadbury, who has a horror of cock-crowing and military men. One of his best lines, by the way, was : 'I wish every soldier

would kill a lawyer, and take the legal consequences.' His daughter Mary enacted Cadbury's
niece Fanny, who is secretly in love with Captain
Damer of the 19th Dragoons. Damer was played
to perfection by Leigh Murray, who was, of
course, one of the most accomplished actors of his
day. His duties on the stage were not, however,
always punctually performed, and after a long
spell of irregularity, his manager was compelled
to discharge the otherwise excellent comedian
and engage another to take his part.

It need hardly be said that Mr. Murray was
greatly distressed at what had happened, and
asked to be taken back. But Webster, who had
already overlooked the same offence more than
once, could not be persuaded. Then, in despera-
tion, the actor went to the stage-door of the
theatre, and begged the attendant to let him pass,
saying that he wished to see Mr. Keeley and
obtain his intercession. But the man's strict
orders were to let no one through, except those
engaged upon the stage. However, upon his
undertaking to go only to Mr. Keeley's dressing-
room for a moment, Mr. Murray was admitted.
So the actor entered and went at once, not to
Mr. Keeley's room, but to the stage itself, arriv-
ing there at the very moment when his great
scene was on. Being ready attired in military

dress, he threw off a large cloak, which had hitherto concealed his uniform, and just as his substitute was about to leave the wing he pushed him aside and went on in his place.

The teller of this story said that Leigh Murray never acted so well in his life as he did that night, and that the whole house rang with loud plaudits when their old favourite appeared. Whether the actor turned over a new leaf from that night history does not say. But Webster was so pleased by the good impression created in the house, that he took the comedian back, and for a time, at least, 'The Camp at Chobham' went merrily as a marriage-bell.

Mrs. Keeley, who was not in the cast of the play just referred to, witnessed it more than once from the front of the house, and speaking of Leigh Murray from that point of view, she said :

'He was the most perfect man I ever met. He was excessively handsome, with an elegant figure, graceful movements, and a most fascinating voice. When playing Captain Damer, I remember Sir William de Bathe, who was present, saying to me, "He would be a credit to the army. We should be proud to have such an officer in our own camp." But poor Murray died prematurely.'

My valued friend, Mr. G. Manville Fenn, kindly contributes the following reminiscence of the play-going days of his youth :

' My recollections of Mrs. Keeley are very vivid, though few, the first standing out, in spite of the lapse of time, right in front of the others, impressed as it was upon the eager fresh imagination of a very small boy, who was taken, somewhere about the year 1838—before or after I cannot say for certain—to see the dramatization of the work written by an author who had suddenly flashed into the full light of fame, and whose name was upon every lip. "Nicholas Nickleby" was to be played at the Adelphi Theatre, and, as a great treat, I was taken so that I might see the breaking-up scene—literally breaking-up scene of the school at Do-the-boys Hall. There it all stands out clearly as ever, with the various striking characters which most took my attention—Squeers, his wife and daughter, Ralph Nickleby and his nephew, bluff John Browdie ; but, above all, from its genuine pathos, that of poor Smike. As a child the first impression at the sight of the pitiful, grotesque figure excited a desire to laugh ; but as laughter is so nearly akin to tears, my young sympathies were soon aroused, and Mrs. Keeley's Smike became my hero of the night. My wrath was aroused by Squeers' brutality, and my love and admiration for Nicholas by his brave defence of the boy, while the triumphant Nemesis of the tremendous thrashing of Squeers, and the glorious revolution of the boys, and tumbling together of the forms and desks, have never passed away. But above all stands out the calm, silent scene where Smike has the stage to himself in the silence of night, and there Mrs. Keeley's pathos held the house as she depicted the boy's desolation and agony, and, trembling at the imaginary enormity of his offence, shows him escaping from the window by moonlight. It must have been by moonlight, for no stage-carpenter would have omitted that effect ; but, to be honest, I cannot recollect the moon. But another scene stands out of the past, and that must have been the next, or nearly the next, where, having joined Nicholas, Smike encounters the bluff, manly Yorkshireman, John Browdie, whose hand, I remember, went deeply into his breeches pocket to supply the funds to help the fugitives upon their way.

'I have to take a leap of a dozen years spent mostly in the country before I come to my next recollection of Mrs. Keeley, when, in company with her husband, she convulsed her audience in Bayle Bernard's clever farce, " Platonic Attachments." The Keeleys played Mr. and Mrs. Thistledown to the Tom Rawlings and Miss

Millman of Alfred Wigan and Miss Murray. To
my mind Keeley was always genuinely droll in
his impersonations, but Mrs. Keeley possessed
the power of being serio-comic, and she has, to
my way of thinking, rarely been equalled, seldom,
if ever, surpassed, in her acting of the scene with
Thistledown, whom she has convicted of a
" platonic attachment " to a lady who proves
to be his wife's bosom friend.

' Passing over another lapse of years, the scene
is a drawing-room in Bayswater, and I find myself
one of the actors in a pleasant duologue of real
life, when a friend has introduced me to a lady
whose face seems to belie the fact that it is fifty
years since she first impressed me in her personification of Smike, and I believe gave me the great
love for the stage which I have always since possessed.'

CHAPTER XVII.

ALBERT SMITH.

A BOOK about the Keeleys would be incomplete without some reference to their two distinguished sons-in-law. Montagu Williams has indeed left reminiscences which can be seen at any time, but no personal recollections of Albert Smith exist, except what may be contained in his novels, which record a few of his experiences as a medical student.

Nor has there, so far as I am aware, been published any detailed account of Albert Smith's entertainment at the Egyptian Hall, Piccadilly, 'The Ascent of Mont Blanc,' which was for six years as popular in its way as the Tower of London or Madame Tussaud's. The last performance of 'Mont Blanc' was given in the July of 1858.

Before 'Mont Blanc' was produced, as it was on March 15, 1852, Albert Smith gave a similar 'lecture' at Willis's Rooms, called 'The Overland Mail,' being an amusing account of the route to

India, interspersed with topical songs and stories, and illustrated by some beautiful scenery painted by William Beverly.

' Mont Blanc' at once took the Metropolitan public by storm. No such entertainment was ever given before, or has been since, and it was one that could be seen over and over again with increased enjoyment. It was also sufficiently varied every night, more particularly in respect of the topical song known as ' Galignani's Messenger,' with the memorable refrain,

' Beside our press, you must confess, all other sheets look
    small,
But *Galignani's Messenger's* the greatest of them all !'

Any passing event of the day was introduced into this ditty, whose respective lines were so long drawn out that you thought you were never going to get to the end of the so-called melody, the monotony of which formed one of its most amusing features. Albert Smith had no singing voice, but had he been another Mario he would not have been listened to with more rapt attention or ap- plauded with greater warmth. It was, however, the words of the song rather than its tune that took the public fancy.

But one of the greatest charms of the whole ' lecture,' as it was called, consisted in its natural-

ness and air of spontaneity. The lecturer had
apparently only just thought of saying the things
he was relating, and when he sat down to tell
those marvellous yarns of the celebrated engineer
of the lake steamer with a water-pipe in his mouth,
which he took out now and again to sing a quaint
song, the audience were almost afraid he would
forget some of the story, or break down in the
middle of it, which he most assuredly never did.

Then, what a treat it was to be seated in that
picturesque auditorium, completely surrounded,
not by bare walls and gas-lamps, but by Swiss
châlets, the windows of which formed private
boxes, where the select few could witness the show
and fancy they were really seated at a window in
Switzerland! At any rate, such was the impression from the three-shilling stalls, or from the
shilling balcony. The wall at the back of the
platform was similarly built up as a Swiss châlet,
and near the centre was a wide shutter, which was
occasionally withdrawn to disclose a brilliantly-
lighted scene from the dexterous brush of Beverly,
who had accompanied Albert Smith to Switzerland
to take views of Chillon, Martigny, the Convent
of the Great St. Bernard, Chamounix, Mont Blanc,
and similar places.

In an old woodcut of the 'Mont Blanc' auditorium are depicted some real 'properties' in the
shape of Swiss hats, jars, hunting-horns, utensils,

ALBERT SMITH.

To face p. 227.

and bits of bright drapery, together with the lecturer's knapsack and alpenstock, placed in picturesque disorder on the walls or in spare corners.

But the lecturer himself is not to be seen on the platform, which was tastefully decorated with flowers and plants ; so the spectator of the sketch must fancy that Mr. Smith is, as yet, inside that delightful châlet. There was a clock on the proscenium which struck the hour of eight very deliberately and distinctly, and precisely at the eighth stroke the little door to the extreme right of the spectator opened, and a big, burly, well-bearded man, attired in evening dress and looking the picture of health and contentment, stepped into the hall without fuss or theatrical display, and, placing himself at his covered table, close at hand, began to talk to us about his travels as if he had only just arrived from the Grand Mulets. We also saw his St. Bernard dog, a splendid creature, of which he was not a little proud, and which was a great pet among the audience.

Albert Smith opened his entertainment without any preface or preliminary remarks whatever. He plunged at once into the subject of his discourse, with a rattling and rapid description of the journey from town to Dover ; then the run across the channel and the Continent, till in a few minutes he brought the audience to Switzerland itself. Here he seemed to pause and take breath, and

proceeded more deliberately to describe the scenes
he witnessed and the various characters he met
on the road—Mrs. Seymour, who was always
losing her little black box ; the three Simmons
girls, with baby Simmons the youngest, who had
to wear her sisters' cast-off dresses ; undecided
Mr. Parker, who never knew where he was going
or what he was going to do ; the typical Yankee,
with his curious new readings of Byron, such as

> ' Mont Blanc is the monarch of mountains,
>   They crowned him long ago ;
> But who they got to put it on
>   We don't exactly know,'

and many others.

While the ' Mont Blanc ' season lasted Albert
Smith issued a periodical of the size and shape of
two leaves of this book, called *The Mont Blanc
Gazette and Illustrated Egyptian Hall Advertiser.*
It was ' published occasionally ' at ' price—thank
you,' and was full of comic sketches and literary
tit-bits, chiefly by the editor, and apropos of his
travels, together with the latest news of the day
very much condensed, and printed in red ink.
Thus, on ' Friday night, Jan. 15, 1858,' we had a
diminutive column headed :

' THE ATTEMPT TO ASSASSINATE THE
EMPEROR NAPOLEON.

'OFFICIAL ACCOUNT.

'As their Majesties arrived at the opera, three explosions of shells were heard. Three persons were killed ; sixty wounded ; and the Emperor's hat was smashed by a splinter. General Roguet, who was in the carriage, was also wounded. Many arrests have taken place. As the Emperor returned, the boulevards were spontaneously illuminated, and the cheering was most enthusiastic.'

An interesting item in this miniature publication refers to the performances before royalty of 'Mont Blanc.' The hall was visited by Prince Albert in 1853 ; by Her Majesty and the 'royal children' in 1854 ; while private performances were given at Osborne in 1855, and at Windsor Castle in 1856 before the Royal Family and the King of the Belgians. In the January of 1858 'Mont Blanc' had been presented for the eighteen-hundredth time, and it had still to run for another six months. Nine performances took place every week, so that when 'Mont Blanc' was announced for the last time it had been repeated upon more than two thousand occasions.

We saw the last of 'Mont Blanc' in the July of 1858, when the lecturer went to China to collect materials for another entertainment of the kind, which he gave at the same place in the winter. As before, the hall was fitted up in Chinese fashion, and even the approaches to it showed tokens of the traveller's latest trip, as the staircase walls were completely covered with imitation portmanteaus, trunks and boxes, duly labelled with tickets corresponding with the Celestial places visited. There was also a separate exhibition of curiosities and odds and ends picked up in China in a smaller apartment, and these were usually inspected by the audience between the parts, or at the end of the lecture, without extra charge, as was the case when ' Mont Blanc' was in the bills.

Everyone now living who was present at those performances will remember the wonderful act-drop, representing a gigantic plate with the famous willow-pattern painted upon it. Small willow-pattern plates, with a likeness of Albert Smith in the centre, were also sold in the hall at one shilling, and after his death some of the fortunate possessors of these souvenirs re-sold them for as much as three guineas apiece.

The trip to China ran very successfully till the end of July, 1859, when Albert Smith, who was then in his forty-third year, took unto himself a wife in the person of Mary Keeley, with whom he had been on terms of affectionate regard for no inconsiderable period. After the wedding, the happy pair went for their honeymoon to the Alps, where they remained for a couple of months, and upon their return to town in the winter, 'China' was repeated.

The Albert Smiths took up their residence at North End Lodge, Walham Green, and I am told that Mary's husband, who prided himself upon his robust health and iron constitution, was in the daily habit of walking from his home to the hall in all weathers. Unfortunately, he had to give up this habit and rest altogether for a time through illness caused by a partly epileptic, partly apoplectic stroke, with which he was seized on the day before Christmas Eve. After three weeks' confinement to the house, he recovered sufficiently to resume his duties at the hall, but he was never quite himself again.

On Saturday, May 12, 1860, when the Albert Smiths had been married only ten months, after giving his usual entertainment, in spite of a bad cold from which the lecturer was suffering, he walked from the hall in Piccadilly to the Garrick Club, though it was then pouring in torrents, and of course he got wet through. But instead of going home or changing his clothes, he remained at the club. The result may be easily imagined. He was almost immediately laid prostrate by a severe attack of bronchitis. He, however, persisted in giving his entertainment just the same, merely leaving out the songs, till at last he was forced to close the hall, which he did on Monday, May 21, nine days after his attack.

Next day the invalid became insensible, and Dr. Burroughes was sent for. But the physician could then do no good, and on the Wednesday evening, at half-past eight, Albert Smith, in presence of his wife, his brother Arthur, who had conducted his business for many years, and a medical man, breathed his last.

On the Saturday following, all that remained of our dear old friend—of everybody's friend, 'from the Queen of England to the humblest check-taker at the Egyptian Hall,' as Mr. Sala wrote at the time—was buried in the Brompton Cemetery, without the least pomp or circumstance, in accordance with his wishes, the chief mourners being his brother, Arthur Smith; his father-in-law, Robert Keeley; A. P. Barlow, his sole executor; Edmund Yates, and Mr. Lane, A.R.A., the engraver. It is not too much to say that outside and far away from that burial-ground were some tens of thousands of mourners of both sexes and all ages, who felt keenly the loss of the genial friend whom they were never to see again.

In commenting upon Albert Smith's demise, in an excellent memoir of his old friend and colleague, Mr. Edmund Yates remarked :

'His death occurred in the prime of life, at a time when the sun of his fame and fortune had reached its meridian—at a time when he had begun to find the joys of a new existence in home and domesticity. Not ten days before his death, he was expressing to the writer of these lines his perfect happiness in the tranquillity and repose of his home, his constant anxiety to get back to it, and his wonder that he had been able for so long to live a celibate and aimless life. Throughout the entire winter he was engaged in adding to and ornamenting his house and grounds, building a conservatory, vinery, etc., and arranging the gardens according to his own taste. The last words he spoke to the writer were, when bidding him farewell in a little arbour on his lawn : " When you come down next week this place will be lovely, for the pink may will then all be out ;" and curiously enough,' adds Mr. Yates, 'that pink may showed its blossom on the day of his death.'

As an author Albert Smith is best remembered by his successful novel, 'The Adventures of Mr. Ledbury,' which, before its appearance in book-form, was run as a serial in *Bentley's Miscellany*, to be followed in the same popular journal by his ' Scattergood Family' and the ' Marchioness of Brinvilliers.' If I mistake not, the novelist afterwards became one of the editors of *Bentley*; at any rate, he contributed very largely to its pages in many ways, as he also did to *Punch*, which had then no exclusive staff, and to the *Illustrated London News*, of which Albert Smith was for some time the dramatic critic.

In addition to these literary labours he wrote the words of several of John Parry's humorous songs, together with a novel, 'Christopher Tadpole,' which came out in monthly parts after the style of the stories by Charles Dickens, whose 'Dombey and Son' was then appearing in this fashion. Smith's 'Pottleton Legacy' was also issued in monthly parts, and then it was that he and Angus Reach started a sixpenny magazine called *The Man in the Moon*, which had on its permanent staff of writers Tom Taylor, Shirley Brooks, John Oxenford, Dion Boucicault, and Charles Lamb Kenney, with such outside contributors as Robert Brough and G. A. Sala. The latter states that he was 'then a raw lad, employed in the humblest artistic capacities, and frequently had to go to and fro between the residences of the two editors.'

One of those editors resided at 14, Percy Street, Bedford Square, and his name in full was Albert Richard Smith. He was born at Chertsey on May 24, 1816, and he died on Wednesday, May 23, 1860—the eve of his birthday.

CHAPTER XVIII.

IN THE JUBILEE YEAR.

MRS. KEELEY had a rather long rest from her labours as sitter for my first likeness of her, as it was not till 1887, or three years after the completion of the Garrick portrait, that she posed for a second pictorial venture, which, in the year following, figured at the Royal Academy summer exhibition.

It goes without saying that during the progress of this last work we conversed, as before, upon many topics of interest to both of us, and it being Jubilee Year when the new picture was begun, my sitter touched upon a few topics bearing upon the early years of Her Majesty's reign. She and her husband were not in England at the time of the Queen's accession, as this event happened two months before their return from the United States; but they were present at the coronation in the year following, and in referring to that ceremony Mrs. Keeley said :

' I little thought at the time that I should live
for another half-century to tell the tale and be
present also at these Jubilee festivities. I have
already been to the Mansion House, and if all's
well, I hope to go to Westminster Abbey on
Tuesday to see the celebration ceremonies. Mrs.
Stirling, Mrs. Sara Lane, and myself, have been
all three specially invited, so we shall perhaps
meet there. By a strange coincidence, the man
who drives me to the Abbey is the same who
used to lead the Queen's pony, when she was
quite a girl and took lessons at the riding-school.'

The Keans and the Keeleys were the first
comedians to perform before Her Majesty and the
Prince Consort. Upon the first occasion, in 1848,
the piece presented was ' The Merchant of Venice,'
with something like an ideal cast, in which Kean
was the Shylock ; Mrs. Kean, Portia ; Miss Mon-
tague (Mrs. Compton), Jessica ; Webster, Gratiano ;
Alfred Wigan, Bassanio ; Leigh Murray, Lorenzo ;
Keeley, Launcelot Gobbo ; and Mrs. Keeley,
Nerissa. In referring again to this event, the
Nerissa of the piece remarked by way of postscript :

' The room was not full, but it was a fine audience to play to, and I could see them all as distinctly as if we were amateurs at private theatricals.
The Prince of Wales and Duke of Edinburgh,

who were then little boys in short frocks, were
seated upon a raised place at the feet of the
Queen, and they all seemed quite at home and at
their ease. I myself felt dreadfully nervous, cold,
and half-scared. But I managed to get through
the part somehow, and when the Shakespearian
play was over, Mr. Keeley and I appeared as
Fanny Pepper and Euclid Facile in John Oxenford's farce of "Twice Married," which made
them laugh in the most natural way possible. In
fact, they seemed to enjoy the performances
thoroughly. But I think, on the whole, I got on
much better at the next one before royalty.'

Upon my speaking presently of her Nerissa,
she said :

'It is not considered much of a part as played
in the acting edition, though that, of course, de-
pends a good deal upon how it is performed. I
myself never thought the part small. But then I
am one of those who consider all parts good, if
their players make them so. I remember the
time when the whole of Nerissa's lines were introduced. When acting under my maiden name,
I spoke them exactly as they were written by
Shakespeare. But once, when playing to the
Gratiano of Farley, the pantomimist, some audible
hisses were heard after one of the long speeches,
and ever since then many of such speeches were

cut down. I think I must have played Nerissa to nearly all the Portias of my time, and once I played it when Edmund Kean was the Shylock. It was just before his death, and I remember he felt faint and I got some brandy-and-water for him. When acting it with his son at the Princess's, the play was beautifully mounted and dressed, as with most of the Charles Kean revivals and productions. Nothing better is done nowadays at any theatre. Oscar Byrne made the designs for some of these productions, and Mrs. Charles Kean assisted in the carrying out of his plans. In one of the productions I recollect that Miss Violet Cameron's mother and the latter's sister appeared in vocal parts.'

After further talk of the Charles Kean days and of the lavish manner in which his plays were put upon the stage, we spoke of the Macready productions and their wonderful casts. Mrs. Keeley said that no such casts were ever seen before or since his time, and that, with but few exceptions, they were composed of star performers, any two of whom would have been sufficient to draw crowded audiences at the playhouse of to-day. But, of course, the salaries then paid to star performers were not nearly as great as now. In fact, it was quite possible to secure the services of half a dozen of them at about the same price received to-day by a single one, and in some cases at less than that. However, in spite of the vastly superior casts, taken as a whole, of the Prince Consort days, many a fine piece, though superbly acted and fairly well staged, was a financial failure, notably in the case of ' As You Like It,' already referred to in these pages, and of which Mrs. Keeley said :

' It went very well for a few nights, and our Drury Lane audience thoroughly appreciated the performances, as they couldn't well help doing with such comedians in the leading and minor parts as Macready, Phelps, Anderson, Ryder, Compton, Mrs. Nisbett, Fanny Stirling, myself and Mr. Keeley. But, for all that, I remember Macready came to my husband one night and said, " There is only fourteen pounds in the house, so the piece will have to be withdrawn." '

While upon this topic, the lady who played Audrey in this unfortunate piece said that when first the part was offered to her, she felt very reluctant to accept it, as she considered herself unfit to play the character as it is usually repre- sented, and said as much to her manager, who replied :

' " But you are already down in the cast." " Well, Mr. Macready," I said, " you are my chief, and I am bound to obey orders. But I warn you that unless I play the part in my own way it will be a miserable failure." " Then play it in

your own way," answered my trusting chief. And
I did. I played it in a stolid, stupid manner, and
Macready complimented me upon it in high terms,
saying that I was the very best Audrey he had
ever seen.'

One of the great charms of Mrs. Keeley's conversation upon such topics as we touched upon in
the course of the sittings, was that while speaking
in praise of the players of her time, she by no
means ignored those of the present day, or made
odious comparisons. You never heard her say,
' Yes, Irving is all very well, but you should
have seen Charles Kean in the part;' or, ' Terriss
is certainly strong, but he is nothing to what
Walter Lacy was in the same character.' She
spoke of each player, whether living or belonging
to the past, exactly as she found him or her.
There were no such expressions in her vocabulary
as ' the good old times,' and so forth. Only in
referring to certain revivals of standard plays
was she sometimes tempted to recall the acting of
her time, as was the case when ' Twelfth Night '
was presented at two of our theatres, when, after
witnessing both performances, she would remark :

' I have seen many Violas, and perhaps every
one of them, since I was born. But the best of
all, in my opinion, was Mrs. Charles Kean, and
after her Ellen Terry, whose conception of the

character is so tender, joyous, refined, womanly, and altogether charming. But I don't care much for Miss Ada Rehan's version—clever actress though she undoubtedly is—and I am surprised that the critics should have praised it up to the skies. It may be an American Viola, but' (with a comic look) 'it isn't Shakespeare's.'

Jubilee year being also the year of the American Exhibition, with the first appearance there of the Wild West and Buffalo Bill, our conversation naturally turned upon American topics, and as I had hitherto heard but little of the Keeleys' visit to the United States, this was a good opportunity of sounding Mrs. Keeley upon the subject. Much the same idea occurred to an American lady who happened to visit my sitter at about the time I was engaged in depicting her again, so that between Miss Annie Wakeman's interview and my own, I have more than enough material for the last half of the present chapter.

If I am not mistaken, I was the first to find out that our subject entertained the highest opinion of American acting, beginning, say, with Edwin Booth and E. A. Sothern, and ending, maybe, with Joseph Jefferson. Speaking of the last-named player and his Rip Van Winkle, she remarked to one or both of us :

'Ah, he is what I call a real actor. And I

hear he's coming to London again this year, so I shall certainly go and see him, or perish in the attempt!'

I have already mentioned that it was about a year before the coronation that the Keeleys set sail for the United States. They did not, however, go thither as star performers, but simply to try their fortunes, and appear in their old pieces. In those days Transatlantic steamers were, of course, unknown luxuries, so that instead of a trip of five or six days across the ocean, it was a voyage in a real sailing vessel, and it lasted something over a month. And when the stormy winds did blow, the ship's decks were not quite as level as the stage of Drury Lane upon the night of a nautical drama. After briefly describing their first experiences of life on the ocean wave, Mrs. Keeley remarked :

'We went over just to try our luck at the Park Theatre, New York, then under the management of Mr. Simpson. At first the prospect was not at all encouraging. In fact, for the first two nights the house was half empty, and Mr. Keeley said : "This won't do ; we had better go back to the place we came from. They evidently don't care for us." You see, we had not been previously "boomed," as you call it, and the American public knew nothing of us, and next to nothing of English acting generally. But Simpson appeared more confident of our success, and said : "Wait till Thursday." So we did, and from that time we were a great success."

At that period the Keeley repertory, though sufficiently extensive, was scarcely as varied and striking as was the case later. Still, the Keeleys did very well with their old farces and Adelphi dramas, and on the whole the American public had reason to remember their visit with satisfaction. The comedians themselves carried back with them many pleasurable memories of their visit, and in speaking of the various cities they played at, Mrs. Keeley remarked :

'Philadelphia is very dear to me and Boston also, though in the latter place we did not have as good a chance as in New York and other cities. But we spent a very happy time there, as we did everywhere else, and Mr. Keeley was greatly amused by the queer characters we met, and the odd manners and customs of the different places we went to. I think it was partly on account of the interest he took in these things that our visit was prolonged. But it was not all plain sailing. In Mobile I had rather a curious experience. The houses there were built like barns, with a small pile of bricks placed under at intervals to keep them from the ground, for, I suppose,

drainage purposes. Once when we were at
dinner the floor began to heave up in one part,
which gave me an awful fright. But they said it
was nothing ; only a pig rubbing his shoulders
under the boards! My life was saved in Mobile
by a Jewish family, named Jones or Wolffe, if I
am not mistaken. I had a bad attack of fever
and ague, caused, I think, by rats. It was supposed that the vermin had got into my room and
on to my bed, where they bit me severely. This
led to blood poisoning, and I was sick unto death
in lodgings among people I did not know. But
those good souls took me to their home and
waited upon me like slaves. They were not
wealthy, but they did what they could for me,
and I recovered under their constant care. God
bless them! say I, and if any are still living, tell
them so from me.'

These last words were, of course, addressed to
the American interviewer, who took occasion to
ask at this point whether it was true, as reported,
that Mrs. Keeley had Jewish blood in her veins ?

' Quite true,' was her prompt reply ; ' my great-
great-grandparents were of the Jewish persuasion,
and I am proud of that fact. The Jews are a noble
race—God's chosen ones, perhaps—the beloved of
the Father. The Hebrew people have given some
brilliant names to music and the drama—right

royal names, I think. And the list seems never-ending.'

Asked what recollections she had of Boston, the actress replied with some enthusiasm :

'Ah, I remember every street and square in it ; Boston Common, Bunker's Hill Monument, and Boston's great hotel. I can't help laughing at the mention of Bunker's Hill Monument. At that time it was not finished and money was needed for its completion. Not being strong in American history, I proposed to Mr. Keeley that we should put our shoulders to the wheel and try and raise the money by a monster benefit. But my husband exclaimed with horror : "You fool! Why, don't you know that Bunker's Hill Monument was put up to commemorate the awful licking we got from our Yankee friends?" I was always chaffed un-mercifully about this mistake, and one day a young man belonging to our company presented me with a sketch of Bunker's Hill to remind me of it.'

In explanation of the big hotel, previously spoken of, Mrs. Keeley said to her Boston friend :

'I could find that hotel with my eyes shut, and though you say there are many others in your city, I don't believe there is one to compare with it. It was called Tremont House, and I

remember that everything, including the furniture,
the food and the cooking, was simply perfect.
I should just like to go there again, if only to
taste their wonderful lobsters.   One night a fire
broke out somewhere, and my maid, who was
eating a plate of lobster salad, took it up and
went to the corridor at the end of the dining-
room.   Seating herself in a rocking-chair, she
said that if we were to be burnt alive she would
like to have just one more rock and a final lobster
salad.   Rocking-chairs were then a new experience
for both of us.   I shall not forget, either, the
flowers of Boston, with their acres of columbines
—I can see them now in my mind's eye.'

Asked presently whether she had any message
for Boston, she said :

'Tell them that old Mary Anne Keeley sends
her love to the Tremont House, where they treated
her so well.   Oh, those lobsters! those oysters!
those canvas-back ducks!   In fact, everything
and everybody, down to the bell-boys, who nearly
ran their legs off to wait upon me.'

Among other places visited by the Keeleys
before their return to England was New Orleans,
and while sauntering along the street with some
friends an incident occurred which forms a sort of
companion picture to the Bunker's Hill episode, as
it remained a standing joke against the actress for

some considerable period. In relating the story to me, Mrs. Keeley said that one of the things that struck her most in New Orleans was the large number of parrots flying freely overhead.

'I never saw so many in my life,' she remarked. 'The sky seemed quite black with them, and they looked such little specks high up in the heavens, that it was impossible to judge of their beautiful plumage. But one day I saw one quite close. It was running and flying along the road in front of us. So, thinking it was either a wild bird or had escaped from a cage, I ran after it, and continuing to run down a side street, I soon lost sight of my husband and our party. The bird kept flying steadily ahead of me, as if it meant me to come very near, but not quite near enough to catch. However, presently the pretty creature took refuge in an open doorway. So I thought to myself, "Now I shall catch it!" And I did. But, alas! not in the way I thought. An older bird, in the shape of my husband, came panting along with his fellow-actors, and seeing me enter the house, they were struck dumb with horror and amazement. For the house was—well' (with a look that spoke volumes) 'not quite as respectable as Buckingham Palace. And the parrot was—well, they called it a decoy-bird.'

Mrs. Keeley spoke with enthusiasm of the

scenery along the coast of the Mississippi from
New Orleans to Pittsburgh, and had a few amusing
stories to tell of their journey in the canal boat.

' I took some sketches of the scenery as we
went along,' she said, ' but I think I have given
them all away.   There were some wonderful trees
close to the water's edge with roots exposed in
large masses, and picturesque bits everywhere.
The canal boats were rather primitive then, and
I shall not easily forget them.   There was only a
curtain of division between the ladies' and gentlemen's sleeping compartments, and we had to repose upon shelves placed one over the other.
They gave me the lowest one, as it would have
made me giddy to sleep so high.   But at one of
the stations a lady with a baby got in, so I was
obliged to give up my place to her and sleep above.
This gave me the nightmare, and I must have
been shouting pretty loud all night, as at last I
felt a hand shaking my head from the gentleman's
side, and heard a voice saying, " My good lady,
pray calm yourself."   I don't know who it was,
but he was evidently sleeping with his head to
mine.'

While in the South the Keeleys saw something
of slave life, and attended one or two slave sales
to see what they were like.

' White slaves were put up for sale,' she said,

'as well as black and brown ones. But I think there was some sign to show that the white slaves were of coloured origin. It was chiefly in the finger-nails and eyes. Some of the poor creatures were marked on the shoulder, and the bidders examined them there. Mr. Keeley nearly got us into trouble by his open expression of indignation at the traffic in human flesh, and once he re-marked, loud enough for everyone to hear, "Dam shame!"'

In returning to England the Keeleys brought with them many little souvenirs of their American tour, and among them a cage of squirrels. These were in charge of Mrs. Keeley's maid, an old Ipswich servant who had been for some years in her service, and accompanied her to the United States. During the homeward voyage the maid got dreadfully sea-sick, and as she lay helpless on deck her nose somehow found its way between the bars of the cage she had hitherto fondly clasped. But the squirrels could not resist the temptation of playing with her proboscis, with the result that it soon became as well tattooed as that of any North American Indian.

The American tour came to an end in New York, where it had begun, and the Keeleys re-turned to London, where they were warmly wel-comed back upon their appearance, early in the

October of 1837, at the Olympic, which had been opened for the season by Madame Vestris.   The first pieces they played in were a new burletta by Planché, called ' The New Servant,' and another one entitled ' Advice Gratis,' by Charles Dance.

The Jubilee year also recalled one very sad event in the history of Her Majesty, which Mrs. Keeley had more than one reason for remembering, as it happened in 1861, shortly before the actress's retirement from the stage.   In referring to the occurrence in question, she said :.

' We were living at the time at Mary's house in Walham Green.   I had broken a bloodvessel and had not been feeling well for some time.   So we thought that a complete change would do me good, and we went to live with our daughter for an entire year.   But it was a great mistake. While there an old friend, whom I have now known for forty years, looked in one day and said, " This is a sad thing, is it not ?"   " What is sad ?" I asked, wondering what he meant.   " Why, the death of the Prince Consort.   Haven't you heard of it ? He died to-day."   The news came upon me like a blow.   I was dreadfully shocked and upset, and the suddenness of the news gave me another attack.'

CHAPTER XIX.

WILD MEG AND THE WILD WEST.

THOUGH not chronologically following the last chapter, the present one may be said to form a sequel to its predecessor from the fact that it deals mostly with the famous entertainment known as Buffalo Bill's Wild West ; and, as I have already spoken of the American Exhibition while referring to the leading events of the Jubilee year, the reader will naturally expect to hear something of Mrs. Keeley's visit to the Earl's Court show and want to know what she thought of it.

The actress had seen something of the rough side of American life on the stage when ' Uncle Tom's Cabin ' was produced at the Adelphi. Not that the humble exploits of little Topsy, at a West End theatre, could in the least compare with the daring deeds of Buffalo Bill at West Brompton. But ' Uncle Tom's Cabin ' was not without its blank-cartridge firing, its swarthy heroes, and its scenes of intense realism. Real animals were

also introduced into the drama, and real danger
attached to the performances, as was sufficiently
shown by at least two occurrences which took
place in the course of the play's action.

One of these happened in the scene where
Topsy escapes with the boy George upon her
back, followed by her fellow-slaves. For, while
going up some steps at the back of the stage, a
pack of live bloodhounds were let loose, and one
of them, who appears to have overacted his part,
went for Topsy savagely, and Mrs. Keeley being
flimsily attired, the actress could easily feel the
animal's claws against her flesh. She might have
also felt his teeth but for the interposition of the
dog's trainer, who came to the rescue. The dog,
which was not a bloodhound, but a rather large
black-and-white retriever, had formerly belonged
to the actress, and she had to part with him on
account of his ferocity to strangers. Not recog-
nising his late mistress as a runaway negress, the
dog attacked her in the manner described.

A far more serious accident happened to Miss
Woolgar while enacting Eliza, the runaway quad-
roon. In the scene where Eliza escapes with her
child from the banks of the Ohio river, leaping
from one block of ice to the other till she reaches
the opposite shore, the actress's foot slipped, and
she fell on her face, saving the child in the fall,

but fracturing her own nose. The effects of the disaster remained for years after, and when, as Mrs. Alfred Mellon, she sat to me for her portrait, the disfigurement to her features was still plainly perceptible.

The Adelphi drama 'Sea and Land' may also lay claim to more than a distant relationship with the realistic dramas of the Wild West, by reason of its thrilling incidents, its rough scenes with smugglers, its firing, and, above all, its Wild Meg, who was as wild in appearance and habits as any untutored Indian.

Those who may have seen Mark Lemon's stirring play will not easily forget the Wild Meg of Mrs. Keeley as it was performed by her in 1852 and again in 1855, when produced at Sadler's Wells. And methinks I see her now in the smuggler's cave, attired in ragged vestments, with bare feet and unkempt locks, or standing defiantly upon the ruins of the old castle overlooking the sea.

Mrs. Keeley visited the Wild West in 1892, when Buffalo Bill and his 'outfit,' as the troupe was called, visited us for the second time. I was then acting as manager of the press department of the exhibition, and I remember that there was quite a little commotion in camp when I mentioned that the oldest living actress was coming to the show.

As for burly Major Burke, the general manager, he was so delighted at the prospect of seeing so distinguished a lady, that, in accordance with his custom when any notability was expected, from a royal princess to a member of the press, he proposed all manner of things for the proper reception of our visitor, including a champagne luncheon, with speeches, at the Logwood Cabin, and an extra policeman or two to keep the crowd back while her ladyship should go the round of the camp. But I assured the hospitable man that Mrs. Keeley would be quite content with a private box for herself and escort. So the best box in the auditorium was reserved for our honoured guest and her niece, Miss Alexander.

When the last shot had been fired in the ' Attack upon a Settler's Cabin,' and the last dead Sioux Indian had briskly remounted his gallant charger, we got our ladies safely out, and, assisted by Inspector Foster of the L Division, escorted them through the camp, pausing on the way to show the Indian wigwams, the Russian Cossack's tent, the Guacho's retreat, Annie Oakley's snug quarters, and most of the other side-shows, with which they were greatly interested.

Then we took them to the Hon. Colonel W. F. Cody's comfortable quarters, as it formed part of our programme that Mrs. Keeley and

Buffalo Bill should interview one another. And
I shall never forget that first meeting between
the tall, dignified, handsome hero of the Wild
West and the little lady who, if old enough to be
his grandmother, was quite as upright, graceful
and firm on her feet as Buffalo Bill, while the
tones of her voice were, if anything, clearer and
more powerful than his.

'Proud and honoured to shake hands with
Mrs. Keeley,' said the crack shot and hunter of
buffaloes, warmly greeting his visitor.

'I met you once, Colonel Cody, at some civic
festivity in the City,' remarked Mrs. Keeley, when
we had all seated ourselves around the well-
appointed tent. 'It was only at a distance, and
I don't suppose you noticed so insignificant a
person as myself.'

'I can't say I did,' he replied in rather
pronounced American accents. 'And I don't
remember seeing you on the stage, Mrs. Keeley.
I reckon you kinder retired before my time. I did
not begin my career properly till the fall of 1861,
when I was a Government scout and guide. But
your honoured name is well known in my native
city and in all parts of the States, as I guess it is
everywhere else.'

'I have, of course, heard much of you, Colonel
Cody, and your various achievements,' said the

actress; 'but till this afternoon I had no idea that you were so good an actor. But you are all actors—born actors, and it is the most wonderful performance I have ever seen.'

'You do us proud, madame,' answered the big man with a little smile of incredulity; 'but with all due deference to your opinion, Mrs. Keeley, I think you do your profession kinder injustice by calling us actors. I guess we're no actors. What we do comes natural like. We can't help it; that's so. We have been used to it all our lives, and we don't know any different.'

'But that is the very perfection of acting,' said the original Wild Meg in her emphatic way. 'Study and tuition are all very well, but they won't make an actor, and never did. One of the best things I have seen to-day was that horse-stealing and lynching business. Though mostly in dumb-show, it was intensely dramatic and easy to follow. I have seen nothing better on the stage. When that wretched man steals the horse while the owner of it is calmly sleeping, and creeps off, afraid of disturbing him, it was like the real thing, and therefore like acting of the highest order. Every movement was a study. Some parts were also extremely funny, and I laughed till the tears came to my eyes. Those two men are what I call born actors.'

'Glad you approve of our new feature,' said the Colonel, who appeared quite as interested by the actress's eloquence and energetic manner as by her professional opinion.

'The fighting with the Indians was also good,' she continued, 'but I shouldn't like to have been in it. And I wouldn't like to drive in that ramshackle coach, though I am told that the audience are sometimes invited to do so.'

Someone here remarked that Mrs. Langtry had been round upon two occasions in the famous Deadwood coach, and was coming again to drive in it, at which Mrs. Keeley said :

'Well, let Mrs. Langtry go in it as often as she pleases ; I much prefer a good old London growler, and even then ' (in an aside to me) 'I must have my faithful Brown on the box.'

Then, after complimenting Colonel Cody upon his sharp-shooting while riding on horseback, and speaking in praise of Annie Oakley and the other crack shots, the guest of the occasion exclaimed with rapture :

'But one of the most marvellous sights that I have witnessed to-day is that expansive arena, with its endless crowd of human beings around it. What a wonderful scene ! That alone was well worth coming to see. I have never beheld anything like it anywhere, and I am surprised that it

17

is not spoken of more.   Before coming to-day I
had no idea it was such a large place.'

'Yes, it is pretty big,' the Colonel said dryly,
and as if just awakening to that fact.   'And I
reckon it was a fairish attendance to-day.   But I
guess it's bigger on a Bank Holiday.   You should
see it then.'

'No, thank you!' said his guest, with a characteristic look in her face ; 'no Bank Holiday sight-
seeing for me!'

'But I hope this won't be your last visit here,
Mrs. Keeley,' remarked her host, as his black
valet proceeded to hand round glasses of champagne.   'I trust to see you here pretty often.'

Mrs. Keeley thanked the Colonel for his polite-
ness, and after partaking very sparingly of his
proffered cup, she said in a semi-confidential tone :

'Now, Colonel Cody, I want to ask you something, and hope you won't be offended or think
me too inquisitive.'

'Why, certainly not,' promptly answered the
courteous gentleman, with a look half of inquiry,
half of amusement.   'Pray proceed, Mrs. Keeley.'

'Well, then,' continued that lady, 'are the buck-
jumpers trained to buck, or are the poor creatures
really wild ?'

'That is a question,' replied Buffalo Bill thought-
fully, 'pretty often asked in these parts, and our

answer is that it's kinder impossible to train them. But there's no need to, because "once a bucker always a bucker," as we say. And that's a fact.'

I forget what was said after this. But I remember that before Mrs. Keeley took her departure Colonel Cody asked whether it was true that she was more than fourscore years. For after what he had seen and heard of the lady that day he was in great doubt whether she was much past fifty.

' I shall be eighty-seven in November,' was, however, the prompt reply, and with this statement the interview came to an end.

Buffalo Bill would have been more astonished still if he had seen with what a firm step the octogenarian walked from the Wild West to the main building, along the lengthy bridge and down the lofty steps leading to it, when, in spite of the fatigue and excitement of the afternoon, she sat out another performance by the Zulu choir.

CHAPTER XX.

THE ACADEMY PORTRAIT.

WE called it the 'Academy Portrait' to distinguish it from the one exhibited at the Institute of Painters, and now in possession of the Garrick Club. The posture chosen was a standing one, with the face inclined to the right side and a hand lightly resting against it. It was an attitude which Mrs. Keeley naturally assumed, and was among many graceful poses that she unconsciously threw herself into while conversing with a friend. It was not necessary that my subject should remain erect during the whole period of the sittings. She, however, remarked :

'I would much rather stand than sit at any time. This comes, perhaps, of my old habits on the stage, which I have not yet got over. I had plenty of standing then, and often more than was good for me. When playing Jack Sheppard I found the part so exhausting that I was glad of a brief rest now and then. So, whenever not

wanted on the stage, I sometimes threw myself
full length upon a sofa. But one night I fell
sound asleep, and they only just managed to arouse
me in time to go on before the curtain rose for
another act. Those were fatiguing days, if you
like. I remember Webster once made me play
Topsy and Jack on the same night ; and I thought
it would be the death of me.'

The tendency of Benjamin Webster to over-
work the actress was apparently a family failing,
for I remember that in my Sadlers' Wells days
his nephew, George, prevailed upon Mrs. Keeley
to play in ' Pas de Fascination ' and ' Jack Sheppard ' on the same night, and again in ' Sea and
Land ' and ' Uncle Tom's Cabin.' Upon my reminding her of those events, she said :

' Yes, I remember them well. I also remember
when his uncle Ben asked me to act the Fool in
' King Lear ' for Macready's benefit. The part
is a long one, as you know, and though I was
always a quick study, it seemed to me quite impossible to learn it at only a day's notice. However, there was no one else to play the part, and
Webster at last persuaded me to have a try. But
I had to sit up all night to do it, and I think I
acquitted myself with credit, for after the performances Macready complimented me highly—a thing
he never did with anyone unless he meant it.'

But if 'uncle Ben' was rather exacting as a manager, he was apparently an easy person to play with on the stage, for Mrs. Keeley observed :

'As a comedian it was a treat to act with Webster. While thinking of his own part he never forgot yours. He was the most suggestive actor I ever knew. He saw in a moment when you wanted to make your effects and helped you in a most surprising way. Macready, Yates, Charles Kean, and my husband also possessed this quality, but not to the extent of Webster. When playing " The Roused Lion " everyone noticed how well we acted together, and I'm sure that was the reason. In that favourite piece I did a ci-devant opera-dancer, and there was a scene in which we had to dance a minuet and gavotte. I told a friend the other day that if Webster were now living, I think, old as I am, I'd get up in the middle of the night to play that part with him.'

During the sitting my subject's fine Persian cat, who was as devoted to his mistress as she to him, would sometimes enter the apartment uninvited, and stare like a two-legged critic at the picture, and from the picture to the living original. Whether tabby recognised the likeness I do not know ; but as he invariably sprang upon my sitter's shoulders, after a long contemplation of my handiwork, I presumed that he much preferred the work of nature to the work of art. The cat's presence in the room one day gave rise to a little talk on domestic animals generally, and it began :

' Mr. Keeley was fond of tame animals of all kinds. At one time we had a lovely cock canary, who sang beautifully, and a little dog called Fusia ' —the dog mentioned in the farce of ' Keeley worried by Buckstone.' ' The bird was often allowed his freedom, and would then fly about the room. But one day he was left alone with the dog, and the dog attacked the poor little creature. Mr. Keeley came in only just in time to save it.'

This little domestic incident was followed by a story of a raven named Grip, which the actor had bought, thinking it might be useful to his wife in ' Barnaby Rudge,' which was then in rehearsal at the old Adelphi.

' But birds,' she explained, ' are not easy to manage on the stage, so the idea was abandoned, and we kept Grip for our own private purposes. Mr. Keeley and his feathered companion became devoted friends, which is more than can be said of our neighbours, who considered the bird a nuisance, as it screeched and talked from morning till night. We were then living in Brompton Square, close to the church, and Grip, who had no respect for holy days, was heard distinctly to

call out in the middle of the sermon, " Keeley !—
Keeley !—Bob !—Bob Keeley !—Cook !" or some
other disrespectful words.

'One fatal day our little pet was heard no
more, which, if a blessing to our neighbours and
the Sunday devotees, was a source of infinite
sorrow to ourselves. We had reason to suspect
that the people next door, who hated the
bird, had got over the garden wall and made
away with it. Some time after our sad loss I
happened to go to the Zoological Gardens with
my brother Fred and my grandchild, Jessie, and
while strolling about, Fred came up to me and
asked, with some excitement, " Didn't your raven
have a broken claw ?" " Certainly," I said.
" Then," said he, " I think we've found him.
He's here in one of the cages." I went, and
there, sure enough, was a bird very like our poor
Grip. I thought it must be the same, because
he struggled so hard to get at me.

'When we got home I told Mr. Keeley, and
said : " Do you know, dad, I think our Grip is
at the Zoo." He would scarcely believe it. So
to make sure he went the next day, and directly
the raven saw my husband, he shrieked with
delight, and called out, " Keeley !—Keeley !—
Bob !—Bob Keeley !—Cook !" His master was
quite overcome, and told Mr. Bartlett, the super-

intendent of the gardens, that it was a bird that belonged to him and was once lost or stolen. Mr. Bartlett was, of course, quite satisfied with the evidence of the bird and his master that it was ours, and he said that Mr. Keeley might take the raven away. But my husband would not risk having him stolen again, so thought it safer to leave Grip at the Zoo. Mr. Bartlett also said that he remembered some time ago a lady and gentleman coming to the gardens to present the raven, though who they were he could not tell.'

This led to a story of Vandenhoff, the actor, who had a horror of cats, and could not remain in a place where one was to be seen. In speaking of this, Mrs. Keeley said :

'Once he called to see us when we happened to be out, and as we would not be long in returning, he was shown into the parlour, where he would have waited but for the presence of a black tom, which so terrified our visitor that he rushed wildly upstairs and locked himself in a bedroom, where he remained till we came back.'

I have good cause for remembering when my second likeness of the actress was completed, as the finishing touches were put to it in the same week that the fire at the Islington Grand took place, which, most playgoers will

know, was on the night of December 28 in the
Jubilee year. The very day that the distressing
news appeared in print Mrs. Keeley, who felt it
acutely, as she did every human disaster, at once
sent a cheque for £5 towards the relief of the
sufferers, together with a characteristic letter to a
private friend, of which this is a copy :

'Last night's fire at the Grand means misery
and hunger to a large body of people. Of course
there will be a fund organized for their relief, but
immediate relief will be necessary to a great many
of the sufferers. They say, " A rolling stone
gathers no moss." I don't believe it. I send a
very small stone ; but if you, with your usual
energy, will set it going, I believe it will soon be
too heavy to lift.'

Mrs. Keeley's portrait appeared in the Royal
Academy in 1888. She was then in her eighty-
third year, and by an odd coincidence the catalogue
number was 880. Before being sent to Burlington
House the picture had been privately 'on view'
in a small gallery at 88, King's Road, Brighton.
There it was purchased by a private collector of
theatrical celebrities on February 8, 1888.

At the private view I had the pleasure of
accompanying the original to the Academy and
escorting her through the different galleries.
This was, I believe, one of the very few occa-

sions on which Mrs. Keeley had then been seen within those walls at a private view.

She also went the round of the studios on Show Sunday—a thing that she had not been in the habit of doing ; for, although the Keeleys had been on intimate terms with many of the leading artists of their day, including Stanfield, the scene - painter, Beverly, Roberts, Maclise and Sir Edwin Landseer, studio visiting was then not as common as it has since become. But they went not unfrequently to the Gower Street atelier of Abraham Solomon, and, if I am not mistaken, one of the Keeley sisters—I think it was Louise—sat more than once to that artist for subject-pictures.

Mrs. Keeley was also intimate with Mr. Frederick Goodall, Mr. W. P. Frith, Mr. Keeley Halswelle, who was not related to or called after her, and other distinguished painters of our own time.

The actress, being herself a promising amateur with the brush, naturally took a lively interest in everything appertaining to fine art, and her criticism of pictures was often as sound as were her views of the drama. She had a preference for historical works, and those which told a story or appealed to the sympathies. She likewise adored landscapes when these reminded her of what she had seen in nature, and, as a general rule, she preferred realistic works to more suggestive ones. This is sufficiently exemplified by the little landscapes which Mrs. Keeley has produced from time to time for presentation to friends, one of these being in the possession of the Savage Club, where it is greatly prized.

Mrs. Keeley was not less candid and plain-

From a Watercolour Drawing by Mrs. Keeley, March, 1895.

spoken in her observations when viewing a work of art than when seeing a play. I remember once accompanying her to Mr. Frith's studio when he lived in Pembridge Villas. Among the canvases on the artist's many easels was one of a historical nature with several figures in it, all carefully finished with the painter's usual close attention to detail. Of course, the actress singled out this dramatic work from the rest, which, I think, were mostly portraits, and the instant she looked at it, up went her hands, and in a voice loud enough for everyone in the studio to hear, she exclaimed :

'Oh, how wonderful! I never saw anything so marvellous in all my life !'

The artist, who was one of the first to hear these flattering remarks, was naturally gratified to find that his picture had created so favourable an impression. But, in coming up to thank his critic, he noticed that she was gazing intently, not at the figures in the composition, but at the extreme top of the canvas, close against the frame, and upon his asking what it was that she particularly admired, she pointed to a rather obtrusive candelabra, a portion of which was alone visible. With the quick perceptions of an artist, Mr. Frith saw that in this case his realism detracted somewhat from the merits of the rest of the picture, and, being grateful for the timely suggestion, he said :

'Yes, I think you are right ; the candelabra does attract the eye too much, so I shall tone it down a little.'

But his critic, not quite understanding the nature of his remark, looked rather alarmed, and upon leaving the studio she asked :

'What have I said ? I thought I was praising the picture. But Mr. Frith didn't seem to think so. I hope he wasn't offended ?'

CHAPTER XXI.

PICTURES ON VIEW.

IN 1888 the Academy cast of theatrical celebrities was unusually scanty, for, with the exception of a fine portrait by Mr. Pettie of Mr. Charles Wyndham as David Garrick, the drama was unrepresented on the walls. The *Era* complained of their absence, saying that out of two thousand and odd exhibits only two were associated with the stage. Those it proceeded to describe, and in speaking of one of them said :

' It is full of interest for all lovers of the theatre, for its subject is a dramatic artist who has long since endeared herself to the hearts of all the elder generation of playgoers. It is No. 880 in gallery No. IX., by Mr. Walter Goodman, a head of " Mrs. Keeley in her 83rd year !" Yes, there it is in black and white in the catalogue, ' 83rd year '! But look at the picture and your faith in the veracity of catalogues will be for ever gone. The lady's locks are gray, to be sure, and here and there the crow

has set his foot. But "83rd"—pooh! We would
not believe it for a wilderness of catalogues. Look
at the pink, fresh-coloured, almost ruddy complexion, the bright eyes, the lively, youthful smile.
With much discretion, whether of sitter or artist,
or both combined, the delicate pink and gray of
face and hair are set off by a dress of plain
black stuff, relieved only by the dull red stone
of a circular brooch at the throat. The head is
lightly resting on the right hand, and in the painting of the eyes and mouth the artist has successfully caught the expression, at once genial and
intellectual, of the famous heroine of many an
"Adelphi screamer" in the old days when the
world went to the Adelphi for laughter instead of,
as now, for thrills and tears.'

Many other prominent journals had a kind
word to say of the picture and similar personal
compliments to pay concerning the original, while
a few used the portrait as a sort of dramatic peg
for descanting upon the histrionic triumphs of the
lady represented.

The interviewer also took occasion to call again
at Pelham Crescent, perhaps to ascertain, by personal observation, whether the living picture was
really as youthful looking as the artist had made her,
in which case they found that he had by no means
flattered his sitter. One of the callers, who may

have possibly thought that an octogenarian, who could sit every day for her portrait, was qualified to take the chair at a public dinner, asked if there was any truth in a printed statement to the effect that Mrs. Keeley had consented to preside at the annual banquet of the Royal General Theatrical Fund. But she answered by a positive :

' No ! There is not the slightest truth in the report. I will speak any number of addresses in the cause of charity, or to oblige an old friend, and have indeed done so repeatedly. But I draw the line at taking chairs at public dinners.'

And Mrs. Keeley was as good as her word, for it was just two days after the opening of the Academy of 1888 that she spoke an address at the complimentary benefit to Mrs. Leigh Murray, and towards the end of that year she recited some verses at the Great Ormond Street Hospital for Sick Children.

Mrs. Keeley continued to be seen at theatres, music-halls, and similar places, till the nineties were well on in years. She has been also seen by her many friends at her old home in Pelham Crescent. One of her visitors being much struck by Mrs. Keeley's retentive memory, gives an instance of it :

' Happening to remark that some fifty years or more ago my mother had heard Mrs. Keeley sing in a song a line which had always haunted her,

the line being, " A tear—a tear shall tell him all "
—" Ah," said Mrs. Keeley, " that was in a piece
called ' The Devil and Dr. Faustus.' The song
was ' The Moonlight by the Cross,' " and on my
remarking that when my mother heard it it had
brought tears to her eyes, Mrs. Keeley, with her
usual good nature, promised, if my mother called,
she would sing it again for her. So I brought
her one day, and Mrs. Keeley sat down to the
piano, and accompanying herself to the old song,
sang it again with such clearness and expression
that the interval of more than fifty years was forgotten, and the tears came to my mother's eyes.'

To another visitor, who remarked, ' There must
be an enormous store of interesting matter connected with your life and work which is written
on no printed pages, and which you alone can
supply,' Mrs. Keeley replied :

' That is true ; and sometimes when I look
back, one picture or another will come up with
wonderful reality. For instance, when I heard of
the death of Mrs. FitzGeorge (Miss Fairbrother)
a week or two back, it was as if I lived through
everything that happened fifty years ago. I did
not train her, as has been stated in some papers,
but she was for some time in my company. Yes,
she was very beautiful—very beautiful indeed—
and not only her face, but her head and figure

18

were just as fine. Indeed, she was physically as nearly perfect as it is possible for a human being to be. But what attracted far more than her great beauty was her sweetness and amiability. It was always the same, and a more charming woman it was difficult to imagine. No wonder the Duke of Cambridge was so proud of her.'

'And was she a great public favourite ?' asked the guest.

'Oh yes! of course she was. And weren't they delighted when she danced the polka as Abdallah in Mark Lemon and Gilbert à Beckett's " Forty Thieves "! It was the first time the polka was danced on the stage in this country, and she introduced it and was triumphantly successful. When I heard that Mrs. FitzGeorge was dead, I would have liked to follow the natural impulse to send her a pretty wreath, as a last greeting and tribute, but I did not like to appear intruding. It is difficult to know what to do in such cases, where people in a high position are concerned.'

Asked about the playhouses of to-day, as compared with those of the Keeley times, she said :

' Theatres were not as popular as they now are, and the critics and connoisseurs went to the pit instead of the stalls, as is now the fashion. It wasn't the wealthy so much who, in my younger days, came exclusively to the theatre, but the

lovers and connoisseurs of the drama, whereas
now everybody goes. This is the golden age of
the theatre, as it is of all the arts ; painters, musi-
cians and actors are paid better and honoured
more highly than they have ever been before.
At present there are so many theatres that I don't
even know where to find them all. I am going
to the Garrick next week to see " La Tosca," but
I haven't the faintest notion where it is. Yes,
I've seen " The Dead Heart," and done my duty,
and cried my eyes red over it. It is a fine but
gloomy piece of acting, and when it was over I
said, " Now let us go to the Gaiety and see bright
Nelly Farren," and it was a great relief to have a
good laugh.'

Of callers who were much impressed by Mrs.
Keeley's youthful manner and comparatively
youthful appearance, was a 'fellow Arcadian'
(understood to be Mrs. Stannard, better known as
John Strange Winter), who afterwards wrote a
rather long article upon the subject, from which
I make the following extracts:

' She is so young, so fresh, so happy ; above all,
so sweet and womanly, that I am more than justified in speaking of her as a young and womanly
woman. . . . There is something in the spectacle
of a woman who, having far outreached the allotted
span of life, yet retains all that makes life worth

living, which cannot fail to make one think more reverently of a woman's life. . . . So there is, to myself at least, something infinitely touching in the thought of this lady, who, after nearly ninety years of vivid and varied experiences, has kept her illusions intact, has not lost that *foie de vivre* of which we have no longer the secret.'

Then, after touching lightly upon Mrs. Keeley's early triumphs as an operatic vocalist, the writer goes on to say :

'Even to-day you may hear her humming brightly to herself snatches of old songs ; and to me was granted the rare privilege of hearing her hum a bar of " Che faró." Our talk had fallen upon the opera of to-day, and Mrs. Keeley told me with what delight she had witnessed Giulia Ravogli's superb performance of " Orfeo." And speaking of that divinely pathetic lament, she fell to humming a few notes of it in a voice wherein there was no touch of age. . . . She told me, in what I thought a very happy phrase, that if Orpheus had sung half as sweetly as Giulia Ravogli, the fiends would never have let him leave hell.'

Mrs. Keeley considered that Giulia Ravogli was the nearest approach to Pasta that she could remember. She did not much care for 'Orfeo' taken as a whole, but she thought it well worth sitting out, if only to hear 'Che farò' at the end.

Whenever a musical friend called to see the lady who had sung with Malibran, Braham, and other great vocalists of the day, she had plenty to say on the subject of modern minstrelsy in all its branches. Mrs. Keeley was, of course, a warm admirer of the Gilbert-Sullivan operas, and thought that nothing like them had been ever done before, except as regards the libretto, which she considered equal to, though by no means better than, the best burlesques or extravaganzas of such dramatic humourists as Planché, Gilbert à Beckett, Frank Talfourd and the brothers Brough. While on this topic she once said :

'There ought to be an Act of Parliament to compel Gilbert and Sullivan always to write pieces together.'

At the head of living English song-writers she placed Mr. Charles Salaman, and whenever asked which was her favourite melody, she at once named that composer's 'I arise from dreams of thee,' saying :

'I think that is one of the most lovely songs ever written. It is so well wedded to Shelley's words, which are as beautiful as the music. But I have never heard the song sung to my complete satisfaction. I have often tried to sing it myself,

and I think, if I possessed the vocal power, I
might have done some justice to it, as I know
and feel how it ought to be sung.'

The musical enthusiast once had an opportunity
of hearing her favourite melody rendered to her
liking, and also accompanied to her liking by no
less a person than the composer himself. This
event happened in the year that her Academy
portrait was on view, and Mrs. Keeley was at
Mr. Salaman's house upon the occasion of his
seventy-fourth birthday, which fell on March 3,
1888. There was a large gathering of musical
and dramatic celebrities, among whom was
Miss Macintyre, and, if I mistake not, it was
that charming vocalist that did justice to Mr.
Salaman's masterpiece, greatly to the delight of
Mrs. Keeley and the rest of the company.

I think it was upon this occasion that she heard
also Mr. Salaman's more recent song, 'My Star,'
set to words by Sir Edwin Arnold, and rendered
to perfection by Mr. Ben Davies, who has sung
not a few of Mr. Salaman's best compositions.

In a pleasant chat upon old times, which Mr.
Salaman afterwards had with his guest, he informed her that the song of her preference was
written about a year before the Queen came to
the throne, and was published in the same year
that Mrs. Keeley made her début as Smike.   It

was sold 'for a mere song,' if not actually given away, as at that time the young composer attached no pecuniary value to his early efforts. Both ' I arise ' and ' If thou wert mine own love ' were among many that Mr. Salaman wrote in his youth.

Mr. Salaman showed an old programme dated April 7, 1829, in which Miss Goward and Mr. Keeley's names figure in the list of artists who contributed to a musical and dramatic entertainment given in memory of Charles Dibdin, and under the patronage of the Duke of Clarence (afterwards William IV.).

But, if a warm admirer of high-class music, Mrs. Keeley cherished no prejudices against the popular style. She was equally warm in her praises of the best ballads of the day, and fully appreciated comic opera of the ' Madame Favart ' or ' Madame Angot ' stamp. She did not even disdain music-hall minstrelsy of the genuinely humorous kind without vulgarity. She delighted in Chevalier's coster ditties, and after hearing them for the first time I remember her saying :

' I have a profound admiration for Mr. Chevalier, and consider that he has done more to raise the standard of music-hall singing than anybody else. I could see him over and over again. I could also see Madame Réjane as Madame Sans-Gène more than once. But I didn't see any fun

in F——, though the audience seemed to like
him much and applauded him to the echo.   And
I don't approve of all the lady artistes of the
variety stage.   But, on the whole, I think that
the burlesque of to-day is not a bit better than the
music-hall business, and in many cases not so good.'

Of burlesque singing-actors Mrs. Keeley gave
the palm, without hesitation, to Arthur Roberts,
and thought that he stood alone in his particular
groove.   Mr. Roberts' ready wit on the stage
was, in her opinion, far preferable to many of
the lines carefully prepared for him by his author,
and Mrs. Keeley tells an amusing story in reference to his ready wit off the stage.

' I was once made an honorary member of the
Bohemian Cycling Club.   Arthur Roberts, who
is a great cyclist, took the chair at one of the
annual dinners at which I was present, and he
had, of course, several speeches to make.   In one
of them he was told to say something about me.
But when it came to the point he stumbled and
stuttered in his dry way and with his funny look,
till at last he said, " I really don't know what to
say about the lady, except that she is like an old
bicycle with all the latest improvements." '

Mrs. Keeley's impartial views of music did not,
of course, extend to street-minstrelsy, though her
repeated generosity to the self-appointed seren-

aders of Pelham Crescent would seem to show
that she also patronized them.   Once, when we
were seated together at her drawing-room window,
an itinerant harpist planted himself in the road
and serenaded us with some doleful strains.   This
caused my companion to remark :

' I don't care much for the harp, and never did.
I like it in the orchestra, but not alone ; though I
once heard it played to perfection by Thomas,
who performed piece after piece for my sole benefit.
That man is, of course, performing for his own
benefit.   He expects to get something out of me.
This is his day for visiting my street.   He always
comes on Tuesday, and knows that he will not go
away empty-handed.   I declare I spend quite a
small fortune in pennies to street minstrels.   But,
when out the other day for a stroll in the neighbourhood, I was accosted by quite a respectable-
looking man who said he remembered me well in
the old days, which was more than I could say of
him.   That's how they always begin.   They seem
to think I like to be reminded that I once had an
audience.   Well, this one said that he was brother
to the leader of the band at the Strand Theatre
under the Swanborough management—a further
inducement, I suppose, for me to relieve his wants.
But it was not a few pence that he wanted, or
even a small silver coin, but exactly seven and

sixpence to get his fiddle out of pawn.   So, as I happened to have only two shillings in my purse, I couldn't oblige him.'

Mrs. Keeley continues to reside at her old home in Pelham Crescent, and at the moment of writing she is to be seen also on the walls of the Grafton Galleries in the exhibition of 'Fair Children.' This picture of the actress was painted at the age of fourteen, and represents her in a straw bonnet, trimmed with poppies and blue ribbons.   The complexion is ruddy, and the hair is a dark-brown with touches of auburn.   The artist was J. Smart, a pupil of Sir Joshua Reynolds, and was over eighty when the picture was painted.

At the same gallery is a small, daintily-touched likeness of Mrs. Keeley's mother, Miss Plannen, at the age of fifteen, painted by the same hand, and in both of these portraits a striking resemblance to Mrs. Keeley's great-grandchildren may be traced.

CHAPTER XXII.

WITH MRS. KEELEY AT THE PLAY.

THE first time I went with Mrs. Keeley to the
play was shortly after her recovery from her accident in 1884. We dined together at her house
and then went to Drury Lane to see the 'Canter-
bury Pilgrims.' My companion had heard much
of Professor Stanford's new opera, and had expressed a desire to see it. But I am afraid it did
not come up to her expectations, so that her first
evening out since her illness was on the whole
rather a failure.

Far more successful was our visit to the theatre
in Coventry Street, then called the Princes', upon
the occasion of a professional matinée of 'Called
Back,' which had been running successfully there
for some little time. The principal characters
were enacted by Miss Lingard, Mr. Kyrle Bellew,
Mr. G. W. Anson, and Mr. H. Beerbohm Tree,
and the performance was warmly applauded by an
audience composed for the most part of members

of the theatrical profession.   Many of these came
to pay their respects to their sister in the stalls,
including the Bancrofts, the Kendals, Mrs. Billington, Mr. Henry Neville, and Mr. J. G. Taylor,
and those who were not personally acquainted
with Mrs. Keeley, except by sight and reputation,
asked to be introduced to her, among these being
Mr. and Mrs. George Rignold, Mr. Charles Kelly,
and Mr. Brandon Thomas.   The actress had seen
the last-mentioned gentleman upon the stage and
thought highly of him, and was very pleased to
meet him in private life.   Seated in the stalls next
to us were Miss Violet Cameron and her mother,
whom Mrs. Keeley knew well.

Respecting the performances, Mrs. Keeley spoke
in praise of the adaptation, though disapproving,
as a rule, of dramatized stories, as she thought
that, without reading the original book, it was not
always easy to follow the incidents upon the stage.
She was also enthusiastic about the acting, more
particularly as regards the Maccari of Mr. Tree,
who she considered played and looked the part to
the life.   She also thought the other characters
well represented, and was altogether delighted
with the performance, and applauded everything
worthy of applause.

We also went, about that time, to the Opera
Comique, to see the American actress, Lotta,

in 'The Old Curiosity Shop,' which Mrs. Keeley had already witnessed, and desired to see again on account of Lotta's excellent performance of the Marchioness. The clever impersonator of the Marchioness evidently took it as a great compliment that the original impersonator of Little Nell should come to see her again in the same piece, and she acted mostly to my companion. At the end of the second act, when Lotta was loudly called before the curtain, the actress kissed her hand in our direction in a most unmistakable way, while the lady by my side showed by the expression of her face and her continued plaudits that she was thoroughly pleased.

We went the round of the theatres together at that time, among those we visited being the Lyceum, where Modjeska was then the sole attraction; Her Majesty's Theatre in the Haymarket, where the wonderful Italian ballet of 'Excelsior' was performed; the Princes', where 'The Great Pink Pearl' was in the bills; the Princess's, with 'Hoodman Blind' running there. Mrs. Keeley thought highly of Mr. Wilson Barrett's performance in that piece, as she also did of Mr. James Fernandez and Mr. Coghlan, when we went to see them in 'Enemies' at the Princes'. She was also much struck by Mr. Terriss and Miss Milward's vigorous acting in 'The Harbour

Lights' at the Adelphi; and when one of the authors of that piece, Mr. Henry Pettitt, came up to our box between the acts to pay his respects to the actress, she told him that his drama was one of the best constructed pieces she had ever seen.

Mrs. Keeley had always a good word to say of our deserving players and pieces, and nothing of merit escaped her notice. But no modern actor stood higher in her opinion than the late David James, whom she went to see night after night when he was engaged at the Strand under the Swanborough management. In speaking of him, I remember her saying :

' He was the best Dolly Spanker I have seen since Mr. Keeley played the part. Of course David James did not play it as my husband did ; but he was quite as good in his way. And how good he was in " Our Boys "! Nothing better was ever done on the stage, or has been since.'

She also thought highly of Mr. Harry Nicholls, of Mr. Penley, of Mr. Harry Paulton, of Mr. Weedon Grossmith and other light, or low, comedians who have come to the front within the past few years.

After these and similar experiences with Mrs. Keeley, I was not surprised to hear that managers of theatres and the 'profession' generally always looked forward with delight to her appearance in front of the house. When she was present they could be pretty sure of an appreciative audience, and one, moreover, who by look, gesture, and sometimes by a spoken word, often quite unconsciously led the applause. Mr. Paulton once told me that it was always encouraging to an actor to see the veteran actress in the front, and more still to hear her hearty laugh. When Mrs. Keeley expressed a wish to see 'Olivia'— then being enacted with the greatest success at the Lyceum—a box was at once sent to her, in spite of overcrowded houses, and with it this note from the manager :

'MY DEAR MRS. KEELEY,

'It will be a delight to have you with us to-morrow (June 29, 1887); I only wish you would come oftener. This house is your home, when you care to make it so.

'Ever yours sincerely,

'HY. IRVING.'

'Fancy, how attentive of him!' exclaimed the recipient of this note. 'And what a nice, kind letter, too!'

When Mrs. Keeley wrote to the editor of *Punch* for places to witness his successful burlesque, 'Black-Eyed Susan,' her request elicited the following reply :

' My dear Mrs. Keeley,
    D'ye want to go reely
    To see " Black-Eyed Susin "?
    There is no refusin'
    Your gentle request.
    Box B is the Best,
    This you understand?
    Yours, F. C. BURNAND.'

The actress, though as fond of the theatre as
a child, and ready 'to travel a hundred miles' to
go to one, was always reluctant to ask for an
invitation, in case the request might be difficult
to grant.   But upon the occasion of Mr. Irving's
expected return to England, after his first visit to
America, she wrote to Mr. Hurst, the box book-
keeper, in the following amusingly desperate terms :

' Do you think, by any possibility, you could
secure me a stall for Mr. Irving's return?   I feel
all the time I am writing that my chance is hope-
less ; but, oh! if by any means—holy or unholy,
lawful or unlawful—you can do this for me, I
will for ever pray for you.'

It is needless to say that her offer to pay for
the stall, in accordance with her habit when business at a theatre was too good to justify her in

asking for a free admission, was not entertained by that management.

In speaking once of a pit and gallery melodrama which I had lately witnessed at one of our West End theatres, Mrs. Keeley, who had been twice to see that piece, was quite angry with me for 'spoiling the pleasure' which she took in it by pointing out its weak points.

'I should be sorry,' she said, 'to go with you to see it again. I am like a child at the theatre, and can't bear to have my pleasure spoiled by too much criticism. When I go to see a melodrama I don't expect to see a Shakesperian piece, and when I go to a pantomime I am not prepared to witness a tragedy in blank verse. I dare say you may be right, but I enjoyed the piece and could see it for a third time.'

But Mrs. Keeley was not always as lenient in her views of the modern melodrama; for I remember once going with her to see a spectacular sporting piece, with which she was thoroughly disgusted, and said :

'If it had not been for Mrs. John Wood, whom I adore, I could not have sat out the performance.'

It was, of course, to be expected that a lady who was once the very best female low-comedian upon the stage should have a keen sense of the ridiculous and a love of genuine humour, and Mrs.

19

Keeley's laugh was one of the heartiest and most
infectious ever heard in a playhouse. In the
same manner anything pathetic touched her
deeply, and often brought tears to her eyes.
There was, however, one drawback to the actress's complete enjoyment of any entertainment,
whether at the play, at a theatre of varieties, or
at a circus, and that was her extreme nervousness
at any performance attended with danger, or risk
of life and limb to the performer.

Once, when Mrs. Keeley was taking a holiday
at Goring, near Worthing, I recollect receiving a
letter from the daring ex-highwayman, in which
she said : ' I have just returned from (to me) a
most interesting and exciting amusement—horses
leaping over hurdles and water-jumps ! I dare
say it was all vastly entertaining ; but I carefully
shut my eyes when the creatures jumped, so you
may imagine my enjoyment.'

The same nervousness also showed itself in
driving to and from a place of amusement. As a
general rule, Mrs. Keeley would go only in a
conveyance that was driven by a careful Jehu,
named Brown, whom she usually employed. But
when her ' faithful,' as she called him, was not
available, her terrors on the road were not inconsiderable, for she was in constant fear lest the
vehicle should run over someone in the narrow

and crowded thoroughfares, or that another chariot
should run into hers.

Mrs. Keeley's nervousness and sense of fun
were never better exemplified than when she
went one evening to Astley's, in the early days of
Sanger's Circus, accompanied by Miss Ada Swanborough and Arthur Sketchley, the celebrated
author of 'Mrs. Brown.' She loved domestic
animals of all kinds, and when convinced that no
cruelty or unfair means had been used in training
the performing ones, she delighted in their clever
tricks and laughed heartily at their comic antics.
She also appreciated juggling, conjuring, and
similar performances of dexterity without danger ;
but she drew the line at acrobatic feats of skill. So,
when at Sanger's a strong man stood with a long
pole on his waist in readiness for another man to
climb it and balance himself, head downwards,
on the top, the lady covered her face with both
hands, and cried out :

'No, no! I can't look at that. Tell me when
it's over, Ada.'

The vaulting over bars and horses' backs was
not less terrible to behold, and Miss Swanborough,
to whom I was indebted for this account of Mrs.
Keeley at a circus, informed me that when an
'indiarubber man' doubled himself up backwards
to pick up from the ground a handkerchief with

his mouth, her horrified companion closed her
eyes tightly, and felt faint with affright. It was
quite a relief, she said, for all parties when, the
first part being over, the manager of the show
came up to pay his respects to his illustrious
visitor. He was a rather illiterate man, and occasionally misplaced his *h*'s ; so, when in an elabor-
ately polite manner he said : '' Ighly gratified to
be *h*onoured by the presence of so distinguished
a person as Mrs. Keeley,' the distinguished person
nearly had a fit, not of fright this time, but only
of suppressed laughter ; and not knowing exactly
what to say in reply, she hazarded the remark :

' The last time I was here, Mr. Ducrow, who was
then at the head of affairs, invited me to supper.'

But this only made matters worse, for, after an
awkward pause, the present manager said :

' Oh, indeed ! What will you have to drink ?'
which so amused the lady that she gave one of
the squeaks which usually preceded an outburst
of merriment.

Fortunately for all persons concerned, she was
still able to keep her laughter under control, and
turned the conversation by extolling the performances and expressing her complete approval of
them. This was, however, scarcely wise on her
part, for, with his most insinuating smile and a
low bow, the manager said :

'Praise from Sir Isaac Newton!' and this perfectly unconscious misquotation and the manner of its utterance so tickled his hearer, that, after another squeak and a stolen glance at her companions, she fairly exploded.

Arthur Sketchley was greatly amused by these little incidents of real life, and doubtless made a note of them at the time.

The next incident happened after the party left the theatre. All three drove home in a four-wheeled cab, and on the way Mrs. Keeley exhibited rather more nervousness than she usually did when driving in a strange vehicle. Somewhere on the road Mr. Sketchley, who was one of the stoutest and heaviest of men, alighted, and when he was gone and the cab drove on, Mrs. Keeley gave a sigh of relief, and said :

'Thank goodness, he's got out! I was in mortal fear every minute that the axles were going to break. And I gave him two fat chops for lunch to-day!'

An occasion upon which Mrs. Keeley felt something like at home in a cab was when she accompanied me to the Adelphi to see the 'Bells of Hazlemere.' This happened on a Friday, and on the following Wednesday the actress was to appear at the Haymarket to speak an address upon the occasion of a complimentary benefit to her old

friend and colleague, Mrs. Leigh Murray (a sister
of Mrs. Edward Swanborough). While driving
to the theatre, by way of Brompton and the Park,
my companion rehearsed the lines with suitable
gestures, which must have astonished any passers-
by who happened to see and hear her. The verses
were by Mr. J. Ashby-Sterry, and began :

'Which is the way ? My good man, where am
I ? Where's my stall ?'

The actress is supposed to have come by mistake
to the stage, and the first line is spoken 'off.' But
for the moment this dramatic outburst in the four-
wheeler rather perplexed me, and my name having
been distinctly pronounced, I was on the point of
answering the query by informing her that it was
a private box and not a stall, when she went on :

'A thousand thanks to all my good old friends,
A greeting such as this doth make amends !

'For if I have been somewhat put about,
Your kindly welcome compensates, no doubt :
I thought this afternoon I'd see your play,
I found the playhouse—but I lost my way !
By some mischance, by some untoward means,
I missed my stall and got behind the scenes !
Then smitten with the spirit of the age,
I felt compelled to go upon the stage.

'And here I am ! And yet it would appear
That clearly I can have no business here ;
No business, p'raps, but pleasure without end,
If coming here can serve a good old friend !

' I don't feel shy—for, thinking matters o'er,
    I fancy I've been on the stage before ;
    Why, yes ! Of course I have ! Let me reflect !
    As if 'twere yesterday I recollect
    The old Adelphi actors and old plays,
    That may be half-forgotten nowadays ;
    " Nicholas Nickleby " was then the rage,
    And I, as *Smike*, then trod Adelphi's stage ;
    Our *Noggs*—O. Smith, our *Mantalini*—Yates,
    And our dear friend, the bonniest of Kates !
    Though many of that band have passed away,
    Smike's here to plead the cause of *Kate* to-day !

' A long dramatic life our friend has seen,
    For she in Shakespeare played with Edmund Kean ;
    Played with Macready and with Robson, too,
    Charles Mathews, Webster, and I know not who :
    So many parts she's played that 'tis confest,
    She's tired of play and wants a little rest !

' I plead for hands to well assure our Kate
    She's not forgotten yet, nor out of date :
    I feel your pulse ! Its throbbing doth portend
    The public favourite's the public's friend !
    She cheered you in her youth, and, I'll engage,
    You've helped to cheer her in her young old age ;
    To-day she makes her final bow to you,
    Takes " rest with honour," bidding you adieu :
    Our dear old friend will find she's not forgot,
    You won't forget her in " Forget-me-not "! '*

' I went over this address yesterday with Fanny
Stirling,' remarked the reciter, as we got out of
the cab at the theatre door, 'and she was oh! so
pleased.'

                    * The name of one of the pieces.

CHAPTER XXIII.

BENEFIT ADDRESSES.

FROM the earliest period of Mrs. Keeley's professional career till long after her retirement from the stage, she has been famous for her public addresses. More than one example of her powers in this respect has already been given in these pages, including her maiden speech at her native town, in 1824, and the one she delivered at the Lyceum, as manageress. Those which I now propose to present to the reader were delivered since Mrs. Keeley's retirement, and on behalf either of a friend's benefit or for the benefit of some charity.

The first address on my list was delivered at the opening of the Lyceum on January 22, 1870, under the management of the brothers Mansell. The theatre had been redecorated, and there were produced for the first time Frank Marshall's comedy drama, 'Corrupt Practices,' and, for the first time in England, Hervé's opera-bouffe

'Chilperic.' Between the new comedy and the opera Mrs. Keeley was announced to appear, and the audience were on the tiptoe of expectation to see her. When she came on the stage she was greeted with the utmost enthusiasm, while a storm of applause followed her admirable recitation of these verses from the pen of John Oxenford.

'When some of us were young—and as you know
  That could not be so very long ago—
Folks talked of press-gangs ; men, we heard, were press'd
Against their will, to fight, and do their best,
  On the broad ocean, for their country's sake ;
  In vain were all objections they might make.

'"Thank Heaven ! Those horrid press-gangs are gone by,
  Says some kind soul. "Nay, not so fast !" say I.
Were there no press-gangs left, it is most clear—
Saving your presence—I should not be here !
There sat I by the cosy winter's hearth,
Watching the coals that gave fantastic birth
To dear old faces, till I seemed to gaze
Upon the dear old Drama's palmy days ;
But as for treading these hard boards—why, bless me,
No thought of that kind ever could possess me.

'No ; someone called on me—no matter who,
And said 'twould be the proper thing to do,
If to this old familiar house I came,
A house where I am known—at least by name.
Thus was I pressed, but still I gravely doubt
Whether 'twas all a pressure from without ;
Whether some voice within me did not speak,
And bid me this same old Lyceum seek—

And with a smile, temper'd, perchance, with tears,
Lost 'midst the monuments of bygone years—
Where wits, who since have earned a high renown,
First lisp'd in infant accents to the town.

‘ But of the past enough.   'Twill be more pleasant,
Doubtless, to drop a word about the present.
My young successors beg me to explain
'Tis not their notion to revive again
The British Drama in the common sense ;
To be reformers they make no pretence.
Admitting that the age is most dramatic,
They still will venture to be operatic ;
And, what is marvellous, they do not blench
To own their play is taken from the French.
For, though there's nothing novel in the loan,
'Tis rare the debt of gratitude to own.
Not only a French opera they do,
But bring before you the composer too ;
And hope to win your plaudits when they serve ye
With a rich dish flavour'd with sauce by Hervé.’

The next address was delivered in March of the
same year, at a morning performance given at the
Queen's Theatre, in Long Acre, for the benefit of
the Royal General Theatrical Fund.   In the
course of the programme Mrs. Keeley, in her
admirable manner, recited the following address,
written by Mr. Tom Taylor :

‘ Ladies and Gentlemen,—I wish to know
If my part was not played long, long ago ?
But, if old birds may e'er hop off their shelves,
'Tis to ask help for those who help themselves.

They say the Drama's dead, the critics do,
And what the critics tell us must be true.
But the more dead the Drama, it would seem
With more new theatres her ashes teem.
The cry is still they come, six at a go born—
East, West, North, South, the New Queen's and Holborn,
The Globe, the Gaiety, Montagu's, Charing Cross,
All entered for the race of gain—or loss.
But, though new theatres be so the rage
That all the Strand, like all the world's, a stage,
Not less the critics' sentence hath been said
That dooms the British Drama dead, dead, dead.
Blackedge your acting edition, Mr. Lacey ;
Write large on stage-doors, " Requiescat in pace ;"
Or epitaph of cheerfuller complexion,
" Hic jacet," in the hope of resurrection.
But if dead Drama take up all this room,
Must living Drama vainly seek a home ?
As her old " maid-of-all-work " I say " No."
Call for her, and, like Topsy, spec's she'll grow.
But one thing's clear, be Drama quick or dead,
The actors are alive, and must be fed ;
And from the summer harvest store away
'Gainst Age's winter and Fate's rainy day.
For this, our bantling Fund, stout, if 'tis small,
Opens its plucky little arms to all ;
Says, " Give your mite—that mite we'll save for you,"
And add what friendly hands may put thereto.
As "many little's into mickle creep,"
Pile mites enough, they'll make a mighty heap,
Till in our bankers' book at length we grow
To four fat figures, in imposing show.
Thalia's eyes in time will lose their twinkle,
Melpomene be put up to a wrinkle.
See the town's favours ebbing tide forsake her ;
All must grow old, even to " Betsy Baker."

Then comes life's quiet eventime.   How blest
If, soothed by comfort, it lead on to rest !
To crown that comfort, and the rest to cheer,
We on these boards, you on those seats, are here.
For that a moment I resume my art ;
No !   These aren't acted thanks ; they're from the heart.'

At the benefit to Benjamin Webster, at Drury
Lane, on March 2, 1874, Mrs. Keeley delivered
an address by the late John Oxenford, to the
following effect :

' Old friend, in numbers we are met to day,
Gladly our homage, where 'tis due, to pay ;
Here plainly writ in many a well-known face,
The record of an early time you'll trace,
Some who, with you, commenced a life's career,
Now, towards their journey's end, salute you here.
Others, more youthful, in your presence stand,
Led to success by that kind, fostering hand—
For Webster's work fills many a brilliant page
In the strange history of the modern stage.
Strange history !   When you began your reign
In Foote's old house, and bade it thrive again,
Artist yourself, inviting to take part
In your great task all who could further Art,
King of "Strong companies" (one small play then
Comprised the talent now spread over ten),
You stood on ancient laws and ruled a home
Where lived a drama, then untaught to roam.
Beneath your sway the Haymarket remained
As Foote designed it, and new glory gained.
Those were the days when Knowles and Bulwer came
To you, and thus acquired increase of fame.

When Wildrake to his love the chase resigned
And Mr. Graves for lost Maria pined.
We hail you, patron of "legitimates"
Yet will not overlook the house of Yates ;
The work commenced by him you took in hand,
Our Porte St. Martin's shines upon the Strand.
There melodrame has flourished through your aid,
There grew "Green Bushes," never doomed to fade ;
There did you clearly make it understood,
The word Adelphi points to brotherhood.
Authors and actors, whether grave or gay,
Heavy or light, revered your double sway.
Chief of the great and ruler of the small,
I ne'er should end tried I to name them all.
Now times are chang'd ; with every coming year
New theatres on some new ground appear ;
Wherever we may turn we're sure to meet
The Muses lodged in some unheard-of street.
Patents are gone—whether for good or ill,
We'll not discuss—one feeling binds us still.
Though to the North, South, East or West we go,
The name of Webster is our friend we know—
The drama's pillar in a wav'ring age,
The pride and honour of the British stage.'

After the address, which was most rapturously
applauded, a rather amusing incident occurred,
thus described by Mr. John Coleman, who witnessed it :

'When the curtain drew up the stage was
crowded with every lady and gentleman of rank
in the profession. Webster led Mrs. Keeley
forward. Now, the great point of her speech
was that at the end of it she had to turn round

and embrace the *bénéficiaire*. When Webster
stepped back he was surrounded by a mob of
ladies. It was a moment of effusion ; who began
it I don't know. But, alas ! the wind was taken
out of poor Mrs. Keeley's sails, and her great
point utterly destroyed ; for, lo ! the beloved
Master Ben was kissing and being kissed *coram
populo* by all the ladies right and left of him.
Strange to say, there appeared nothing incon-
gruous or improper in the business. I am sure
many ladies who were amongst the audience
would have been glad to give the dear old boy a
parting salute, and the younger men only envied
the gay young dog. Upon this osculatory tableau
the curtain fell.'

At Mrs. Swanborough's benefit at the Haymarket, on Thursday, June 19, 1879, to which
reference has been already made, nearly every
leading member of the profession was present,
and the programme consisted of single acts from
' Madame Favart,' ' Les Cloches de Corneville,'
' The Ladies' Battle,' ' The Girls,' and ' The New
Babylon,' together with songs and recitations by
Mr. Edward Terry, who gave ' My Art, my
Hangelina ;' Miss Lydia Thompson, who sang
her new song from the burlesque of ' The Lady
of Lyons,' called, ' I've been Photographed like
this ;' Mr. T. Swinburne, who recited ' The

Charge of the Light Brigade ;' Miss Genevieve
Ward, who, assisted by Mrs. Vere, recited
Buchanan's ' Nell ' ; and Mr. Lionel Brough, who
sang 'The Muddle Puddle Junction Porter.' Then
Mrs. Swanborough held a reception on the stage,
and Mrs. Keeley spoke the following verses by
H. J. Byron :

'Some years ago—the number never mind—
To my tuition was one day consigned
A slim and graceful girl, who soon became
An apt aspirant for artistic fame.
So, on Haymarket boards, with beating heart,
" Miss Swanborough " appeared in her " first part."
Her figure my mind's vision passes by
(For still I have my " pupil " in my eye) ;
And her warm welcome of resounding cheers
Rings at its recollection in my ears.
Soon upon management's tumultuous sea
She launched with something like audacity ;
She took the " Strand," and no less is it true,
At the same time she took the public, too.
And when she left the stage, she also left
One in her place as skilful and as deft
In pleasing that same public and her friends ;
To her is due the fortune which attends
Her stage, which perhaps is limited for show
(Her company's un-limited, we know),
Though she beside her, in her task for years,
Has had another daughter, who appears
To have fulfilled the duties to the letter—
Forgive the pun—of Ada and abettor.
The well-known saying is the tritest thing,
That "great events from little causes spring ;"

'Tis no less true that from a tiny building,
Boasting not much of ornament or gilding,
When 'neath its present guidance it was young,
Great actors and great actresses have sprung.
Those who may gaze upon the "passing show,"
With the experience of a year or so,
Can little realize the fact profound,
As of the theatres they "go the round,"
How wide and varied is the Thespian band
Who first grew famous at the " Little Strand."
'Twas there so many did at first evince
Gifts which have grown—expanded—ripened—since ;
'Twas there so many of our best comedians'
Efforts—I don't think I can add "tragedians,"
Ladies and gentlemen—"low comic "—" high,"
" Eccentric," " musical," " effusive," " dry."
All styles—your welcome plaudits gave a zest,
And spurred all on to try to do their best,
The writer of these lines among the rest,
To add an extra pleasure to the town,
At which the veriest purist scarce could frown ;
To give an entertainment in which mirth,
At frequent intervals, of English birth,
Or, if of French, has with no double sense
Or double meaning, caused the least offence.
For one and-twenty years to never cease,
What with a Christmas or an Easter piece,
Or autumn novelty, with many a play,
By all the merriest writers of the day,
To while our evenings pleasantly away,
Has been this lady's aim ; the day's work done,
To offer a few hours of simple fun,
Wholesome and genial, which, upon the morrow,
May serve to leaven something of the sorrow,
The care, the anxious toiling and the strife
That go to form the sum of daily life.

That is her object ; fearlessly I ask
If to do this is not a worthy task ?
And if to one who's kept this aim in view
The public's thanks are not most justly due ?'

The recitation over, Mrs. Swanborough was led across the stage by Mr. Byron, accompanied by Mrs. Keeley, amidst the greatest possible enthusiasm.

CHAPTER XXIV.

CHARITY ADDRESSES.

MRS. KEELEY was ever ready to lend a helping hand to those in need of her assistance. An exception to this rule was, however, made when early in 1890 she was asked to preside at a ladies' dinner, to be given to her old friend 'Johnny' Toole. At any rate, this statement appeared at the time in print, but when the lady herself was personally approached in reference to it she smiled and said :

'No ; it is a huge joke, and there is not, as far as I know, a word of truth about it. I suggested it jestingly the other night, and proposed that I should head the ladies as the mother of the Gracchi, but I would not for the world have a ladies' dinner, for the simple reason that it would be so deadly, deadly dull ! Not that I would not do almost anything for Mr. Toole, whom I consider one of the most admirable among the

present-day actors. The good he has done in
the profession and out of it only a few persons
know, and those who do, know it only im-
perfectly. He is a fine actor and a fine man,
but I don't think a dinner of ladies would be
the best way of showing him our admiration.
And for me to preside over this " dream of fair
women "—no, thank you !'

I think that the first charity recitation was given
when Mrs. Keeley took part in an epilogue with
Mrs. Stirling at a performance at the Criterion
for the benefit of the National Aid Society,
on March 25, 1885. As I was among those
fortunate enough to get places in the densely-
crowded three shilling pit, I can testify to the
great success of the matinée, and to the enthusiastic reception of the veteran actresses, who
were never seen and heard to better advantage.

The performances began with Mr. C. S. Chelt-
nam's comedy, ' A Lesson in Love,' in which Sir
Charles Young, Mr. Charles Wyndham, Mr.
Blakeley, Lady Monckton, Mrs. Phelps and
Miss Wyndham took part. When this was over
Mrs. Keeley stepped lightly upon the stage and
was greeted with a perfect storm of applause, in
which the Prince of Wales, who was present,
cordially joined. Then, in her clearest accents
and with her old dramatic power, she began the

following epilogue, expressly written for the occasion by Mr. Clement Scott :

> 'Is this a stage ?   Before me there is cast
> A happy vision of my bygone past !
> I've wandered back, as in a dream, to trace
> Some old-world echo in each happy face.
> It is a stage !   I feel it, for your cheers
> Lighten the burden of my lengthening years.
> Why am I here alone in this dear land ?—
> Where I had hoped once more to grasp the hand ;
> To hear the voice, and meet the laughing eye,
> Of some companion of the days gone by. ·
> Someone to lead me, with your sweet assent,
> Back to the meadows of our merriment,
> Where we had played—until my friend and I,
> At life's cross road, we kissed and said good-bye.'

Here a knock was heard, and Mrs. Stirling's
well-known voice was heard to ask, ' May I come
in ?' Mrs. Keeley continued :

> 'Who's there ?   A friend for choice.
> I vow I thought 'twas Fanny Stirling's voice !'

On her opening the door another burst of
applause greeted the entry of Mrs. Stirling.   It
was some moments before the plaudits subsided,
and then Mrs. Stirling began :

> ' Dear friend ! come, dry your eyes,
> I've just looked in to give you a surprise ;
> Since no one hears us, and we're quite alone,
> I want with you to pick a little bone.

Fanny Stirling.

Mrs. K. : With me!

Mrs. S. : With you, most certainly.
Your conscience, dear, now search!
You've left me in the lurch—
You come at night, familiar plays to see,
And leave th' old ladies of the stage to me.
Why in the stalls should Mary Keeley shirk,
Whilst Fanny Stirling has to do the work?
It isn't fair.

Mrs. K. : To lose you would be worse;
Why, where would Juliet be without her nurse?
Stay where you are and charm this modern town,
Link past and present! Come and sit you down,
As in the green-room in dear Drury days,
Discussing actors; in what different plays!

Mrs. S. : Macready! What an actor; could one find
More force or pathos in a mellow mind?
How he could melt to tears, the heart's blood freeze!

Mrs. K.: Stop! you're the actress. I'm the critic, please.

Mrs. S. : No better Jaques lived in such a play.

Mrs. K.: They're playing "As you Like It," dear, to-
day.

Mrs. S. : (Musing) Elton and Mrs. Nisbett! (Suddenly)
Mrs. Keeley.

Mrs. K.: Celia!

Mrs. S. : And Audrey. Ah, we acted freely
In those old days! But we shall never stop!

Mrs. S. : Dear Betsy Baker!

Mrs. K. : Mrs. Malaprop!
But best of bygone plays for me and you,
'Twas Congreve's "Love for Love." I was Miss Prue.

Mrs. S.: Ah! "Love for Love." That title sweet and
kind
Starts an idea to my active mind.
'Midst din of battle and of war's attack,
One common cause leads two old ladies back—

Back to the stage, where they have spent their lives,
To aid our soldiers and our soldiers' wives.
'Tis Love for Love that women, young and old,
Feel in the battle for the soldier bold !

MRS. K. : 'Tis Love for Love when dear ones far away,
Suffer in silence, and we kneel to pray !

MRS. S. : 'Tis love the noblest that in dire distress
Leaps to the heart of peasant and Princess !

MRS. K. : 'Tis love for sick, and wounded, and betrayed,
That wakens women to our National Aid !

MRS. S. (to audience) : Let us not ask in vain. Give what
you can.
No woman pleaded vainly to brave man.
Mothers and maidens, give a helping hand,
Think of the boys who fight for motherland.
Fathers and brothers ! timely help to-day
May save brave lives in deserts far away.

MRS. K. : All hearts are full when love and duty call,
A soldier's cause we've pleaded.

MRS. S. : That's not all.
We still await when we have played our parts,
A loving echo from your honest hearts ;
Do say we've tried, and have not tried in vain,
To soothe the pillow of brave men in pain.

MRS. K. : A woman's mission ! Woman-like appears,
A Princess President !

BOTH :   Give her your cheers.

MRS. S. : Now, one cheer more ! Right royally I mean.
Prince and Princess God bless ! God save the Queen !'

The conclusion of the epilogue was greeted with
bursts of applause, and then the two actresses retired to the back of the stage.

The object of the National Aid Society was to
collect funds for the provision of comforts for the

British troops in the Soudan, especially the sick and wounded.

At the concert preceding a doll show, given at Great Ormond Street, on November 9, 1888, for the benefit of the Hospital for Sick Children, in which Mrs. Keeley took a deep interest as in every other charity of the kind, she recited these verses from the ever graceful pen of Mr. J. Ashby-Sterry :

' You asked me here to come and see your Show—
I thought I'd done with Dolls some years ago !
I've given up the dolls of childhood's age,
And said good-bye to puppets of the stage.

' I've done with skipping-ropes, and hoops, and toys,
With all the simple sport of girls and boys :
And as for hoops !   I scarcely one have seen
Since those extensive days of crinoline !
Some toys remain !   But disillusion comes
With sawdust stuffing and with broken drums !

' And yet I count my warmest friends among
The bright, the merry, and the laughing young.
The children's laughter does me good ; and I
Have made their grannies laugh in days gone by
Their grandchildren repay me with their glee,
And make me feel Eighteen at Eighty-three.
So here I stand, the Children's Advocate,
To plead their cause in Eighteen Eighty-eight !

' We talk of children's happiness ; but who
Can picture half the sorrow they go through ?

Pain's hard for *us* to bear—'tis doubly so
For those poor tiny mites, who do not know
Why they should suffer, as they listless lie,
To dream and ponder of the reason why.
And so I thought just now.   I chanced to stray
Within a Ward not very far away :
A well-warmed, homish room—so clean and light,
So cheerful, quiet, flower-deckt, and bright.

'In one snug corner, in a cot, I note,
Propped up by pillows—in a scarlet coat—
A little girl, who ne'er for many a day
Has had a hope, or thought, or strength for play ;
Though pain now slumbers, she is ill and weak—
Too feeble e'en to move, or laugh, or speak :
A pair of little wasted hands still keep
In close embrace a well-worn woolly sheep.
A sweet, sad smile half flickers o'er her face,
And in those big gray eyes you'll clearly trace
The sorrow that this little one has seen—
The weariness her little life has been !
Those eyes could better plead, in silent grief,
Than *I*, who for our Children hold a brief !

'I plead for them, I beg you each to bring
A tiny feather for our big New Wing ;
Let each one use his thought, his means, his might,
To aid us in our new successful flight !

'I crave for them your sympathy untold,
Your love, your help, your pity—and your gold !
The last I'm bound to have, for, you must know,
I played " Jack Sheppard " many years ago !

'I've not forgot his impudence, his dash —
His rare persuasive power when seeking cash !
Stand and deliver—sovereigns, fifties, fives—
We want *your* money, for we want *their* lives !'

This admirable address was delivered again at the farewell supper given to Mr. Toole before his departure for Australia. Mr. Henry Irving, Miss Ellen Terry, and many other personal friends of the comedian were present, and after Mrs. Keeley's recitation, which brought tears to the eyes of not a few of the company, a collection was made on behalf of the Children's Hospital.

In connection with these verses and the occasion of their delivery, it may not be uninteresting to reprint here a characteristic letter which Mrs. Keeley wrote some three or four years ago to the editor of a popular magazine in response to a request on his part for an account of the favourite dolls of her childhood. This strange application rather puzzled the actress at the time, as she found it difficult to understand why she, above all persons, should be called upon to describe things which, with one solitary exception, she never possessed. However, with her usual good nature, she replied to the editor in the following strain :

'To quote Ashby-Sterry :

> ' " I thought I'd done with dolls some years ago ;
> I've put away the dolls of childhood's age,
> I've bid good-bye to puppets of the stage."

And yet you ask me in my eighty-seventh year to remember the dolls of my childhood. Well, I'll try, but fear the description will be very uninteresting. I never had but one doll, a great heavy wooden doll : no stuffing, no nice soft leather arms and legs. No; its limbs were strongly wedged and pegged into its body—it was so big and heavy, I could scarcely drag it about (I was four years old only); its name was "Lummox." It was a nuisance to everybody in the house, and one unlucky day I let it fall upon my mother's foot, and in her pain and anger she put it on the kitchen fire, and there was an end of "Lummox." As near as I can remember, the enclosed is a faithful portrait.

'MARY ANNE KEELEY.'

For some reason, best known to the editor of the magazine from which this letter is 'borrowed,' the 'faithful portrait' of the writer's only doll, which she took the trouble to sketch from memory, was not reproduced. That it was worth reproduction was to be seen in a replica of it, which Mrs. Keeley was good enough to show me.

On Mrs. Keeley's entering her eighty-sixth year, on November 22, 1890, she received as usual a large number of telegrams, letters, flowers and gifts. There were also many callers during the day, and among them a tiny deputation of seven of the youngest patients of the Hospital for

Sick Children, Great Ormond Street. They had brought the actress a handsome bouquet in recognition of her kindness to them on many occasions, together with an address written by Mr. Ashby-Sterry, which one of the children presented to her :

' Dear Mrs. Keeley, pray, have you the time
This day to list to children's simple rhyme ?
'Mid birthday gifts and birthday odes can you
Bear with your little friends whose words are few ?
Will you forgive the trembling word that trips
From grateful hearts and halts on baby lips !
And kindly think what eloquence can rest
Within the thought that may be unexprest ?

' How oft at eventide, with lowered light,
When tender nurses watch us through the night,
And sweet-toned whispers strive to soothe our pain,
Oft has the tale been told and told again—
How the Good Fairy came two years ago,
And brought her subtle spell within our Show ;
And how she spoke and pleaded till she drew
Bright tears from eyes—bright gold from pockets, too !
She worked such wondrous charms, she made them
    bring
So many feathers for our brave New Wing :
She made it grow—'tis now almost complete—
And feathered such a nest in Ormond Street !

' Two years ! 'Tis half some children's lives—but yet
The Fairy's visit we can ne'er forget !
We wished to take a trip to Fairyland,
To hear her voice again—to kiss her hand :
To thank her for her gracious, gentle arts,
To tell her how she lives within our hearts !

We thought, we planned, we plotted—all in vain :
'Twas far too much for tiny strength and brain,
The project nearly failed—so in this fix
We sought our kindly Matron, dear Miss Hicks :
She, to our troubles, lent a willing ear,
And swiftly, flower-laden, brought us here !

' And now, dear Mrs. Keeley, good old friend,
We'll bring this childlike chatter to an end !
One moment—let us ask you but to take
These simple flowers and wear them for our sake !
A pledge of the good wishes we'd convey,
And all bright blessings on your natal day ;
Though flowers may fade, your little friends keep true,
And ne'er will fade the love they bear for you !
We wish you all good luck, and may you thrive,
As happy always as at Eighty-five !'

CHAPTER XXV.

JANUARY 4, 1870, will be long remembered by every playgoer in connection with one of the most remarkable benefit performances of modern times. Mr. and Mrs. Charles Mathews were on the eve of departure for the Antipodes, there to fulfil a farewell engagement, and a complimentary benefit was organized by their friends at Covent Garden Theatre, which had been lent for the purpose by its manager, Sir Augustus Harris.

Nearly every actor and actress of note willingly gave their services on behalf of their old and valued friends, and among those who took part in the entertainments were several well-tried veterans of the stage, some of whom figured in minor characters, as will be seen by the wonderful cast of 'The Critic,' which formed the *pièce de résistance* of the performances. Chief of these was Mrs. Keeley, who had been prevailed upon for the first time since her retirement from the stage, some nine years before, to reappear at the house so closely associated with her early triumphs as an operatic vocalist.

Here is the cast in full :

Dangle	...	ALFRED WIGAN.
Sneer	...	BARRY SULLIVAN.
Puff	...	CHARLES MATHEWS.
Under Prompter ...	...	CHARLES MATHEWS, JUN.
Lord Burleigh ...	...	J. B. BUCKSTONE.
Governor of Tilbury Fort	...	FRANK MATTHEWS.
Earl of Leicester ...	...	J. CLARKE.
Sir Walter Raleigh ...	...	LIONEL BROUGH.
Sir Christopher Hatton	...	J. H. PAYNE.
Master of the Horse ...	...	J. W. STOYLE.
Beefeater	...	J. L. TOOLE.
Whiskerandos ...	...	WM. COMPTON.
First Sentinel ...	...	F. PAYNE.
Second Sentinel ...	...	HARRY PAYNE.
First Niece	...	MRS. KEELEY.
Second Niece ...	...	MRS. FRANK MATTHEWS.
Tilburina	...	MRS. C. MATHEWS.
Confidante	...	MRS. CHIPPENDALE.
Prompter	...	ARTHUR SKETCHLEY.
Stage Manager ...	...	AUGUSTUS HARRIS.

Each favourite was greeted with a round of applause, and Mrs. Keeley was received with deafening cheers. Though she had undertaken only a small part, the old actress, like a true artist, made the most of her opportunities, throwing as much vigour and spirit into the character as if it were a leading one ; so that it was afterwards said of her that she 'acted with becoming tragic grandeur, to the intense delight of the audience.'

Her next public appearance was early in the following year, when, upon the occasion of the farewell benefit at the Adelphi of her old friend and sometime manager, Madame Celeste, Mrs. Keeley was prevailed upon to play Betsy Baker. Nearly twenty-one years had elapsed since Maddison Morton's farcical gem was first produced at the Princess's, and at that time her husband was the Marmaduke Mouser and Mr. J. Vining the Crummy. It was, therefore, the coming of age of Betsy Baker, and more than three coming of ages of her exponent, Mrs. Keeley, who was then in her sixty-fifth year.

But to a person who aspired to the nineties, sixty-four was, of course, middle age, or what is indefinitely described as one's 'prime'; so it is scarcely surprising to hear that, when just a quarter of a century ago Mrs. Keeley reappeared as Betsy Baker, she never played better in her life, and that she deserved far more praise than she and her spouse were favoured with by the first-nighters of 1850, when one of them said, of the new farce :

'The incidents comprised in the plot afforded full scope for the histrionic capabilities of Mr. and

Mrs. Keeley, who performed the prominent characters in the piece ; and it is scarcely necessary to
observe they availed themselves with their usual
ability of the opportunity to give effect to the
conceptions of the author. Keeley makes the
most of his part, and in the most comic manner
gets through the scenes in which they occur.
Mrs. Keeley was most happy in her performance
of the laundress, and displayed the awkward
attempts of her love - scenes with admirable
humour and facetiousness. The farce was perfectly successful. It was announced for repetition
until further notice. Mr. and Mrs. Keeley had to
make their acknowledgments to the plaudits of
the company upon the falling of the curtain.'

Mrs. Keeley had also to make her acknowledgments at the Celeste benefit twenty-one years
after. The successful farce was announced later
in the same year by the enterprising management
of the Gaiety, who were giving a series of highly-
successful matinées, with some special feature of
attraction in each programme, and Mrs. Keeley
was prevailed upon to repeat Betsy Baker on
Saturday, March 4. In describing the event a
dramatic critic wrote :

' The admirable finish of her style, the thorough
truthfulness of her acting, and the wonderful expression of her features, received once more the

keenest appreciation, whilst no evidence of diminished power was in any respect perceptible. The intense gratification which Mrs. Keeley afforded the audience should be considered a strong reason for an extension of the privilege to those unable on the first occasion to share in the enjoyment of one of those rare histrionic treats long cherished in the memory. Stimulated by the presence of such an accomplished mistress of her art, Mr. J. L. Toole acted Marmaduke Mouser in his best manner, and he was excellently supported by Mr. R. Soutar as Crummy, and Miss Rose Coghlan as Mrs. Mouser.'

Mrs. Keeley did not appear again in public, except to deliver addresses, for eleven years, when, in deference to the wishes of her old and valued friend, 'Johnny' Toole, she was once more persuaded to enact Betsy Baker for his benefit on Saturday, July 1, 1882.

Mr. Toole's programme was an attractive one, beginning with the farce of 'Your Life's in Danger' and 'Good For Nothing,' in which Mrs. Bancroft appeared as Nan. Mrs. Keeley played her original character with the old freshness, vigour, and keen sense of fun; and, as before, the actress received a most cordial greeting, together with many floral tributes. Mr. Toole assumed his old part of Marmaduke

21

Mouser to the Mrs. Mouser of Miss Effie Liston
and the Crummy of Mr. John Billington, and
with Mrs. Keeley on the stage all three performers were inspired to play their very best.
The performances ended with 'The Waterman'
and 'Robert Macaire,' and in the intervals recitations were given by Mrs. Kendal, Mr. Irving,
and Mr. Edward Terry, together with a song by
Mr. Santley.

Perhaps the most important event in the whole
history of the 'retirement' performances, was
when, on March 29, 1891, Mrs. Keeley revisited
her birthplace, Ipswich, after an absence of more
than half a century, to take part in the opening
of a new theatre, called the Lyceum, which had
been recently erected there.

The theatre was built by Mr. Walter Emden,
and the dramatic feature of the opening night was
Mr. Pinero's comedy of 'In Chancery,' played
by Edward Terry and his London company, all
of whom appeared in their original parts. When
this was over, after having been thoroughly enjoyed by a very appreciative audience, Mary
Anne Keeley stepped lightly upon the stage with
all her old ease and grace and, without any indication of lost dramatic force, delivered before the
enthusiastic spectators, composed for the most
part of her townsmen and townswomen, the following verses by Mr. J. Ashby-Sterry :

' (MRS. KEELEY *heard speaking outside.*)

' Thanks, my good man, I ought to know the door,
  I've often been upon the Stage before!

' Enter MRS. KEELEY.

' It's very odd!   It's strange!   Beyond a doubt
  In Ipswich I should know my way about!
  Perchance I've lost my way!   I half suspect
  'Tis not the playhouse that I recollect ;
  Where Garrick first appeared, and where were seen
  Blanchard and Bannister, Incledon and Kean ;
  The house whereat—it seems but yesterday—
  I made my first appearance in a play!
  You've moved your house!   Yes, it looks very nice,
  I've moved a house myself—just once or twice !

' The house *is* changed—more spacious and more smart—
  But *you* are just the same, in energy and heart !
  As, when a girl, I ventured to express
  My grateful feelings in a brief address.

' For, in the Veteran's welcome do I hear
  An echo of your grand-dads' hearty cheer ;
  That thrilled the young recruit and made her glow
  With ardour, Six and Sixty years ago !

' 'Twas June the Nineteenth—Eighteen Twenty-four ;
  Why, bless my heart, that must have been before
  Dear Pickwick to the Great White Horse came down,
  And made things lively in our good old town !
  Or Peter prosed, or Weller went to search
  For Job, and found him near Saint Clement's Church.
  Ere Dickens—my true friend in after-years—
  Had lured your laughter and compelled your tears !

' Then further back—when baby songs were sung—
  When I, and this Good Century, were young,
  The brightest pictures of my childhood's days
  Are Ipswich people, Sparrowe's House, and Plays.

Where childish reminiscences reveal
A dream of Kemble and of Miss O'Neill.

'And now I heartily enjoy to-day
Dear Mr. Terry's most amusing play.
You kindly asked me here ; but goodness knows,
You did not ask me here to come and prose
With recollections of a bygone age—
Though "Reminiscence" is just now the rage.

'I've shaken Henry Irving by the hand
And Edmund Kean's I've clasped, so understand
I feel I hither come with mission vast,
A link between the present and the past !
Full of traditions of the Ancient Rule,
A warm admirer of the Modern School !
I come to wish you, in my brief address,
Most heartily, unqualified success.

'And so, with these two lines my mission ends—
The Veteran says Good-bye to all her friends !
Good-bye—but stop ! Before we close the scene
We'll sing with heart and voice "God save the Queen !" '

In a long account of the proceedings which an
Ipswich journalist wrote at the time, and a copy
of which he has been good enough to send, he
says :

'Only those present can realize the beauty and
the pathos with which the words were coloured
by Mrs. Keeley's rendering of the lines by the
author of the "Boudoir Ballads." To reveal
something of a professional secret, a reporter
who had seen the lines in printed type not five

Mary Anne Keeley
Oct 15" 1893

From a photograph by Walery (the last taken).

To face p. 325.

minutes before brought out his note-book under the momentary impression that Mrs. Keeley was saying something not "in the bond," as it were. It was an involuntary tribute to the marvellous skill in that "art which conceals art" shown by Mrs. Keeley. Her elocution was perfect; her gestures most admirably suited to the words, yet " husbanded in modesty " withal. . . . " You've moved your house !" she said, in a tone of real surprise. And then she moved the house again by throwing a distinct, and rather a proud emphasis, too, upon the clever play on words, " I've moved a house myself—just once or twice," whereat the audience cheered again and again, as was only to be expected.

' In referring to her first appearance, "six-and-sixty years ago," there was an undertone of pathos, not altogether assumed . . . and at last when the "veteran said good-bye to all her friends," and bouquets were showered from the boxes, and little Miss Ghita Colchester went forward to present Mr. Emden's floral tribute, and friends pressed around, why, then the old lady broke down unaffectedly, her playful assumption all gone, and completed her conquest over the hearts and sympathies of every true man and woman in the house. Most people saw the stage through a mist at that moment. . . . Then the audience rose, the players formed a picturesque group on the stage around Mrs. Keeley, and, led by the band, "God save the Queen" was sung literally with "heart and voice," none joining in with more spirit than the venerable lady to whom general homage was paid as the "dear old heroine" of the afternoon.'

The *Daily Telegraph* thus records another gratifying incident which took place four years later, on March 6, 1895 :

'Some time ago Her Majesty, who always shows the greatest interest in the drama and in the actors and actresses who have performed in her presence, inquired after Mrs. Keeley, and was informed that she was well and in her ninetieth year. The Queen expressed a wish to see her, and Colonel Collins, than whom there is nobody more popular with the profession, arranged for Mrs. Keeley to have the honour of being received at Buckingham Palace yesterday afternoon, when she was presented to Her Majesty, to the Empress Frederick, and to Princess Louise. The welcome given to the gifted lady, who so wonderfully preserves her health, intelligence, and vivacity, was most graceful and cordial ; and the Queen was pleased to recall to mind several interesting incidents of the past, and to refer in truly flattering terms to the impression made upon her mind by

the acting in former days of Mr. Keeley. The
Empress Frederick also reminded the aged actress
of performances witnessed many years ago in
which she had interpreted the principal parts.
In Mrs. Keeley's very long life there have been
many memorable incidents. There could never
have been one more memorable, more honourable
to her personally, or more indicative of the perfect
tact and kindness of the Queen, than the interview
accorded to the universally-respected actress by
one who had known her from the early days of
her remarkable career.'

On the memorable day referred to, I happened
to look in at Pelham Crescent to make enquiries
concerning Mrs. Keeley's health, as she had lately
been confined seven weeks to her house with a
severe bronchial attack caused by a chill ; and
pleased indeed, for her sake, was I to hear that
the convalescent had gone for a drive. But I was
surprised as well as pleased when I found that
she had driven to Buckingham Palace, to be presented to the Queen of England.

Remembering that I had not long since been
in correspondence with the Queen's private secretary, Sir Henry Ponsonby, upon the subject of
these memoirs, it occurred to me that this might
have suggested the idea of a personal interview
with Mrs. Keeley. It appeared the more likely

because in one of the letters received from Sir Henry he said :

'The Queen tells me she has plenty of re-collections of Mr. and Mrs. Keeley,' etc.

In my own missive I had enclosed an extract from the chapter relating to the 'command performances' at Windsor nearly fifty years ago, together with a note concerning the representation on December 28, 1848, of the 'Merchant of Venice' in presence of the Queen, the Prince Consort and the Duchess of Kent.

In Mrs. Keeley's interview with the Queen forty-seven years after, reference was made to that performance, and Her Majesty was pleased to recall also the farce of 'Twice Married' which followed, and in which both Mr. and Mrs. Keeley excited the hearty laughter of the Royal audience. The Queen spoke in terms of high praise of Mr. Keeley, saying that she entertained the greatest respect and admiration for him, and the old actress was quite touched by this kind and gracious tribute to her departed husband.

She was also much struck by Her Majesty's simple and perfectly unaffected manner, and while describing her impressions of the interview, she said :

'I was rather nervous before I was shown into the Queen's presence. It was like the first night of a new play ; and I said so to Colonel Collins, or Miss McNeil—I was in such a flutter of excitement that I really don't know who it was I spoke to—but somebody reminded me that upon the first night of a play the performers knew what they were going to say ; to which I replied, " That's the worst of it ; I don't know what I am going to say on this occasion. I wish I did. I don't even know what I ought to do upon entering." So they told me I should have to curtsey to the ground. But " No," I said, " I can't do that ; I am at present suffering tortures with my rheumatic leg, and stooping would be impossible. I will bow as much as you like, but I can do no more." '

No more was, however, necessary, as upon the Queen's hearing privately of Mrs. Keeley's infirmity, she at once consented to her entering as she best could.

' When I did so,' the actress continued, ' nearly all my nervousness disappeared. It was like being in the company of an old friend. The Queen rose and took my hand, and her voice was so soft and sweet, her words so kind and encouraging, that I was placed at my ease directly. And what a charming smile! I could have embraced her there and then. As it was, I could not help saying before leaving, " May I kiss your hand, madam ?" And I did so.'

' I hope I was not too outspoken,' she remarked in answer to an inquiry as to what passed at the interview; ' but the dear lady encouraged me to speak freely, saying, " I dare say Colonel Collins has told you the Princesses have taken part in some amateur acting ?" to which I replied : " I'm sure they act well, madam, for they are so accomplished in every way, madam." And I spoke of Princess Louise's paintings and sculp- ture. Upon my reminding Her Majesty presently of the Royal visit to the Lyceum many years ago, when my husband and I were playing in " To Parents and Guardians," she appeared amused when I said : " I'm afraid, madam, you were rather shocked at my behaviour as Bob Nettles ; for it was reported at the time—I don't know with what truth—that your Majesty had said you would take care the children didn't come to see me in it." '

No one was in the room except the Queen, the Empress Frederick, Colonel Collins and Mrs. Keeley.

After leaving the Queen's presence, Mrs. Keeley was shown into a room where an equerry was in attendance to request that the actress would write her name in Her Majesty's birthday book.

When first Mrs. Keeley heard from a friend that the Queen desired to see her, she treated it as a joke on the friend's part, and in referring to this circumstance, she remarked :

' I thought, perhaps, she was only going to take me for a drive, as usual, in the Park, and made Buckingham Palace an excuse to persuade me to go out. But when next day I got a letter direct from Colonel Collins to say that Her Majesty had appointed Wednesday afternoon at three o'clock to see me, I was never so staggered at anything in all my life! So I sent for my doctor and asked if I might go. He said "Yes"; though I had already made up my mind, saying : " If the Queen commands me, I am bound to obey." So when Colonel Collins called for me at a quarter to three in my friend's carriage, I was ready and went.

'And I shall never forget the Colonel's kindness and attention. From beginning to end he took the greatest care of me and made things easy and pleasant. What I should have done without him I really don't know. He was my guide, philosopher and friend. And I needed a guide, I can tell you, in walking along those never-ending passages of the Palace ; for the Queen's private apartments seemed a mile off from the entrance.

'What did I go in ? Well, I wore my best black silk ; for there was, of course, no time to order a new dress. I also put on a mantle, intending to keep it on in the Queen's presence ; but at the last moment I changed my mind and took it off before going in. I don't think I looked bad on the whole, and as the Empress Frederick and Princess Louise were attired quite plainly and unpretentiously, I experienced no sensation of discomfort in the matter of costume. In fact, I felt as much at home in that respect as I did in all others, and I shall never forget it.'

Nor will Mrs. Keeley forget the Queen's kindness and attention in afterwards sending her an excellent photograph of Her Majesty signed by herself, as a souvenir of an event which to the illustrious giver of the portrait must have been scarcely less interesting than it was to its proud recipient.

The Queen was also graciously pleased to grant her patronage to the complimentary *matinée* at the Lyceum Theatre on November 22, 1895, in celebration of Mrs. Keeley's ninetieth birthday.

POSTSCRIPT.

SINCE penning the last chapter of these memoirs, which, as regards their leading lady, are not yet ended, the writer has received so many additional notes bearing upon his subject that he ventures to place a few of the best at the disposal of the reader.

The first item of interest comes from Mr. G. Manville Fenn, who has been good enough to show me, in his home at Isleworth, a large number of old playbills which once belonged to the late Jonas Levy, who was a great collector of souvenirs of the stage, and a very old playgoer indeed. Most of these bills are neatly bound in huge square volumes, for in the old days a bill of the play was a rather formidable document, measuring in some cases about three-quarters of a yard in length, by nearly two feet in width when open, presenting something of the appearance of a small poster.

Those in Mr. Fenn's possession date as far back as the latter end of last century, and contain printed records of a vast number of performances at leading theatres in town. But the first to interest a Keeley researcher is naturally the one referring to Mrs. Keeley's *début* upon the stage. This is dated July 2, 1825, and contains the full cast of the two pieces in which she made her first bow before a London public. Her proper maiden name is also printed, so that this affords sufficient evidence against the statement of a modern writer that Miss Goward originally appeared under the *nom de théâtre* of Miss Gray, and that it was not till the 'Shepherd Boy' was produced in the following September that the name of Miss Goward was published. Miss Goward's name is found in every bill on and after July 2, so that Miss Gray was probably one of many pupils that Miss Kelly had at the time.

The musical farce, in which Miss Goward acted Little Pickle, is printed 'The Spoil'd Child,' and I find that it was founded upon a Spanish comedy, written as a satire on the hoydenish pranks of Princess Charlotte of Spain.

In a bill dated July 24, 1827, is announced the first night of 'The Sergeant's Wife,' with Miss Kelly, Miss Goward, Mr. Keeley, O. Smith, and Bartley in the leading parts. 'In Act I. will be introduced a new quadrille; after which the comick operetta "Lying made Easy." To conclude with "The Cornish Miners." Music by Rodwell. Bobby Redruth, Mr. Keeley, Anne Oswald, Miss Goward.'

The next programme of interest is dated
June 27, 1829, and refers to the opening for the
summer season of the 'Theatre Royal English
Opera House,' with the 'comick' opera 'Tit for
Tat; or the Tables Turned,' altered and adapted
from 'Cosi Fan Tutte.' At the end 'God save
the King' was played, and after that 'The Middle
Temple' was enacted, with Mr. Keeley as Brutus
Hairbrain, and Mrs. Keeley ('late Miss Goward')
as Penelope. The Keeleys had been married
only on the previous day, so that their honeymoon must have been passed mostly upon the
stage, for in addition to the evening performances
there were rehearsals every morning, and often
all day long.

Beethoven's overture to 'Prometheus' and
Mozart's overture to 'Figaro' were played on
this occasion, and the performances concluded
with a new operetta, 'The Quartette; or, Interrupted Harmony,' in which Mrs. Keeley enacted
Justine, a *femme de chambre*. The stage-manager
was Mr. Bartley; the 'Director of the Melo-
dramatick department' was O. Smith, and it is
interesting to note the prices of admission, which
were: Boxes, 5s.; second price, 3s. Pit, 3s.;
second price, 1s. 6d. Lower gallery, 2s.; second
price, 1s. Upper gallery, 1s.; second price, 6d.
There were also 'Private and Family boxes.'
The doors opened at 6.30, and the performances
began at 7; and in those days it was found

necessary to announce, 'No money returned.' In those days, also, a bill of the play cost the public one penny, and contained no trade advertisements to cover the expense of printing, etc.

The bills of 'Jack Sheppard' and 'Nicholas Nickleby' were to be found in the volumes relating to the Adelphi doings of 1838-39, while among printed records of Drury Lane, the first to attract notice is one relating to the opening of that theatre on Monday, December 29, 1841, under Macready's management, when 'The Merchant of Venice' was revived with a cast which included Macready, Anderson, Phelps and Compton. The Portia was then Mrs. Warner, and the Nerissa Mrs. Keeley. Miss Poole and Miss Gould—two famous vocalists of the day— were specially engaged as 'minstrels to Portia,' so that the piece and its cast apparently required strengthening by the introduction of a little music.

But 'The Merchant of Venice' was perhaps regarded by that fastidious audience as a kind of curtain-raiser to play the people in, as we find, upon reference to the programme, that the great attraction of the evening was a new Christmas pantomime, called 'Harlequin and Duke Humphrey's Dinner; or, Jack Cade and the Lord of London Stone.'

Here is a copy of the bill for the only benefit which the Keeleys took in town, and to which brief reference has been made :

THEATRE ROYAL, DRURY LANE.

LAST WEEK OF PRESENT SEASON.

BENEFIT OF MR. AND MRS. KEELEY,

THURSDAY, MAY 19, 1842.

HER MAJESTY'S SERVANTS WILL PERFORM THE COMEDY OF THE

PROVOKED HUSBAND.

Lord Townley ...	...	...	MR. MACREADY.
Manly	...	...	MR. PHELPS.
Sir Francis Wronghead	...	...	MR. COMPTON.
Squire Richard	...	...	MR. KEELEY.
Lady Townley	...	...	MISS HELEN FAUCIT.
Lady Grace ...	...	...	MRS. STIRLING.
Miss Jenny ...	...	...	MRS. KEELEY.

AFTER WHICH (NEVER ACTED), A NEW FARCE, CALLED

AN ATTIC STORY.

Gabriel Poddy ... MR. KEELEY.   Mrs. Poddy ... MRS. KEELEY.

TO CONCLUDE WITH THE OPERA OF

ACIS AND GALATEA.

ADAPTED AND ARRANGED FOR REPRESENTATION FROM THE
SERENATA OF HANDEL. POETRY BY GAY.

In aid of the endeavour to establish upon the English stage
the works of the greatest composers of the English School,
the pencil of

MR. STANFIELD, R.A.,

has been engaged to furnish the scenic illustrations.

22

From another quarter comes a thick volume of
prompt copies of several favourite pieces in which
the Keeleys took leading parts. A few of the
plays once belonged to Miss Louise Keeley, and
her name is inscribed upon them. Among these
are 'Still Waters run Deep,' in which she enacted
Mrs. Mildmay; Mr. Burnand's farce, 'In for a
Holiday,' 'The Loan of a Lover,' 'Sweethearts
and Wives,' 'Our Wife; or, The Rose of Amiens,'
John Courtney's 'Time tries All,' and a one-act
comedietta by Montagu Williams, called 'A Fair
Exchange,' which was produced at the Olympic
under the Robson-Emden management in 1860,
and in which Miss Louise Keeley was cast for
Mabel Gray.

Douglas Jerrold's 'Prisoner of War,' with a
large number of its pages and lines cut down,
also figures in the book, as does also the same
author's famous nautical drama, 'Black-eyed Susan;
or, All in the Downs,' originally produced at the
Surrey in 1829. This is also cut unmercifully in
some parts, while on page 23 there is a marginal
note in pencil to tell the reader to 'go on to
page 26.' Not a few of the plays are cut and
scribbled over in this fashion, and one of them—a
one-act burlesque called 'The Sphinx, a "Touch
from the Ancients,"' by the Brothers Brough,
written expressly for the Keeleys, has inscribed
upon its fly-leaf in pen and ink, 'To Robert
Keeley, Esq., to whose exertions this little

piece is so largely indebted for its success, and
whose personification of the "hero" has been so
completely all that they could desire. With the
most grateful thanks of the Authors.' In this
little extravaganza Keeley was the Sphinx, and
his wife Mercury; while Miss P. Horton enacted
Œdipus. Another piece of the kind, by the same
authors, 'Camaralzaman and Badoura,' is similarly
inscribed.

The same volume contains Mrs. Keeley's
marked copies of 'Our Clerks' and 'Betsy
Baker,' together with a cleaner copy of Planché's
delightful fairy extravaganza 'The Invisible
Prince'; Stirling Coyne's spectacular piece 'Sata-
nas and the Spirit of Beauty,' in which Mrs.
Keeley was the Jannetta, with a song, 'A Maiden
I am'; and H. J. Byron's 'Jack the Giant-killer;
or, Harlequin King Arthur,' which he wrote expressly for Louise Keeley, who was the Jack, and
which was produced at the Princess's in 1859
under the direction of Sir Augustus Harris's
father, who was then manager of the theatre in
Oxford Street.

A friend gives the following sketch of an old
burlesque extravaganza:

'The production of "The Alhambra; or, The
Three Beautiful Princesses" was one of the
brightest events in the history of the Kean-
Keeley management. It was written by Albert
Smith, and was at least as clever as anything of

the kind ever composed by his contemporaries, Frank Talfourd, Planché and the brothers Brough. It was splendidly cast. The three Princesses Zayda, Zorayda and Zorahayda were played by Miss Murray (afterwards Mrs. Brandram), a fine, stately woman, Miss Carlotta Leclercq and Miss Mary Keeley. The three knights, their lovers— Sir Desperado the Dauntless, Sir Rupert the Ready, and Sir Toby the Timorous—were represented by Alfred Wigan, Mrs. Keeley and Mr. Keeley. Harley was a renegade chamberlain, and Agnes Robertson (afterwards Mrs. Dion Boucicault) a bewitching little waiting-maid, his sweetheart ; Wynn (a brother of Mr. G. A. Sala) was the Moorish king, and Flexmore a wonderful monkey named Al Djaco.

' There was a prologue in which Mrs. Keeley was played " By a Lady (not by any means her first appearance in that character)," and she came on in ordinary walking attire in a scene representing Brompton Square—where the Keeleys lived—by moonlight. Mrs. Keeley's business was to arrange for the production of a new burlesque, and while considering what the subject shall be she summons to her aid Asmodeus (Flexmore), who undertakes to go in his own balloon in search of a subject, saying :

> ' I've one up there : I'll summon it forthwith.
> My passport's made out in the name of Smith.'

This was not an allusion to the name of the author, but to that which Louis Philippe assumed in his flight from France to England.

Mrs. K.—'But if you come to where the Channel waves end,
          Don't make a mess of it, and drop at Gravesend,'

as an aeronaut of that period had recently done.

'The balloon then descends; Asmodeus gets into the car, the clouds fall, and as they clear off, they discover a view of London by night, with the Crystal Palace of 1851—the date of the play ; the scenery then begins to sink continuously, giving the audience the notion that the balloon is constantly rising, and presents a bird's-eye view of Dover and the Channel by night, Calais Harbour, Paris, the Pyrenees, the Amphitheatre of Gavarnie, Seville and the Vega of Granada. Then the balloon drops, the clouds disperse and discover a mountain-pass in Granada, with a view of the city and the Alhambra beyond it.

'Then the play began. There was not much plot in it, and what there was is partly told by Hussein (Harley) in an amusing song to the tune of "The Cork Leg."

'There's a wonderful king who lives up there,
And keeps in a tower three daughters fair,
Whom he never allows to take the air,
Like the pagan girls in Grosvenor Square.
                    With their tooral, looral. etc.

' Now when they were born, an astrologer said
That if ever these beautiful girls were wed,
He might put up his spoon and go to bed,
For the Christians would soon knock his crown from
his head.

> With their tooral, looral, etc.

' For fear that the prophecy should come true,
The old king lives in a terrible stew,
And his beautiful daughters mope and mew,
And all day long they have nothing to do.

> With their tooral, looral, etc.

' But as all young ladies are born to be wives,
And make men happy the rest of their lives,
We hope the enchanter has told a flam,
And that all his predictions are not worth a ——.

> Tooral, looral, etc.

' A war was going on between the Moors and
the Christians, and three knights of the latter
party were captured, and of course fell in love
with the king's three daughters. There were
various vicissitudes, and at last the Moors were
attacked again, Granada was taken, and the knights
rescued and enabled to carry off the princesses.
That was all the story, but the bare outline was
filled up with a wealth of amusing and picturesque
detail, and the dialogue was brilliant. We have
nothing like it nowadays.'

Here is a little note on the author of ' The
Alhambra,' in connection with his ' Mont Blanc '
lecture :

' Among the many jokes that Albert Smith introduced into his entertainment, he had not the

least objection to repeat some that had been made
at his own expense. Thus, in a visitors' book
somewhere he had written a few lines, signing
the entry " A. S.," to which a waggish com-
mentator afterwards added the remark, " A pity
he tells only two-thirds of the truth!" Then,
again, an enthusiastic admirer wrote : " I am
very fond of Albert Smith's writings. They
remind me of Goldsmith." " Yes," observed
another tourist ; " but a good deal of the Smith
and very little of the Gold."'

In an autograph letter from Albert Smith, which
Mr. Dillon Croker has placed in my hands, the
writer gives a list of all his principal literary
works and essays, together with the titles of his
plays. Among the first are ' The Natural History
of the Gent,' ' The Ballet Girl,' ' The Idler about
Town,' ' Stuck-up People,' ' The Flirt,' and ' Evening Parties ' ; ' A Bowl of Punch,' ' A Pottle of
Strawberries ' and ' The Social Parliament.' The
plays include ' Blanche Heriot,' ' The Headsman,'
' The Pearl of Chamounix,' ' To Persons about to
Marry,' ' The Enchanted Horse,' and seven burlesques, among which are ' Valentine and Orson '
and ' Cinderella.' The sketches of Mrs. Keeley
as Valentine and Cinderella, to be found in these
pages, are from water-colour drawings taken at
the time by Thomas Harrington Wilson, who, I
believe, is happily still amongst us. Mr. Smith
adds : ' The only piece of poetry I ever com-

mitted myself in was the translation of Burger's
" Leonora," published in a little shilling book, "A
Bowl of Punch." '   Just before his death Albert
Smith was engaged in the compilation of a volume
to consist of many of his old magazine papers and
some of his more recent *feuilletons*, to which he
intended to give the title ' Wild Oats.'   The
book was, I believe, afterwards published by his
brother Arthur.

Another example of Albert Smith's powers in
burlesque-writing is afforded by an amusing skit
which he wrote ' for the most private circulation ' at
the time of the opening of the Sydenham Crystal
Palace in 1854, and which was never published.
The author, who writes under the name of
' William Jones,' calls it ' Cucumber Castle ; or,
The Sydenham Summer-house,' and says that
the ' songs, duets, choruses and incidental ballads
were *intended* to have been sung before the
Queen.'

The scene is supposed to open with the interior of the Crystal Palace on June 10.   There
are a great many people assembled.   ' Some are
very nice indeed ; more are very commonplace ;
and many excite doubts as to their having paid
their two guineas for the season tickets, bearing
a great resemblance to upper-box orders out for
the day.   Several gentlemen, in evening costume,
are charming ; several more, in unwonted Court
attire, are very uncomfortable.'

Chorus of Discontented People.

'Oh dear ! what can the matter be ?
  Hear, hear ! what can that clatter be ?
  Dear, dear ! each will mad as a hatter be—
    Why are we seated out here ?

'We paid our two guineas to place us in clover,
  But now the baize barrier we may not climb over ;
  For the sight, we might all just as well be at Dover,
    Or sitting on Hungerford Pier !
                Oh, dear !' etc.

In referring to Mr. Whymper's lecture on the Alps, delivered two years ago, Mr. Edmund Yates took note in the *World* of the lecturer's ' kindly mention of Albert Smith and his ascent of Mont Blanc,' adding : ' Although in the eyes of keen climbers A. S. was only a *montagnard pour rire*, making his ascent when a man of middle age, and coming straight from London without any adequate training or condition, there is no doubt that it was by him—through his entertainment at the Egyptian Hall—that Chamounix achieved an extraordinary popularity with the English travelling public, which it sustained for more than ten years, and which was of enormous benefit to the guides, the villagers and the district generally. And at this time, scarcely more than thirty years after his death, the name of Albert Smith is wholly and absolutely forgotten, and not a single Swiss guide-book with which I am acquainted—Murray,

Baedeker, or Bradshaw—contains the faintest reference to him or his exploit.'

In speaking of the Keeleys off the stage, a
writer who remembers them well says :

'At a time when a good deal of coarseness
was practised on the London stage by low
comedians, and tolerated by the public, it was
creditable to the Keeleys that they never indulged
in such indiscretions. The only license which
Robert Keeley ever allowed himself was an
occasional use of the "big, big D." But it could
not be called swearing. The exclamation fell so
naturally from the lips of the little man, and in
such a droll tone, that no one could object to it
or help laughing at it. One who was present at
the Royal Dramatic Fêtes at the Crystal Palace
of 1865-66, remembers seeing Keeley in the box-
office of one of the Richardsonian shows, where
Nelson Lee the Younger's mock melodrama, "The
Smuggler's Doom" and his " Mysterious Monk "
were being played by Robson and other notable
actors. Old Keeley, who was then rather feeble,
did little else beside sit in the box-office, leaving
others to do the more active part of the business.
Presently something went wrong somewhere—
a door was not opened when it ought to have been,
and there was a little confusion. The attendants
were called to account in various ways, but Keeley,
in his grave, dry manner, only observed—he could
hardly be said to have exclaimed—" Dam fools!"'

Mr. E. Nelson Haxell, a native of Ipswich, who has rubbed shoulders with nearly all the theatrical celebrities of the Keeley days and long since, contributes an old letter from Robert Keeley, addressed from 3, William Street, Gordon Square, and dated January 2, 1836 :

' Mary is very busy just now, and desires me to say that we have a spare bed, and the sooner we catch you in it the better. Of course you know you won't be welcome.

' We are all well except the usual complements of the season in the shape of coughs, sneezing, chap'd hands, chilblains, noses which we keep blowing till we don't know whether it is us or the wind outside that makes most noise ; but we don't care.

' By-the-bye, did they write to you about doing some hams for me, and have you remembered it ? Give all our loves to all, and expect a hearty welcome when you come. Answer this. Good-bye, God bless you.

'(Signed)   R. KEELEY.'

Mr. Harrison Weir, the artist, tells me that he remembers seeing Keeley at a charity fair in Brighton or Lewes, and says :

' He and my uncle sold things by public auction. Keeley was the auctioneer, and my uncle his clerk, and they formed a striking contrast in appearance, my relative being six feet four inches in height, and the actor not much over five feet. After haranguing the crowd, Keeley used to end by pointing to his tall clerk and to himself, saying, " And that is the long and this is the short of it !" '

A friend calls my attention to some lines in the ' Ingoldsby Legends,' in which Keeley's name is mentioned. They occur in the humorous poem of the ' Old Woman clothed in Gray,' and are :

' The moment her shadowy form met his view,
  He gave vent to a sort of a lengthen'd " Bo-o—ho—o !"
  With a countenance Keeley alone could put on,
  Made one grasshopper spring to the door—and was gone !'

Mr. Augustus Toulmin, an old playgoer and intimate friend of the Keeleys, tells me that he was present at the opening night of ' Martin Chuzzlewit' at the Princess's, when Keeley appeared for the first time in his famous part of Mrs. Gamp, and that his fellow-players were so amused at his make up for the part, which they had not yet seen, that they were seized with an uncontrollable fit of laughter, and the curtain had to be lowered till they had sufficiently re-covered for the piece to be continued. But Keeley never moved a muscle, or budged an inch, and seemed utterly unconscious of the cause of their merriment.

When Mrs. Keeley went to Ipswich in 1891,

to be present at the opening of the new Lyceum, she was the guest of Mr. Felix T. Cobbold, of Felixstowe, a great-grandson of the actress's old benefactress, Mrs. Cobbold. In referring to the visit, Mr. Cobbold says : ' It was a great pleasure to see Mrs. Keeley here. When we went to Holywells, near Ipswich, where she had lived, I believe, for ten months, with my great-grand-father and his wife, she would not go and see the room where she had slept ; though she described it accurately to me as we looked up at the window. . . . I could not persuade her to drive twelve miles to the ball held at the Town Hall, Ipswich, in aid of the East Suffolk Hospital. But she was very merry and gay, and added much to the life of our party.'

After the performance at the new theatre, Mr. Cobbold escorted Mrs. Keeley to the offices of the *East Anglian Daily Times*, to partake of afternoon tea with the directors and several friends. Among those introduced to the actress were Mr. Peter Bruff, who remembered Mrs. Keeley's appearance on the Ipswich boards fifty years since, and Mr. S. A. Notcutt, jun., whose grandfather she danced with, and of whom she laughingly said that he was just like the Mr. Notcutt she used to know years ago.

Among Mrs. Keeley's many accomplishments, letter-writing may certainly be numbered. More than one example of her readiness with

the pen has been given in these pages, and here
are a few additional ones.   The first was written
some seventy years ago, when the postage of a
letter from London to Ipswich cost eightpence.
It is addressed to Miss Lucy Smart, of St.
Mary's Elms, Ipswich, and says :

'Will you send Ann, in the next parcel, a
bottle of eye-water ?

'Will you pickle a ham for me? and I will
enclose you the money in the next parcel, if you
send word what it comes to.

'Will you send me what stage dresses you
have of mine, including boots?

'Will you accept my best love? and believe
me,

' Yours truly,
' M. A. KEELEY.

' P.S.—Will you burn this scrawl ?'

The next letter belongs to our own times, and
refers to one of many unsuccessful attempts of
the camera to delineate the expressive features of
the actress, who in speaking of it says :

' I received this morning a copy of the photograph.   Good gracious!   The moment I set
eyes upon it I went off to my lawyer, made over
my last property to different hospitals, and have
resolved to quit the world and devote myself to
the service of the " blessed Virgin."   I have no

right to walk about the streets to the danger of
the good looks of the future generation, if I am
so ugly.'

Writing on September 4, 1886, she says :

'Here I am still in town—the "Last Rose of
Summer"; *all* my companions have fled, either
to Margate or Westgate-on-Sea. I wanted to
go, too, but could not get a place to put my
head in, for love or money. I think I shall try
Brighton for a week. I am not very well, and I
think a change of air and scene will improve me.
I am getting tired of my own company. I am
glad you are enjoying yourself. You are in a
lovely part of the Thames. I know Wargrave
very well; but do go to Marlow for an hour or
two. The view from the bridge there is most
beautiful. Edmund Yates has a charming house
there and a steam-launch. Happy man! . . .
Please do not be long before you *do* return, for
I have not a soul to speak to. The Swanboroughs have gone to Brighton, and I am,

'Yours very truly,

'THE LAST WOMAN IN TOWN.'

Writing to decline an invitation from a friend,
she says :

'How cruel of you to put temptation in my
path! I should like, above all things, to go to
you on Sunday; but how am I to get back?
My faithful Brown does not come out on Sun-

days ; it is difficult to find a " growler " late on
Sunday evenings, and I dare not trust my valuable life (at least, what remains of it) to the
mercies of a hansom. And so I must decline.
" Hey willy, waly oh !" '

Here is an invitation *from* Mrs. Keeley :

' What are you going to do with yourself on
Christmas eve ? [1885]. If disengaged, come and
spend the evening and *sup* here. Charles Stuart
and Ada Swanborough are coming. We will
have " cakes and ale " and " ginger ' shall be hot
in the mouth." '

Mrs. Keeley was, of course, among the very
first to congratulate Sir Henry Irving heartily
upon the honour of knighthood conferred upon
the actor by the Queen. After the dinner given
by the Savage Club in commemoration of the
event, Sir Henry received from Mrs. Keeley the
following ' anonymous ' note :

' MOST NOBLE SAVAGE,

        ' It was cruel of you to deprive the
feminine portion of your " tribe " of the pleasure
of hearing you address the assembled warriors on
Saturday evening last. Of course we could and
did read it in the newspaper reports ; but the
reading deprived it of half its worth ; we lost the
gestures—the whimsical expression of your face
—the fun and force of language ; and the disappointment was great.

'I am aware it is not the custom for squaws to feed with their warriors in public or share in the good things they eat; but they might be allowed to listen to some of the good things spoken by the noble and gifted warriors assembled to do honour to their chief.

'Your devoted squaw,

'MARIANKEELEE.'

In reply to another letter from Mrs. Keeley, in which she expressed a wish to see 'King Arthur,' Sir Henry Irving wrote :

'My love and greeting. It will be delightful to make you right welcome, but I am sorry to say that Miss Terry will be unable to act to-morrow. If you would rather wait till next week, when she will be playing, please send one word by bearer. If you will come to-morrow, a box shall be sent by return, and you must please come by private door in Burleigh Street to save you some trouble.'

Mrs. Keeley greatly appreciated this delicate attention and kind consideration, and on the following Monday, when Miss Terry was well enough to appear, she was present at the performance of 'King Arthur.' She also went to see the 'Story of Waterloo' and 'Don Quixote, and was as enthusiastic as most people were at those remarkable performances.

The last letter of interest is one that Mrs.

23

Keeley recently wrote to a friend who was collecting independent subscriptions from 'celebrities' on behalf of the '*Daily Telegraph* Shilling National Testimonial' to Dr. W. G. Grace Some amusing lines were written in response to her friend's request for a small donation ; but only a very brief and inaccurate extract from the letter was forwarded to the newspaper.   Here is a copy of the original document :

'I send 5s. towards Dr. Grace's graceful and well-deserved testimonial.   Not that I know anything of the noble game.   I once sat out an afternoon at Lord's, and when the game was over I wondered what it was all about.   No, dear ; the only cricket I know is the " Cricket on the Hearth."

'Yours ever,

'Dot.'

INDEX.

THE END.

BILLING AND SONS, PRINTERS, GUILDFORD.
G. C. & Co.